STORM RISING

Also by Sara Driscoll

Lone Wolf

Before It's Too Late

STORM RISING

SARA DRISCOLL

KENSINGTON BOOKS
www.kensingtonbooks.com

KENSINGTON BOOKS are published by

Kensington Publishing Corp.
119 West 40th Street
New York, NY 10018

All Kensington titles, imprints and distributed lines are available at special quantity discounts for bulk purchases for sales promotion, premiums, fundraising, educational or institutional use.

Special book excerpts or customized printings can also be created to fit specific needs. For details, write or phone the office of the Kensington Special Sales Manager. Kensington Publishing Corp., 119 West 40th Street, New York, NY 10018. Attn.: Special Sales Department. Phone: 1-800-221-2647.

Library of Congress Card Catalogue Number: 2018944168

Kensington and the K logo Reg. U.S. Pat. & TM Off.

ISBN-13: 978-1-4967-0445-0
ISBN-10: 1-4967-0445-2
First Kensington Hardcover Edition: December 2018

eISBN-13: 978-1-4967-0446-7
eISBN-10: 1-4967-0446-0
Kensington Electronic Edition: December 2018

10 9 8 7 6 5 4 3 2 1

Printed in the United States of America

STORM
RISING

CHAPTER 1

Landfall: Coming ashore after a trip over water.

Friday, July 21, 10:04 PM
Jennings residence
Arlington, Virginia

"Meg, come look at this."

Meg Jennings looked up from packing at the sound of her sister's voice. She tucked several folded athletic shirts into her duffel bag, then jogged out of her bedroom and down the hall.

She found her sister Cara perched on the edge of the sofa, her attention focused on the flat-screen TV at the far end of the living room. Cara's brindle greyhound, Blink, gave a low whine from where he sat on the floor beside her and pushed his nose against her knee. Cara reached out blindly to stroke his head, crooning to him softly, her eyes never leaving the screen.

Meg took in the breathtaking scene splashed across fifty-two inches. The stark white lettering on the brilliant red news ticker labeled the area as Nags Head, North Carolina. Nags Head was unmistakably under attack. The fact that Mother Nature was the marauding force would make no difference to the outcome. Huge waves crashed ashore, trees bent nearly sideways in the roaring wind, and lethal pieces of debris were whipped into the air by the gale.

"It's making landfall now?"

"Yes. And Clay is out there somewhere in the middle of it."

Meg took in Cara's motionless stance and stiff shoulders. Her sister was silent, but her body language shouted her concern. Meg came close enough to rub a hand down her sister's back. "Hey." She waited until Cara tore her eyes from the TV and looked up at her. "He'll be okay. It'll take more than Hurricane Cole to take him down. He survived Iraq and other war zones; he'll survive this. Besides, he's not a storm chaser for The Weather Channel, he's writing a story for the *Washington Post*. TV reporters will be out in the gale. McCord will be undercover, finding the personal interest pieces."

Hearing his owner's name, Cody went from lying prone to standing on his back feet with his front paws pressed to Cara's thighs in a single motion. He jammed his wet nose into the hollow of her throat and Cara pressed both hands to his shoulders in response. "Down, Cody. You know better." The twelve-month-old golden retriever dropped obediently to the ground and grinned up at her, his entire back end undulating with his enthusiastic tail wags. "Did you hear Daddy's name?" Cara ruffled the puppy's ears and sighed. "Cody misses him."

"He's doing fine and you know it." Meg dropped onto the couch beside her sister. They were so similar, almost carbon copies of each other—tall and athletic, gifted with the ice-blue eyes and the long, glossy black hair of their Black Irish paternal grandmother. "Cody loves you and he loves the pack." Meg's gaze drifted over the two dogs sleeping in a pile on the oversized dog bed against the far wall—her own black Lab, Hawk, and Cara's mini blue pit bull, Saki. "He loves to spend time here. The only thing that would make it better is McCord being here too." Meg relaxed back against the couch cushions and cocked an eyebrow at her sister. "Like he did night before last."

Cara flushed up to her hairline. "You . . . knew he was here?"

"Of course I knew he was here. You're an adult. You don't need to justify your relationships to me. I'm not Mom. Not that you'd need to justify them to her either."

"I didn't know if you'd find it awkward. We share this house, so maybe I should have cleared it with you first."

"It's not like you brought home a stranger. It's McCord. And I saw this happening two months ago." Meg regarded Cara, as much best friend as younger sister, and waggled her fingers in a give-it-to-me gesture. "Now stop being stingy with the details. Just because I knew him first doesn't mean I don't want all the sisterly dirt." She leaned in close so she could drop her voice to a conspiratorial whisper. "How was he?"

At that, Cara laughed and flopped back onto the couch beside Meg, turning her head toward her sister. The glint in her eye answered Meg's question before she spoke. "Absolutely fantastic."

Meg grinned at her slyly and sat back. "I would expect nothing less."

Cara turned sideways on the sofa, snuggling into the soft cushions, some of the tenseness relaxing from her frame. "While we're on the subject of sisterly dirt, what about you and Todd?"

An image of the firefighter/paramedic in question sprang into Meg's mind: tall and dark, with the muscular build of a man used to sprinting up stairs wearing sixty pounds of gear with one hundred pounds of fire hose tossed over his shoulder. They'd met last May when a vengeful man had acted on his personal grudge by blowing up government buildings with C-4–loaded drones, uncaring of the innocent bystanders inside who ended up as collateral damage. DC Fire and Emergency Medical Services had been called in along with any available teams from the FBI's Human Scent Evidence Team—Meg and Hawk among them—to rescue the live victims and recover the dead. Together, Meg and Lieutenant Todd Webb had saved the life of a young girl and a bond had been forged.

"Getting close, but we're not quite there yet." Meg's tone was easy. "I've been away so much in the last few months—out in California helping with the mudslides and then in Colorado after that avalanche, not to mention local deployments. Add into that his schedule at the firehouse and things are moving slowly. Which is fine for both of us. We're not in a rush."

"Sometimes that's the best way. Does he know you're headed out of town again?"

"He knew it was likely, but I haven't talked to him since Craig made it official." Craig Beaumont, Supervisory Special Agent for the Forensic Canine Unit's Human Scent Evidence Team, had only called an hour ago with their orders. "I wanted to pack first," Meg continued, "then I'll give him a call and let him know we're headed to Virginia Beach."

Cara shifted to look back at the TV. The scene had changed from the sand dunes of Nags Head to the charming pastel three-story houses of Hatteras. The whitecap-topped, churning sea roared up to smash in front doors while the wind screamed and torrents of rain fell at a steep angle. "This is going to be bad."

"It is." Meg's attention was drawn across the room where Hawk stood up and stretched after his nap, and then wandered over to her. "Hi, buddy. How's my boy?" She stroked a hand down his glossy black fur and he sighed in pleasure. "They're saying this one could be up there with Sandy. The only good thing is this time they had a better handle on the track of the storm from the beginning and got the appropriate warnings out earlier. But you know we're going to lose people despite all the warnings and evac orders."

East Coast weather forecasters had been talking about Hurricane Cole for almost a week, their concerns becoming more strident as the storm approached. It was early in the season for a storm of this ferocity, but the talking heads were already discussing the impact of climate change on extreme weather events. A particularly warm Caribbean Sea and its evaporating water helped produce the dense cloud system that spun into a tropical storm before forming a hurricane. At first, they were hoping the storm would do what nineteen out of twenty Atlantic hurricanes do—curve east and burn out over the Atlantic. However, the usual high-pressure system over Bermuda that blocks and turns those storms hadn't materialized, and the hurricane had hugged the U.S. coast, running parallel up the Eastern Seaboard following the warm Gulf Stream. Then a blocking high over Greenland paired with an undulating jet stream over the continental United States and Canada drove the storm westward, where it rolled over the barrier islands of North Carolina and onto land.

The governors of North and South Carolina and Virginia had given evacuation orders for communities on the coast, but, as always, some inhabitants refused to leave their homes, preferring to take their chances with Mother Nature rather than risk all their worldly possessions to looters taking advantage of a natural disaster. Those who'd opted to stay had been warned that, after a certain point, they were on their own. Emergency services couldn't risk the lives of first responders coming to rescue them if they got into trouble because of their decision to stay.

And yet, they remained.

Those were the people Meg and her teammates would

be sent in to locate and rescue once the storm passed. Or, more likely, recover, because by that time, for many, it would be too late. Meg studied Hawk, who looked up at her with bright eyes full of love and loyalty. "I think the body count is going to be pretty high, and you know how hard that kind of search is on the dogs. I have a bad feeling about this whole deployment."

"They think Virginia Beach will be hit that hard?"

"As long as I lived and served in Richmond, I've only been to Virginia Beach that one time with you and Mom and Dad when we were teenagers, so I don't know that much about it and my visual memory is filtered through the eyes of a teenager. I can tell you what the beaches and the snack shacks looked like; I couldn't tell you about population density, elevation, and emergency services strength or normal response times. But Craig says it's been considered a hurricane risk for a long time. All that low-lying beachfront with no protective barrier islands and nearly forty thousand people living in a floodplain at sea level, within a quarter mile of the water's edge. Hurricane landfall is not their problem. It's being on the side of the counterclockwise rotation of the storm. Landfall gets the eye, but that side of the storm, north and east of the eye, gets gale force winds forcing a wall of water up onto land as the ocean floor slants upward and it has nowhere else to go. They think the storm surge is going to be comparable to Hurricane Sandy."

"From what they were just saying on TV, it's the worst of all possible scenarios, high tide during a new moon, which makes it higher, massive waves and then the storm surge on top of that—that's called the storm tide—all piling onto land with sustained winds near one hundred miles per hour. It's downgraded from a Category Three storm, but even making landfall at Category Two, the storm tide could be thirty or forty feet high."

Meg's hand stilled on Hawk's back. "A three-story wall of water. I can't imagine the terror of that coming right for you."

"It wouldn't be if they left." Cara's voice had an unforgiving edge. "Okay, maybe if you're an adult you can make that choice for yourself and if you choose wrong, you'll pay the price. So be it. But people keep their kids and pets with them. Protecting your stuff is a stupid reason to die. They're things; they can be replaced. The life of a child, or pet, can't."

"I agree one hundred percent. It'll probably be at about one hundred and fifty percent by tomorrow when I'm in the middle of the recovery. But—" She cut off when her cell phone rang. "Hold on. I have to get this. It could be Craig with updated instructions." She picked up her phone and scanned the name on the display. "Not Craig. It's Todd." She accepted the call. "Hey."

"Hey. Have you gotten your orders yet?"

"Yes. We're bugging out early tomorrow for Virginia Beach. They want us there for first light, but not before. We need to let the storm pass, and we're going to need light for searching because I'm sure the power will be out by then. Probably is now, in fact. Cara and I are just watching landfall on TV."

"I'm hearing that power is already out. So . . . can I hitch a ride with you?"

"To Virginia Beach? It's not a great time for a vacation, not there anyway."

Webb laughed. "Not for a vacation, for work. I've been deployed out to the Virginia Beach and Norfolk area for mutual aid."

"Mutual aid?"

"It's the agreement DCFEMS has with Virginia and Maryland. When we need help, they come to us. When they need help, we go to them. No questions asked. Right now, that whole area is short on EMS personnel due to budget cuts."

"And since you're dual-trained as a firefighter and a paramedic, you're the perfect person to go."

"Exactly. They've got equipment, but they're lacking in trained personnel. They're sending a bunch of us, but if I can hitch a ride with you, it'll keep my truck off roads that will already be flooded and clogged with debris and rescue vehicles. You need your vehicle because it's got Hawk's special traveling compartment, but have you got room for another passenger and the gear I need to take with me?"

"Sure. And I'd love the company on the way in. I need to start early though. Probably about three thirty?"

"Works for me. Time for us both to get a few hours of shut-eye. See you about three fifteen."

Meg said good night and hung up.

"Todd's going too?" Cara asked.

"Yes. It sounds like DCFEMS is sending a group of them in, but we're going to carpool to the coast."

"Makes sense." Cara laid a hand on her sister's arm. "You be careful. You *and* Hawk. I know you're a pro at this, but some of these searches can be pretty treacherous. Structures will be unstable, and flooding will be a constant problem."

"Of course I will." Meg gave her a pointed look. "And I don't want you sitting at home here, you and the dogs, fretting about the lot of us. We'll all stay safe."

Cara reached over, picked up the remote and turned off the TV. "I know. It's probably just listening to these news reports about the storm. It's making me twitchy."

"I promise to stay in touch as much as I can. Both power and communication could be iffy, so don't panic if it's radio silence for a while." Meg stood and gave Hawk the hand signal to come. "Now I have to finish packing, then grab a few hours of sleep."

"Get me up before you go. I want to see you off."

"You sure? It's going to be way early."

"I can go back to bed after you're gone. Get me up."

"You got it."

Meg cast one last look at the dark TV screen, but the images were imprinted on her brain. Hundreds of people had died during Hurricane Sandy, and almost two thousand from Katrina. Time would reveal what the impact of Hurricane Cole would be.

Bring home the ones you can.

Craig's words to her just before she stepped through the doors following the bombing at the James L. Whitten Building on the National Mall in Washington, D.C., echoed in her brain. They had a job to do: Whether living or dead, they would bring the victims home.

CHAPTER 2

Deployment: The movement of equipment and people into an area to begin search-and-rescue operations.

Saturday, July 22, 3:22 AM
Jennings residence
Arlington, Virginia

"Is that everything?" Meg asked.

Todd Webb swung two packed duffel bags stamped with the DCFEMS logo into the back of Meg's SUV behind Hawk's compartment. "Just about." He tapped an index finger on one of the duffels. "I've got extra bags of medical supplies, bandages, splints, and so on. Local responders will probably be stripped by the time we get there, so it doesn't hurt to have our own supplies. The other guys are doing the same. I also brought sleeping bags, an air mattress, and basic camping equipment because I assume lodging is probably going to be hard to come by." He stepped back and brushed a hand over his dark hair, cut short to fit comfortably under a firefighter's helmet. "Give me two more minutes."

"You have five. I still need to grab my go bag from inside. Otherwise I'm good to go. When we're ready, I'll get Cara up. I promised her I'd say goodbye before we left."

"No need. I'm right here." Wearing an open silk kimono over a T-shirt and sleep shorts, Cara circled the back of Meg's SUV on bare feet. Her dark hair was rumpled from bed and fell loose over her shoulders. "Mom and Dad just sent me a text, thinking I'd get it in the morning, but I heard you moving around so I was already awake."

Worry slithered through Meg. "Mom and Dad? At this time of night? Is everything okay?"

Cara waved away Meg's concerns. "They're great. They just wanted us to know that they're headed to the coast this morning too. The ASPCA, HSUS, and local rescues are all cooperating in livestock, wildlife, and pet rescue following the storm, and Mom and Dad have volunteered to help. They'll also transport back any animals that need medical care or re-homing that overflow local shelters." She frowned. "And now I really feel useless. The whole family is going except for me."

"Don't discount that you're holding down the fort and watching over our animals. You also have responsibilities here. You've got classes at the training school and your private lessons to deal with. You know Mrs. Wettlafer would pitch a fit if her beloved Trixie missed a puppy class."

Cara groaned. "Don't remind me. I've got two private lessons with her this week on top of the group class."

"And communication may be so bad out on the coast that we may need to use you as a go-between, so keep your phone charged and with you at all times," Meg continued. "Craig made sure we all had our satellite phones, so you should hear from me one way or another. Mom and Dad may be another story. They'll certainly be busy though. It never fails to amaze me how many pets lost during a storm are never claimed." Meg looked down at Hawk, who milled around their legs. "If I lost my dog, I'd be going crazy."

"You'd also have him microchipped, so they'd find you quickly."

"Your parents can manage more animals at the rescue?" Webb asked, referring to Cold Spring Haven, the animal rescue the sisters' parents ran at their home and farm outside of Charlottesville, Virginia.

"Absolutely. That's what they do. And being out in the country means they actually have more room than most shelters."

"Not to mention that they'll take wildlife as well," Cara said. "Inundated local city shelters might not be able to house or manage injured wildlife and might be forced to euthanize simply due to logistics. Those are the animals Mom and Dad will take. They have an amazing vet who is game to take on anything they throw at her."

"If Tina doesn't already know how to care for an animal, she'll find out. Honestly, I think she enjoys it. Small-animal practice is great, but give her a bear cub or bald eagle any day. I'm sure they've already given her the heads-up that they're heading out." Meg glanced at her watch. "We have to get moving. Cara, since you're up, can you grab my go bag, please, while I help Todd with the rest of his gear? It's just inside the mudroom door."

"On it."

Meg and Webb loaded the last of his gear while Cara added Meg's bag. Webb gave the gear a push to settle it and then slammed the hatch of Meg's SUV. "All set. Do we need to stop for gas?"

"Gas, no. Coffee, you bet your life."

"You better stop for gas inland before you get there," Cara suggested. "If they've lost power on the coast, they won't be pumping gas, and it could be in seriously short supply."

"I have an alarm set on my phone for about an hour

out, for just that reason." Meg opened the back door to Hawk's compartment. "Okay, Hawk, up."

"Not before I've said goodbye." Cara squatted down in front of the dog and gave him a quick stroke over his head. "You be good, Hawk. You be careful." She dropped her voice to a stage whisper. "And you take care of Meg. Don't let her be a hotshot."

Meg crossed her arms over her chest and gave her sister the stink eye. "I can hear you, you know."

"Oh, I know." Cara stood and moved closer to give her sister a hug. "I'm making the point to you, after all." She pulled back and looked Meg dead in the eye. "Help those you can. Don't dwell on those beyond your reach." She glanced at Webb, including him as well. "You're both going to see a lot of terrible things between the destruction and loss of life. You've maybe seen it all before, but the weight of it will wear on you. Take care of yourselves and each other and leave it behind on the coast when you come home."

Meg caught her sister up in a tight hug. "When did you get to be so wise?"

"I'm not our mother's daughter for nothing." Cara pulled away, and gave Meg a gentle push in the direction of the SUV. "Call, text, or email if you can when you get there. I promise not to assume the worst if I don't hear from you. Now go."

Meg got Hawk settled into the SUV for the drive, then she and Webb climbed in. Her last sight as she drove out of the driveway was Cara in her rearview mirror, waving madly to speed them on their way.

CHAPTER 3

Cut Corners: Do something in what seems to be the easiest, quickest, or cheapest way, often ignoring risk or laws.

Saturday, July 22, 6:46 AM
I-264
Virginia Beach, Virginia

They'd only been on the road for about a half hour when the rain started, and it got steadily worse as they drove into the storm. They stopped for coffee on the way out of Arlington, and then stopped again at 5:00 AM outside of Richmond just as a Dunkin' Donuts was opening. They traded off at that point and Webb drove the rest of the way toward the coast, dealing with the worst of the driving. At times the rain pounded down so hard Meg thought they'd have to pull off the road, but Webb handled the SUV like he'd been driving it for years. The roads were completely deserted except for emergency vehicles, as the governor's curfew dictated. They were pulled over by the state police as they approached the outskirts of town, but they showed their IDs, explained where they were headed, and were waved through with well wishes for successful searches.

Shortly after that, Webb got a call from his battalion chief. Meg answered the call for him and put it on speaker so he could talk and drive at the same time.

"I'm here, sir. I'm driving in with an FBI handler and her dog. I asked her to answer the phone for me so I could keep driving."

"How bad is it?" The chief's voice boomed out of the speaker.

Used to bellowing commands during fires. Hard to turn that off.

"It's getting worse as we get closer. Do we have our assignments?"

"Yes. You're going to the Virginia Beach General Hospital on First Colonial Road. It's a three-hundred-bed acute care center that's only two and a half miles from the coast and backs onto Broad Bay."

Webb muttered a curse under his breath. "That sounds like a recipe for disaster in a storm like this. Are they flooded?"

"Partly, but power is the real issue. Power is out in the area and their generators aren't able to keep up. They've got to evacuate patients before they fail completely. Cardiac ICU, neonatal ICU, palliative care, maternity, and surgical . . . they've all got to be moved to different hospitals that can take them. That's where they need you."

"I can be there in about fifteen minutes," Webb said. "Can we get right to them? No road blocks?"

"Nothing you won't be able to get through. Report there to Battalion Chief Tucker out of VBFD, he's expecting you."

"Message received. Webb out."

Meg hung up the phone for him and glanced sideways at him. His jaw was set and his hands gripped the steering wheel tighter than required. "You okay?"

Gold-flecked brown eyes flicked in her direction and then back to the rain-soaked windshield. "I'm fine. It's just . . . they knew this was coming, right? They've got a hospital sitting mere miles from the coast, essentially surrounded by swamps or ocean water, and they didn't think to get the worst of the worst out ahead of time, just in case? I understand that incidents can happen that catch you off guard, something you can never plan for. But this . . ."

"They had time to get ready for this."

"Got it in one. You know what it comes down to? Money. The admin boards of these places don't want to offload patients to other facilities, especially if they don't own them, because they'll likely never get the patient back, and that's health-care dollars just slipping through their fingers. They wait, thinking they can weather the storm. Then they can't, and who pays for it? Possibly the twenty-six-week-old preemie already facing a life-or-death battle, even without the risk of his ventilator losing power."

"You sound like you've seen this before."

"Yeah. And it didn't turn out well for some. I can only hope they made this call early enough that we've got the time we need. It's going to take the whole day and every ambulance in the city to move these people, but you know we won't have that many."

"They'll be needed for new EMS calls."

"Yeah. We'll have some helo support, which will help spread the patients out to more distant hospitals, lightening the local load, but there are only so many of those available. What about you? Where are you going?"

"I don't know yet. Craig wants us to call in as we're coming into town. Search-and-rescue in a case like this is fluid. The sun's only been up for about a half hour. Local emergency services need daylight to really understand what areas were worst hit. And they may already have an idea of how many refused to leave their homes in the first place or where those people are concentrated." She shook her head. "Insanity."

"Staying put with a storm like that coming in?"

"Yes."

"I used to think that too. And then I went through a few natural disasters and learned that it's never that black-and-white. You say people refused to leave, but maybe they couldn't. Think back to when Hurricane Harvey hit Florida. People wanted to leave but couldn't because the roads were clogged and there was no gas. Or they had nowhere to go, or no money for a hotel for what could have been days or weeks until they could go home. Some couldn't leave their jobs early to get out of town without risking their employment, the only thing that feeds their family. And for the elderly, or the disabled, not being easily ambulatory is a huge disadvantage. Just keep all that in mind when you're out there. Everyone has their own story, and everyone is making the best decisions they can with the information and the resources at hand." He paused for a moment and sipped his coffee. "Sorry. I'm lecturing and that wasn't the intent. I've just seen too many people stuck without help, and I guess I have a lot more sympathy for individuals who can't get out versus administrations who don't do responsible disaster planning when that's part of their job."

Meg flicked a glance at Webb. "I guess I never thought of it that way."

"It's different once you're in the middle of it. That can really change your viewpoint."

"Sounds like it's something for me to keep in mind over the next few days. We're getting close now, so we'll drop you off and then I'll call in. By that time Craig will know where we're needed." She glanced through mesh screen into the back where Hawk lay in his compartment, snoozing while he could before his day started. "I think it's going to be a hard day for Hawk. I hope to find more living than dead, but I have a bad feeling about what's ahead of us."

CHAPTER 4

Fire and Flood: Structure fires are a common occurrence after major storms because of fractured gas lines and downed power lines.

Saturday, July 22, 7:19 AM
Shadowlawn neighborhood
Virginia Beach, Virginia

Even prepared for the worst, the devastation still caught Meg off guard.

Meg got as close to her assigned neighborhood as she could, until the massive trunk of a toppled tree blocked the road for both incoming responders and fleeing families. She pulled her SUV to the side of Norfolk Avenue behind a string of emergency vehicles, all with lights flashing. She climbed out, circled the hood of her car, and gave herself a moment to stand under the cloud-ridden sky to take it all in.

The destruction was breathtaking. The neighborhood consisted of a grid of single-family homes, bungalows, and two-story structures. While these houses missed the fury of the storm surge and were lucky enough to have an extra ten or fifteen feet of elevation to escape the worst of the flooding, evidence of Hurricane Cole's path was clear. Debris filled every yard, while siding and shingles were ripped from houses, leaving bare spots open to the brutal elements. Trees tipped over, their massive, twisted tangles of roots thrusting fifteen or twenty feet into the air. A luxury motor boat sat at a drunken angle, rammed up against the front door of a clapboard house that looked like it had careened off center and might capsize at any moment. Small branches and twigs covered every surface, mixed with beach sand and sprinkled with pool toys and sheets of wooden lattice. Remnants of wooden fencing and two-foot by four-foot plywood sections from roofs commingled a foot deep in places with street signs and mangled patio furniture.

Meg turned back to the car and opened the door. "Hawk, come." Hawk obediently jumped down to stand at her side on the wet sidewalk, his nose twitching at the overwhelming smells of ocean water, spilled fuel, and exposed earth. At least the rain had stopped, so they didn't have to deal with that too. "Sit. Good boy." Meg circled the back of her SUV and pulled out her go bag, which contained everything they'd need for the day's searches, including fresh water, high energy snacks, her satellite phone, a rain shell in case the weather turned, and Hawk's work boots. It was the last item that she rummaged for in the bag, quickly finding them and pulling out the Velcro boots with sturdy rubber soles. She slipped Hawk's leash from the front pocket of the backpack, shouldered the bag, grabbed the boots, leash, and his vest in one hand, and slammed the hatch shut with the other.

Returning to Hawk, she knelt down in front of him. "Time for your boots, Hawk. One foot at a time." He obediently raised each front paw in sequence, waiting patiently as Meg securely strapped on each boot, then stood so she could reach his back feet. "Good boy. I know you don't like these, but at least until we get to the water, you need to wear them. There are going to be roofing and fencing nails everywhere, not to mention broken glass and torn metal and God only knows what else that could cut you." She glanced down at her own steel-toed boots. "That goes for both of us." She stood and quickly put on his navy-blue working vest with FBI emblazoned on each side in bright yellow block letters, and then snapped his leash to the metal hook in the middle of his back. "Hawk, come."

The dog fell into perfect step with her as they started down the road, but she had to loosen the leash more than usual to allow room for them both to step over and around debris in the road.

Her cell phone rang and she fished it out of the zippered pocket of her yoga pants. She glanced at the display before reading it, and couldn't stop the smile at the name—Brian Foster, her closest friend and ally in the Human Scent Evidence Team. He and his German shepherd, Lacey, were also on their way. "Hey," she greeted. "You here already?"

"I am. You?"

"Just had to abandon the SUV. Hawk and I are coming down Caribbean, according to my GPS. But I can't see a single street sign to confirm. They're all stripped off their poles."

"Too much surface area. The wind picked them all up and tossed them like loose playing cards. Take your next left and come over one block to Cypress. There's an inlet there that the teams are using as a launch site for the search boats."

"Is that how they're sending us out?"

"To start with, yes. They've called in the National Guard and they're providing boats for us. It's a mess down here, Meg. It's an inlet that goes out to the ocean, but it's now easily three or four times the usual size, and the houses that lined it are all under water."

"We knew it was going to be bad. Okay, I'm headed over to—"

The roar of an explosion and a massive blue-white light flashing across the sky had Meg instinctively kneeling down to throw an arm over her dog to both protect and calm. "Brian? You there? What was that?"

"I'm here. Lacey, girl, it's okay. Shhhh . . ." He took a moment to murmur to his dog before returning to his phone. "It sounded like it came across the inlet. Do you see the billows of black smoke?"

Meg stood and looked toward the south. With no large trees standing tall to block the view, dark clouds rose above the housetops. "Damn. That doesn't look good."

"You know how salt water and electricity don't mix. My money is on a transformer blowing. Just what they need, a transformer fire on top of all this damage. Wood debris is everywhere and will just feed the inferno."

Meg turned onto the next cross street, Hawk keeping perfect pace with her. "Too bad Todd already has his hands full or he'd be useful over there. Not that he brought his turnout gear."

"Todd Webb? He's here?"

"D.C. and Virginia have a mutual aid agreement. If either needs help, the other responds. He came in with me, but I dropped him off at the hospital across town. They're without power and have to evacuate everyone. Granted, if they needed him as a firefighter, they'd find him gear, but right now he's more useful to them as a paramedic. He has serious concerns about them losing critical patients if they can't move fast enough. Who else is here?"

"Scott and Theo arrived first, then me and Lacey. Lauren and Rocco are on their way, but she knows someone in the Virginia Search and Rescue Dog Association and they're a few teams short, so they made a request to Craig for her to go to the Fort Story area on the north shore, and he agreed. Basically, he's placing us wherever we're needed. Which is pretty much everywhere."

"I'm just turning onto Cypress now," Meg said. "I see a group of people. Is that where you are?" About forty feet down the road, a single dark-haired man stepped out of the group, waving an arm over his head, a dog at his heels. "Got you. Be right there." Meg ended the call and slid the phone back into her pocket. "Come on, Hawk, let's go see Lacey." Hawk's ears perked at the sound of the German shepherd's name and his pace quickened. Hawk and Lacey were as inseparable as Meg and Brian.

As Brian came toward them, Scott Park's tall, lanky form separated from the group, his droopy-eyed blood-hound, Theo, on a leash at his side.

"Sorry if I'm late," Meg explained. "I got held up dropping off Todd." She looked over to the cops and National Guard soldiers in khaki fatigues clumped in a group down the street. "They're still getting organized?"

"Yes." Scott gave Theo a hand signal and the dog immediately sat beside him. "I've been eavesdropping a bit to get a feel for what's going on. They're mapping out search routes to cover the most ground with the few boats they have, in the shortest period of time. It's worth it to let them get that straightened out. They've brought in Zodiacs to do door-to-door searches. That's where they'll need us."

"Is it bad?"

"Follow me. Theo, come." Scott skirted the cluster of people and headed for the water twenty feet away—the encroaching ocean where it was not supposed to be. The street's single yellow dividing line dove into murky seawater as the surface angled down toward the original sea level. Houses sank into the water until, in the distance, only rooftops showed.

Meg whistled. "This is our search area?"

"Yeah. It's an inlet open to the ocean and split by a peninsula"—Scott pointed out toward where the black smoke roiled darker and in a widening plume—"into two lakes, Rudee and Wesley."

"This area was already wide-open to the water coming in," Brian said. "The storm surge didn't need to cross dry land to get here, so nothing slowed it down."

"Same with the surrounding coastline," Scott said. "We're only about a half mile from the beach."

"Do they have an idea of the size of the combined storm tide?" Meg asked. "I know it would have been dark in the middle of the night and likely no power at that point."

"Apparently some of the people who didn't leave hunkered down in their beachfront apartments. The hotels on the beach closed and evacuated to avoid any risk of lawsuits. But the people who owned apartments made their own decisions. Some of the people who stayed took videos. Based on those visuals, the storm tide is estimated at about forty-five feet."

"My God," Meg breathed. "That's even higher than forecast."

"That kind of thing must be impossible to guess for all areas. It would depend on wind and tides and the shape of the seabed leading up to land. Anyway, some of these hotshots were live-streaming video to Facebook and YouTube as long as they had a data connection on their phones, so that gave the National Hurricane Center at the NOAA all the data it needed."

"Speaking of which, I'm surprised that I'm still connected," Meg said. "I thought we'd be on satellite phones already."

"Depends on where the cell tower is. Parts of town definitely don't have reception. Luckily some still do, so we've had some calls for help this morning, and some maydays were called in last night before they lost reception. Local first esponse has a full list, and the National Guard has the list of everyone in this neighborhood. We'll check everything, but we know some places move up the list." Scott paused momentarily, as if weighing something. "I saw one of those videos."

When he didn't continue, Brian prompted him. "And . . . ?"

"Some people thought it might be fun to stand on their balconies to watch the storm. They couldn't see the wall of water coming toward them in the dark. First they're there, then they're gone."

"God Almighty. Who would be that stupid?" Brian ran a hand through his hair in agitation, setting it on end. "Did they not listen to any of the warnings over the past few days?"

"Some might not have been able to get out for various reasons. But some people think it just can't happen to them," Meg said simply. Her days on K-9 patrol with the Richmond, Virginia, PD had taught her many things, and that was one of them. "They don't think the typical warnings apply to them. They often learn they're wrong, the hard way."

"These people certainly did." Scott looked out across the water. The rain had stopped and the wind had died considerably, but there was still a stiff breeze whipping up small whitecaps across the flooded inlet. "Those are some of the people we're going to find. There's no way they survived being swept off a fourth-story balcony."

"Yeah." Brian knelt down and ruffled Lacey's thick fur. "The dogs are going to have a hard day. The bodies are going to be so fresh, they're going to smell mostly like live victims." He kept his voice light and cheerful despite his words, so none of the dogs would understand the seriousness of the situation. "My money is on finding more vics dead than alive."

"I agree." Meg smoothed a hand over Hawk's head and looked back out over the water. She was about to speak, when movement caught her eye and she froze. Across the inlet, the roofs of houses marched out of the water, but farther inland were homes that had escaped the floodwaters. "Guys, am I seeing flames over there in that neighborhood?"

Shrugging out of her pack, Meg pulled her binoculars out of a pocket and trained them across the water, focusing quickly. At first all she saw was water, then swiveling slightly, she found clusters of houses, battered by the storms. And behind them danced the menacing tones of red and orange. "Damn, that *is* fire. A lot of it." She turned and took a few short steps back to the crowd. "Hey!" The group turned to stare at her. "Someone may have already given the alarm, but there's a mother of a fire starting across the inlet." It only took seconds for radios to come out to report the fire.

Meg turned back to Brian and Scott, who stood staring across the water at the flames, now noticeably brighter.

"Those houses were just soaked in a hurricane," Brian said. "How can they possibly burn like that?"

"You thought a transformer blew, that likely started it," Meg reasoned.

Scott tipped a flattened hand over his eyes to cut some of the glare coming from behind the lightening clouds. "Gas lines could have ruptured, ripped out by shifting tree roots, or by houses themselves moving on their foundations."

"I'll bet some of them on the water got ripped right off their footings. Add in a few ruptured residential natural gas lines and it's a bad setup. But not our problem. We need to focus on what we can do, not what we can't." Meg turned toward the boats pulled up to the roadway as a temporary boat launch. "We need to find whoever we can." She looked over her shoulder at the National Guard soldiers. The group was breaking up and several men in fatigues walked toward them.

A tall man with short salt-and-pepper hair held out his hand first to Scott, then Meg, and finally Brian. "I'm Sergeant Hunt. I'll be coordinating the marine search from this launch point. Are you and your dogs ready to move out?"

"Sure are," Brian said. "How are we working this?"

"We'll send a pilot and two soldiers out with each of your teams in a Zodiac. Each pilot has his search instructions and the lists of any reported calls for help. We'll split up and cover this area as best we can. We're going to be spread a little thin, at least at the beginning, but these first hours are our best chance of finding anyone alive."

"Let's get moving then." Meg looked down at Hawk, all bright eyes and wagging tail. "Ready, buddy? Let's go find them."

CHAPTER 5

No Way Out: In cases of major flooding, the recommended practice is to "shelter" on the roof to avoid being trapped in the attic.

Saturday, July 22, 8:11 AM
Shadowlawn neighborhood
Virginia Beach, Virginia

The boat slid through the inlet, bobbing slightly with the current. Hawk was now free of his work boots and vest; he was an excellent swimmer, but needed the freedom to move safely through the water. He stood in the prow of the boat, head high, eyes focused and nose working constantly, his front paws propped on the rim of the inflated bow, reminding Meg of an old-fashioned nautical figurehead. She sat directly behind him, one hand resting lightly on his back so she could sense his alertness while she scanned the surroundings, looking for any sign of movement.

It was surprisingly quiet after the roar and fury of last night's storm. Now it was just the sound of the breeze skimming the water, ruffling tiny waves. Otherwise, the only sound was the quiet purr of the outboard motor throttled down to allow rescuers to hear any cries for help.

Meg found the lack of ambient noise unsettling, and it took a moment to put her finger on why: There was a complete absence of wildlife, specifically the usual chorus of birds. Under normal circumstancs, the seashore was rife with the squawks and shrieks of ocean birds. Now, the steadily lightening sky was empty and the air was unnaturally still.

A chill of foreboding skimmed an icy finger down Meg's spine.

The two National Guard soldiers—Privates First Class Charles and MacDougall—sat on opposite sides at the back of the boat, Charles scanning the surrounding houses while MacDougall piloted the Zodiac.

It was a neighborhood of mixed homes. Most were bungalow style, or low, rambling, split-levels, but a few were two-story dwellings where the water had receded to nearly the first floor at this point. Even those houses had clearly been overcome by the storm surge as evidenced by sea debris scattered over rooftops.

So far, they'd found nothing, but many of the houses had been underwater to their rooflines. They'd moved the boat in close enough for Hawk to leap out onto the roof to search for any human scents, but they'd found nothing, living or dead.

Meg turned to the commanding officer, who sat just in front of his men. "Corporal Smythe, do we have any idea how many obeyed the evacuation order? Or maybe, more specifically, how many did not?"

"Overwhelmingly, most got out. We were called in early and helped folks get packed and out of town, or at least farther inland. But some just wouldn't go. I wasn't in this area, I was north of here, but I ran into quite a few who weren't going to leave. I had some luck leveraging some into going." From under the brim of his camouflage-patterned cap, he gave her a grimace of bared teeth. "I wasn't above using a little emotional blackmail to do it either."

"Really? How did you manage that?"

"The ones I could talk into leaving had someone or something other than themselves to save. A few had kids, but most of those were already smart enough to be gone or well on their way. Others had pets, and I'd use *Sure, maybe you can swim when the floodwaters come, but how are you going to feel when Rover or Fluffy drowns right in front of you?*" His eyes went to slits. "It wasn't nice, or fair—"

"But it got the job done," Meg finished. "And that's all that matters. Now those owners, and Rover and Fluffy, will survive and will realize you helped them make the right choice. On top of that, you helped them get out of what could be a pretty hefty fine and a misdemeanor charge."

"They didn't see it that way at the time, but hopefully some do now." Smythe raised his head from his list and maps and scanned his surroundings. "Damn." He pulled out his phone, checked their GPS location.

"What?"

"That house there." He pointed at the shallow roof of a bungalow coming up on their right. Water lapped over its eaves, but a ripped and tattered American flag protruded into the air from an angled flagpole at one end of the house. "Private MacDougall, get us over there. We had a mayday call from there last night. An older couple who didn't leave because the wife is bedridden with end-stage cancer. Water was pouring in through their doors and flooding the basement." His eyes were flat as he took in the little of the house that remained above water. "They didn't make it to the roof, so unless they managed to get to an attic that stayed dry, I don't see this ending well. I doubt that design has much in the way of attic space."

"We'll check it out," Meg said. "Get us close enough that Hawk and I can jump off."

A little maneuvering and the front edge of the inflatable craft scraped against shingles over what was likely the front door.

"Hawk, out." Meg sent her dog onto the roof with a hand signal to reinforce the command. Then she climbed out herself, setting her boots carefully on the slanted surface. "Hawk, find them."

Hawk scented the air before trotting up and over the peak of the roof. As Meg followed, she heard Smythe's command to push off and follow them around to the back of the house.

Meg climbed carefully up the slope and then over the peak that ran the length of the roof. She stopped as soon as she saw Hawk. He was sitting beside a skylight that broke the roofline to let light into the house below.

Sitting. He's alerting on a positive scent.

"Hawk has something," she called.

"Nearly there," Smythe called back just as the Zodiac rounded the edge of the house.

Meg crouched down beside Hawk. "Good boy." She fished in a pocket and pulled out a small jerky treat. She held it out on her palm as he stared at her, unmoving, until given the command. "Okay, Hawk. Take it."

With one damp swipe of lips and tongue he swept her palm clean. The treat was gone in seconds.

"I swear you don't even taste them." She ruffled his fur and then leaned over the skylight.

The house below was dark, surrounded by floodwaters, the skylight providing the only light filtering into the gloom. Bending down a little more, she could see the skylight was hinged on the upward edge and latched on the lower. Slipping her fingers under the edge, she tugged hard, but the frame didn't budge. She swiveled around to find the soldiers just climbing out of the Zodiac. "Have you got a pry bar? Or maybe a hammer?"

"Pry bar, yeah." Charles bent low into the boat, rummaged for a moment, and then his hand shot into the air with the metal bar.

"Bring it up."

After quickly dragging the boat a few feet up the roof to secure it, the men joined her. Smythe pulled out a flashlight and shone it down into the waters, but most of the light simply bounced off the glass. "Let's get this open, Charles."

It only took a few moments to lever the skylight up and to push it open on hinges that audibly protested their rare usage.

Water filled the house nearly to the ceiling of the room below.

Meg scanned the walls enclosing the skylight. "There's a good three feet here." She knocked on the wall just inside the frame. "Think this is the attic? There's even more space at the peak of the roof. Maybe they got up there." Meg pounded harder. "Hello? Is anyone here?"

Silence.

"Maybe they got out?" MacDougall suggested.

Meg glanced at her dog. Hawk's gaze was trained on the open skylight and her heart sank. "And went where? The whole neighborhood is flooded. No, they're here. Hawk tells us that."

"Corporal, let me go in." Charles leaned into the gap and surveyed the water below. "There's a couple of feet clear of the floodwater down below. I can go down on a cable and you can pull me back if I run into trouble. I was a lifeguard all through high school. I'm a very strong swimmer."

Smythe hesitated and Meg could read his opinion of the futile situation as if he'd voiced it. His gaze flicked out across the other houses as if feeling the press of the ticking clock.

Charles dragged off his cap to reveal close-cropped blond hair and a face that looked even younger than what Meg guessed to be about twenty-five years. "Please, sir. We can't take the chance they're alive. They might not make it until the waters recede."

Smythe took a moment to stare into the house below before responding. "Lose the boots, but keep the life vest. Take the waterproof flashlight. Be safe, but be quick. There are others waiting."

"Yes, sir."

Charles returned with a duffel bag containing the gear they needed, and the two privates quickly strapped into harnesses. Without a tie-down, MacDougall used himself as ballast, snapping the end of the cable to his own harness, and then handed the other end to Charles.

"Hawk, here." Meg stepped back several paces and waited while Hawk joined her. With a single gesture, she had him sit, then joined the men. "Let me help. I can pitch in as counterbalance."

"Thanks." Charles tossed her a pair of gloves. "Put those on so your hands don't get burned by the rope."

Charles unlaced his boots and set them aside. Then he sat on the edge of the frame. "Ready?"

Meg and Smythe gripped the rope and all three on the roof firmly planted their feet.

"Two tugs on the rope means you need more slack. Three means pull you back in. Go," ordered Smythe.

Charles pushed off and then there was a splash below. "I'm in." Charles's voice was muffled, but his words were clear. The rope vibrated twice in their hands and they loosened off to give him more slack. "I'm going in farther."

The rope moved smoothly through their hands, occasionally going taut, followed by twin tugs. A minute ticked by. Then two.

"I don't like this." Smythe's words were strained between clenched teeth. "He could be running into trouble in there and we won't know it."

"Give him a minute," Meg murmured. "They're there."

Three strong tugs jerked up the rope.

"That's it," Smythe said. "Pull him back slowly."

When Charles got back under the skylight, they pulled him up the cable far enough that Smythe could grab the private's forearm and haul him up to the roof. The younger man staggered slightly before catching his balance, then he sat down heavily.

Meg didn't need him to speak to know what he'd found. It was there in the pallor of his skin and the deep lines carved around his mouth.

Smythe needed confirmation though. "Charles?"

Charles automatically straightened in response to his commanding officer, squinting up into the sky after the dimness inside the house. "They're gone. They couldn't make it out." His head dropped into hands that scrubbed over his face and hair. "They're in the bedroom. On the bed. Holding each other. They died in each other's arms."

Meg's breath caught in her lungs at the mental image of an elderly couple embracing as the floodwaters poured in through every crack and rose to cover them. Did they feel terror in the grip of the raging storm or comfort that in the face of a fatal disease, the darkness would take them together at the end?

"When I got to the bedroom, I thought I could see something underwater in the light of the flashlight, so I went under to check."

"She never had a chance, and he wouldn't leave her, so they died together. If she was that sick, he may have found it easier to find a way to go with her than survive without her." Meg knelt down beside Charles. "You okay?"

The young man swallowed and looked up at her. "I

know I have to get a grip because we're going to see a lot more of this today."

"Is this your first search after a disaster like this?"

"Yeah."

Meg gave his forearm a squeeze. "Then give yourself a break. Take a minute, take a breath, and pull yourself together. We need you for the next one. There are people out there who need you." She pushed off the roof and stood to find Corporal Smythe watching her. "Can we move on, Corporal?"

"Just let me X-code the house." Smythe grabbed a spray paint can with a neon orange lid from the boat and crossed over the roofline and down the far side. Meg followed to stand on the peak as he spray-painted a large orange X on the bottom part of the slant of the roof. In the top section of the X he marked the current date and time, in the left quadrant he marked their squad identification, in the right he marked INT for an interior search and underneath he painted 0-2.

Zero survivors, 2 deceased.

Snapping the cap back on, Smythe trudged up the slope.

Meg stopped him before he could pass her. "Do we report in so someone else will retrieve the bodies later?"

"Yes. They need us to keep going because the clock will be ticking for other victims. We'd waste too much time and it would be too risky bringing the bodies out through the skylight. When the water level drops, it will be safer. I'll radio it in so they know. Come on, we need to move."

Meg followed him down the roof, calling Hawk to follow. He lithely jumped into the boat, but then stood looking back toward the house, his head tilted to one side.

"Something wrong with your dog?" MacDougall asked.

"What do you mean?"

"He looked confused."

Meg followed Hawk's gaze back to the skylight. "He is confused. He found the victims and he doesn't understand why we didn't bring them out. This is going to be hard on him. To search dogs, finding the victim is the winning part of the game. When they are robbed of a live victim, it's devastating for them. Many of them actually get depressed. Depending on how today goes, I may ask one of you to go 'get lost' "—she mimed air quotes around the words—"so Hawk can find you. He has to come out of this day with a win, whether we do or not. Then he'll be ready to take on tomorrow."

Understanding lit MacDougall's eyes. "We'll make sure he gets his find, no matter how the day turns out."

"Thanks." She climbed into the boat. "Where to next?"

"That way." Smythe pointed in the direction of deeper water. "This is when we really need your boy. If anyone's out there, we're depending on him to find them." His head rose and his eyes locked on the fire on the far side of the inlet.

Meg turned to look at it too and couldn't stop the involuntary gasp of shock. They'd been so busy, she hadn't kept an eye on the fire. Now it was out of control, a huge number of houses ablaze, the whole hill that ran up the peninsula seemingly alight.

"Luck is clearly not in our favor today," Smythe said. "It may take a miracle to turn this around."

They pushed off and the motor flared to life.

It wasn't just Hawk who needed the win now.

CHAPTER 6

Inaccessible Hide: An odor source that a scent-work dog can smell and locate, but cannot touch with its nose.

Saturday, July 22, 4:21 PM
The North End
Virginia Beach, Virginia

By late afternoon the waters had receded and the teams were sent out to the storm-ravaged beachfront. As bad as the flooded and battered inlet neighborhoods were, at least they had been sheltered inland, while the exposed coastline had taken the brunt of the storm's fury and the storm surge.

The high-rises along the ocean shore fared best, being constructed of rebar-reinforced concrete built to withstand incoming storms. They looked worse for wear, many of their metal or glass balcony enclosures ripped away by the hurricane-force winds, but they stood tall, spearing up in the now cloudless blue sky, pale columns in the blinding sun.

Devastation spread all around them. The concrete board-walk between the high-rises and the beach lay hidden by sand piled high over any remaining railings. The classic iron-and-glass street lamps bore testimony to the fury of the storm—not a single glass globe remained intact, and only a few posts still stood upright; most tilted drunkenly or had toppled, some obliterated by the sand below. A smattering of the palm trees lining the boardwalk remained standing, but only the odd truncated palm frond remained among the jutting stems. Houses by the seaside had been hollowed out by the combined forces of the wind and the crushing weight of the storm surge, stripping away many of the lower-level supports, leaving precarious, top-heavy, mushroomlike structures. Often, they were only roofs missing all exterior supports, balanced delicately on a few load-bearing walls stripped of nearly all interior possessions.

The National Guard was using drones to search some of the worst of the damage and those areas most inaccessible. They could fly the small crafts over piles of debris, watching intently for signs of human life on their small video displays. They used the flexibility of the remote vehicles to enter houses unsafe for human explorers, darting through rooms via ragged holes on the minuscule chance anyone could have survived the storm. It saved time, safely cleared structures, and created a search list for actual human and dog forays.

Lauren Wycliffe and her black-and-white border collie, Rocco, rejoined the Human Scent Evidence Team for this part of the search. Meg needed only one look at Lauren's face to read how her day had gone so far. Brief greetings, followed by a commiserating hand squeeze—*Us too. It's been awful*—and they were ready to start again.

Craig Beaumont gathered his team around him. Even though he'd only been coordinating the searches and hadn't been in the boats with the teams, the stress of the day's searches was etched into his expression, reminding Meg of the complexities of organizing a recovery of this scale. They were only seeing their own pockets of the search; Craig was liaising with every group on site, trying to make sure that all areas were covered, nothing got missed, and not a single man-hour was wasted. Lives hung in the balance and that weight lay on his shoulders.

Craig snapped open the map in his hands and then passed one end to Scott to hold so he had a hand free. The beach strip ran down one end of the map, the city an organized grid moving inland, away from the water. "This is our search area, here where the commercial part of the waterfront opens out to private homes," Craig said. "Without that line of big high-rise apartments and hotels to shelter the streets behind them from the storm, this area was wide-open to catastrophic damage. Keep in mind that what you see in this map is no longer going to resemble current status. Something as simple as a street grid no longer exists in the same way. On the way here, I passed a house ripped off its foundations and sitting in the middle of a street. Trees are down, telephone and power poles too, but the power's out in this area, so at least that's not a hazard. Dominion Virginia Power is all over the place, cleaning up downed lines so they'll be able to get power back up and running as fast as possible, but it will probably be more than a week before that happens in some areas. Parts of town farther inland already have power restored, so those are the areas where they're using community centers to accommodate evacuees and searchers.

"Now, to put it in perspective, this is where most of you were this morning." Craig circled the Rudee Inlet on the map, then dragged his finger northward. "This is where we are now. This area took the brunt of the storm surge in Virginia Beach, although I hear Norfolk also got hit badly to our northwest. The winds and storm surge followed the hurricane's counterclockwise spin and pounded Norfolk in the extreme. I've already had a request for us to be there tomorrow, but we'll go over that tonight when we've cleared today's searches. Now that it's low tide, they need us here.

The water pulling out has revealed *a lot* of damage. And while the chances of anyone surviving in these areas are beyond slim, this is our chance to make sure. High tide is at 22:11 tonight, so we stick with this area until we lose the light. I'll get food brought in so you can keep searching." He glanced down at the dogs, all lying quietly at their handlers' feet, taking a moment of rest while they could. "It's been a long and discouraging day for the dogs. Will they make it?"

"Yes." Lauren answered for the whole group. "We'll keep them hydrated and give them a full meal when it's time. They'll go as long as we do. And then they'll have a well-deserved rest tonight."

"Okay. One last thing. There's no cell coverage in this area, so it's all satellite phones from here on. Stay in touch with regular updates, even if you have nothing major to report. This has the possibility of being a very dangerous search area, so I need to know you and your dogs are safe. These are the areas we're going to cover." Craig outlined the search areas assigned to each team, describing the challenges as he knew them. He assigned adjacent areas so each handler had another handler relatively close if anyone ran into trouble and first response was tied up. "Keep in mind, this scenario will change on the fly. Do not enter a structure you feel is unstable. X-code any structure you search. If you need assistance from another team or from first responders, call it in, and I'll make sure they get to you. Now, get out there. Sunset is 20:18 tonight and we'll only have at most a half hour of light after that. Clock's ticking."

A half hour later, Meg and Hawk found themselves walking down what had been Highway 60, Brian and Lacey beside them. About two hundred feet ahead, Scott and Lauren trudged down the road with their dogs, headed for their own search areas.

Craig's map had shown a network of streets between Highway 60 and the ocean, and an earlier peek at Google Maps satellite view revealed houses crowding the beach, hugging the grass-topped dunes that looked out to sea. Now her line of vision was unimpeded to the pounding surf. Dozens of houses were simply gone, washed away as if they'd never been.

If anyone had still been in them, there was no helping them now.

"How did the rest of your morning go?" Brian's words lifted Meg from her contemplation. "The last time I texted you, you sounded pretty discouraged." He glanced down at Lacey trotting at his side. "Lacey sure was. She started gnawing at her paw after we found the fifth or sixth deceased victim."

"Poor girl." Meg ran her fingers over Lacey's back, earning her a quick, ear-perked look from the dog. "These kinds of searches are so hard on them. We had a terrible start to the morning, but got lucky later on. There was a family trapped in their two-story house with the water nearly to the roof. Dad drowned downstairs trying to keep the water out, but Mom, her newborn baby, and two other kids made it up to the attic. Then Mom threw a postpartum clot and stroked out, leaving the care of all four of them in the hands of her ten-year-old son. Not knowing what else to do, he stood at their attic window bellowing for help. I couldn't hear him, but Hawk could. Launched himself out of the boat because we weren't going fast enough and swam right to the window where the boy stood in waist-high water. We got them all out."

"Did Mom make it?"

Meg nodded. "We can thank Todd for that. I got him on his cell and told him the symptoms. He confirmed it was an ischemic stroke and told us what we needed to do for her and what meds she needed immediately to save her life. We called in a Coast Guard chopper with a medical team and they got her into the chopper and had meds flowing before they even had everybody off the roof. Then they airlifted the whole family right to the hospital. Her chances for a full recovery look pretty good, thanks to Hawk and Todd. Even another hour or two would have changed her life forever, or ended it."

"A full recovery is crucial now that she's lost her husband. Those three kids are going to need their mother more than ever. Hey, I think this is where we split up." He pulled out his phone and checked the map on the screen. "Lacey and I will leave you guys here. Good searching."

"You too. Be safe."

"Always." He tossed her a saucy grin as he and Lacey continued down the road.

For a few seconds, she watched them go. Then she turned to study the remnants of the once-charming row of houses to her left. Highway 60's divided roadway had created a small buffer zone against the punch of the storm. While many of the houses lining the coast had collapsed, been shredded to bits carried off by the wind, or simply washed out to sea, the structures on this side of the highway were still standing, even though they were piled high with debris and studded with overturned and stacked vehicles.

Meg studied the mass of slivered wood, shattered glass, and tangled metal and wondered where to start.

The dog running that part of the show shifted at her feet. Dressed once again in his vest and boots to protect his vulnerable paws, but this time off the leash and heeling at her knee, Hawk was recharged after the short break, several drinks of water, and some high-energy treats. "You ready to go, boy?"

Hawk looked up at her, eyes bright and tail wagging enthusiastically. *Let's go!*

"Okay, Hawk, find them."

Hawk instantly put his nose into the air, searching for scent, and trotted in the direction of the nearest collapsed house.

A low, insistent buzz crept slowly into Meg's consciousness. Involuntarily, her heart rate spiked and her gaze swung upward, quickly finding the small, dark silhouette streaking through the sky. She forced herself to calm down, pushing against the involuntary jolt. *Not carrying a bomb. Here to save, not kill.* But part of her kept one ear on the craft, tracking it as it flew overhead and past. The scars from their case last May were still too fresh.

Hawk made quick work of the first several structures, searching through and over debris, but with no sign of victims, living or dead. Meg sincerely hoped that everyone in this vulnerable area was smart enough to have fled when they had the chance. She could only imagine what it had been like here last night, totally exposed, one-hundred-mile-per-hour winds and a wall of water twice the height of most of these houses crashing over the area. These houses had been built to withstand a rugged nor'easter, but none had been built to withstand last night's challenges.

The fourth house they approached was on the corner of one of Highway 60's cross streets, although now it appeared more like a sand-covered creek bed. This open conduit had allowed the storm surge to charge up the street from the beach. While the mammoth wave would have been spreading out and losing height at that point, it had momentum on its side and had sliced into the house like a chef's knife, cutting away a huge swath of the lower floor on the street side, along with a smaller piece of the second floor. This left most of the upper story of the house hanging in midair, held in place by only a few shaky bits of crossbeam and a smattering of roof trusses.

The moment Hawk got near the structure, his posture

changed. His tail went up, waving excitedly from side to side, and his whole body took on an air of alertness that spoke of possibilities.

"Do you have something, Hawk?"

Her dog glanced back over his shoulder, the gleam in his eye answering her question.

"Good boy!" Meg kept every ounce of positivity in her voice, but she eyed the house with skepticism. It did not look stable, and the last thing Craig needed was to tie up a team that got into trouble, taking up the fire department's precious time digging out a rescuer and her dog. She pulled out her satellite phone and called Craig. "Craig, we found something. Hawk is giving strong indications, but it's not a good situation."

"Where are you?" Craig asked.

"Corner of what was Highway 60 and 43rd Street. Two-story cedar shake Craftsman-style home. The storm surge hit it and took out half of the first floor. Most of the second floor is hanging in place, but I'm not confident about the stability of the house. How fast could we get a fire team here?"

"Let me call you back." Craig ended the call without a goodbye. He called back less than a minute later. "They're saying forty-five minutes to an hour."

Meg studied the house. As if feeling the weight of her gaze, the structure creaked ominously. "I don't think we have that long. Let me check it out. Maybe just have Brian on alert in case I run into trouble."

"Meg, do *not* get into a situation you can't handle. You have a tendency to sometimes bite off more than you can chew."

"No, I have a tendency to bite off exactly what I can manage. I won't take any unnecessary chances and I'll let you know the status. Meg out." She ended the call and then spent five seconds glaring at the phone in her hand as if it were Craig's face. Then she rolled her shoulders and stuffed the irritation away. Craig meant well and always had his teams' best interests at heart. Sure, his command had bumped up against her stubbornness a few times, leading to a suspension in a previous case when she defied one of his orders, risking her life and Hawk's to save a victim. But when push came to shove, he would always be in her corner if she ran into trouble.

"Let's try not to jam him into that position," she muttered to her dog.

Hawk gazed up at her, and Meg could have sworn he had both brows raised as if to say *Yes, let's . . .*

"Okay, smarty pants, let's get this search going. Find them, Hawk, but slow. Slow."

Hawk put his nose back into the air with the familiar sound of his breathing when he was in odor. Not the longer, deeper inhalations of regular breathing, but a noisier series of short inhalations and exhalations that directed air up into his olfactory recess instead of down into his lungs. It was how dogs were able to detect scents that would need to be up to 100,000 times stronger for any human to smell. It's how Hawk could find anyone in the area. In Meg's experience, his nose was never wrong; the victim might not be alive or even in one piece, but there was always a victim. Eyeing his body language, she was reassured that he sensed something. Someone.

Hawk picked his way carefully through the flotsam that had built up in the yard and even into the footprint of the house under the unsupported second floor—concrete cinder blocks tossed about as if by a giant hand, sheets of corrugated metal, branches with spearlike points, filthy tufts of pink insulation, and sheets of shingles, still nailed to the wood sheathing originally covering roof joists. He moved confidently but set his feet down carefully and with considerably more grace than Meg felt clambering after him

while loaded down with her SAR—search-and-rescue—
pack. Once again, four paws and a low center of gravity
were an advantage.

He moved directly toward the missing section of the
house. Beyond the missing walls, open doorways led into
the rest of the house. There was no basement; Meg knew
from her years living in Virginia that some areas didn't
have basements due to high water tables and coastal living. That suited her just fine since it was one less hazard to
manage.

"Hawk, stop."

Hawk immediately stopped and held in place just outside the corner boundary of the house, but Meg could see
his impatience in the way he nearly vibrated with pent-up
excitement. The game was afoot as far as he was concerned.
Her concern was the structural stability of the house. Now
closer, she examined it thoroughly. She was no engineer
and probably wouldn't be able to recognize a load-bearing
wall from twenty paces, but she needed to be as sure as she
could. She and Hawk were not going to be in the building
when it collapsed.

Inside the house, the inner wall, now wiped clean of any
adornment, held a doorway opening to a center staircase
beyond. Overhead, she could see the exposed joists of the
subfloor, and, at the ragged edge of the far side of the upper
story, broken ceramic tiles dangled on the remains of steel
mesh and scratch-coat mortar near what must have been
originally a sink or shower, but now was merely jutting
pipes.

"If there's an iron tub up there, risk of collapse is high,"
she told her dog. She turned her gaze to the lower floor.
The foyer inside the doorway seemed intact. No more time
to waste. "Hawk, find them."

With one last appraising glance at the ceiling above,
Meg followed her dog across the debris. He nimbly made

the two-foot jump up to the doorway while she scrambled up after him. Once inside the foyer, she took a moment, letting her eyes acclimate to the lack of light. Inside the hall, it looked like a cyclone had swept through and a mix of bedroom belongings—clothing, stuffed animals, and books—mingled with lamps, end tables, and shattered family photos. Water pooled in corners and dripped from the upper floor down the stairwell in a rhythmic patter.

"Okay, Hawk, where are they? Find them."

Hawk was already nosing through the debris inside the house, his nose working furiously. He looked up the master staircase—a place they were well familiar with as being a place for pooling scent to funnel down from above—hesitated for only a fraction of a second and then bolted up the stairs, Meg already primed to dash after him.

"Hawk, slow." The dog immediately slowed to a walk. "I know, buddy, but we have to be careful. This house is in bad shape. Now, find them. I'm right behind you."

Hawk came to the top of the stairs and Meg swallowed a curse as he immediately turned left toward the light. Toward the part of the house with little support. "Of course," she muttered darkly.

The doorways leading off the upper hall to her right all led to jumbled bedrooms. To her left, one open doorway showed a bedroom at the front of the house, a dresser still against the stairway wall, but drawers hung drunkenly or had crashed to the floor. Other pieces of furniture were all gone, swept away by the rushing water. Hawk ignored that room, instead sitting down in the open doorway of the bathroom, his classic alert.

At least one person was in there. But alive or dead?

Meg moved to stand in the doorway and did a quick scan of an apparently deserted room. Small mercy—if there had been a tub, it had been down at the far end and was gone now. A battered toilet missing its lid and the top of the tank teetered at the edge of the abyss next to a sink set over cabinet doors. Shattered wood and shards of mirror gathered in the sink and Meg could see the holes in the wall over the sink where a mirror had once been mounted. Opposite the sink was a double-doored linen cabinet. "FBI search-and-rescue. Is anyone here?"

Silence.

Meg's stomach knotted. *Not another dead victim.* She turned to her dog. "Hawk, find them. Show me."

Hawk, surprisingly, paused, as if unwilling to go farther. *Alerting at the doorway. Stopping now.* What could he sense that she couldn't? At that moment, the house groaned. Meg's gaze snapped to her dog, who was staring intently at the floor. Could he hear something beyond her range? Or sense micro vibrations not detected through her steel-toed boots?

Time to try a different tack. "Hawk, sit."

He sat and looked up at her.

"Stay. Now show me, Hawk. Stay, but find them." His head swiveled to the linen closet. "Good boy. Now stay." She accompanied the command with a hand motion as reinforcement.

She took a single step into the bathroom, paused, then took a second. Nothing. She let out the breath she'd been holding and took a third. Only two more feet to the cabinet. Her gaze flicked to the open end of the bathroom only three or four feet past the cabinet. Ragged walls opened up to late afternoon sunlight and rooftops. Her stomach clutched reflexively and Meg cursed her fear of heights for rearing its ugly head.

Get a grip. It's only two stories up. A toddler wouldn't think anything of it.

Another step.

The house shuddered around her, the wood straining with a shriek, and Meg froze.

Two stories is going to hurt like hell when you land.

She glanced back at Hawk. He was on his feet now, but hadn't moved from where he'd been told to stay. "Good boy, Hawk. *Stay.*"

Keep going.

One more careful step with the most cautious resettling of her weight and she was in front of the cabinet. She grasped one of the two round doorknobs and pulled, but the door didn't budge. She studied the top of the door frame, which seemed like it was at an odd angle, jamming the door into place. "Damn it, the house is tilted and the framing is off." She tried the second door, but it was no better.

This was going to take brute force. Hooking her free hand over the lip of the sink for extra leverage, she gripped the door handle as hard as she could.

One yank.

Two.

Nothing.

She gritted her teeth and pulled with all her might. With a scream of wood tearing against wood the door popped free and Meg flew back against the countertop. Under her feet, the floor jerked, dropping an inch or two, then vibrating back to stillness.

Meg let out a shaky breath and then opened her eyes. Then she forgot all about the house. "Oh my God."

A man lay in the bottom of the linen closet, curled into a ball around a belly wet with blood. Mindless of structural collapse, Meg dropped to her knees in front of him. "Sir? Sir!" She gave his shoulder a rough shake and was rewarded by fluttering eyelashes. *Still with us.* She gently pulled his arm away from his belly and tried not to gasp in shock—a four-inch-long, triangular shard of mirror protruded from his abdomen. God only knew how much was buried inside.

It was a miracle he hadn't bled out yet. The knifelike shard must not have hit anything vital, but even smaller vessels could leak enough blood to cause death.

She fumbled for her satellite phone and dialed Craig, talking as soon as he picked up. "I need help. I have a single male, approximately forty. He's taken a shard of mirror to the gut and he's bleeding out. I need paramedics stat."

"I'll get you what I can, Jennings, but they told me forty-five minutes."

"I'm not sure he'll last that long. He's—" She let out a shriek as the sound of tearing wood screamed around her.

"Meg! You there?"

"I'm here. Craig, remember how I said the second floor was suspended with almost no support. That's where we are. I think I'm going to have to move him."

"You can't do that. You'll slice his guts."

"If we fall, it could sever his aorta and then he'll last only seconds. Call for paramedics. And can you get me Brian? I may need help until first responders arrive, and he's closest."

"Yes. Hang tight." The line went dead.

Meg bent back over the man. "Sir? Can you hear me?"

"Yes." The word was croaked from dry lips.

"Hold on, I have some water." She carefully slithered out of her pack and pulled a fresh bottle of water from it. Uncapping it, she crouched down and set the bottle against his lips, tipping it gently. He took a few sips, but as much drizzled down his cheek as into his mouth. "Can you tell me your name?"

"James . . . Carpenter."

"James, have you been in here since the storm?"

"Thought I could ride it out. Didn't think it would be this bad. Didn't want looters to rob us blind. Sent my wife and kids away. Stayed."

"Help is coming, but I'm worried you've lost a lot of blood. How were you injured?"

"House was flooding. Had to get to the second floor. Winds were terrifying. Hid in the bathroom. Thought it might be the most stable place. All that extra tiling and plumbing. Then part of the house ripped right off. Mirror ripped off the wall, glass in the air everywhere." He had to stop and take a breath to gather himself. "I took a piece in the gut. Didn't want to pull it out. Worried it would bleed worse."

"That was a good decision."

"Crawled into the closet. Thought I'd be safe here with the door closed. Nothing else could hit me. Then I couldn't open the door. No cell phone. Thought I'd die here."

"Not if I have anything to do with it. I—" She stopped. Was that her name being called?

"MEG!"

Brian.

"James, hold on a minute. Don't move, I'll be back, I promise." She planted her feet and rose slowly to a standing position. But the moment she tried to shift her weight, the floor shifted beneath her and she sank back down. "On second thought, I'll stay here. My colleague is outside." She turned to face the open end of the bathroom. "Brian!"

"Meg! Where are you?"

"Inside, second floor. Bathroom at the top of the stairs. Are you looking at the open end of the house?"

"Yes."

"Second floor. That's the bathroom, that's where I am."

"Jesus, Meg. Get out of there. It could go at any moment."

"Brian, I would love to, but I'm here with Mr. Carpenter and he's not up to leaving right now. Perhaps you could come up?" She knew he'd read the formality in her words and tone as *Can't leave, get your ass up here and help!*

"Roger that."

Meg turned back to James. "Help is coming. Hang on."

She heard Brian's boots pounding up the stairs and then he was in the doorway, Lacey at his heels. "Stop. Don't come any farther. I'm concerned about structural stability."

"No kidding." Brian took in the room in a quick study. "What do you need?"

"Mr. Carpenter has taken a piece of shattered mirror to the abdomen and blood loss is an issue." She kept her voice calm and reasonable, knowing that would help keep James from panicking. "Normally I wouldn't want to move him until paramedics arrive, but I'm concerned we may lose this section of the house. I think we need to move him. *Carefully.*"

"Using what? Recommendations?"

"Normally, I'd suggest something solid, like a door, but I'm hesitant to add any more weight in here. What about something light, like material. Curtain, quilt, sheet. Something we can get him onto and then drag?"

"Done. Lacey, stay." Brian whirled and disappeared into a room on the other side of the stairs.

Meg laid a comforting hand onto James's leg. "Do you think you can move? We need to do our best not to shift that piece of mirror."

His voice was getting weaker, but it was still backed by steel. "I got in here, I can get out."

"Good man."

Brian ran back into the doorway. "Hey, what about this?" His arms were full of bedding. "I thought maybe a top sheet to wrap around him, to pack the mirror into place. And then the quilt to drag him."

"Excellent. Toss them here. Sheet first."

Brian's lob landed the sheet squarely in her arms and she grinned her thanks. Slowly and with infinite care, she wound the sheet around his torso, silently concerned about how fast the material turned dark with blood. She tied it off as tight as she could manage, hoping it would give stability as well as enough pressure to stanch the blood.

"Okay, quilt next." The quilt unraveled as it flew through the air, but Meg caught a corner and pulled it toward her. With Brian's help, she flipped it out flat on the floor. "Okay, James, I wouldn't ask this of you if I didn't think it was crucial, but we're going to need to move you now. You have to help us because otherwise we'll hurt you more. We need to get you onto the quilt, then we'll take it from there. Can you do it?"

James nodded. Then, a tiny bit at a time, he started to inch out of the closet, sliding his body along the floor. Every so often, a groan of absolute agony slipped from between his clenched teeth and he'd have to stop, panting to catch his breath.

"Doing great. You're halfway there." Meg glanced at Brian. "I'm going to move backward so he can get into place."

"Wait, isn't that—"

Meg talked right over him. "Once he's in place, carefully start pulling him. When he's inside the hallway, there should be enough stability to leave him there until the paramedics arrive."

Lips tight, Brian gave a curt nod. Just because it was their only option didn't mean he had to like it.

Meg inched backward another foot, the floor groaning and trembling under her weight. They didn't have long now. The floor was going to give way soon. Minutes might be all they had.

It took those minutes to get James onto the quilt. Brian

quietly ordered the dogs on either side of him, then gave the command to pull. Together, Brian, Hawk, and Lacey pulled the quilt with the supine man slowly and steadily over the floor. James groaned when they rolled him over the odd piece of debris, but there was no other way, so they kept going. Meg didn't dare move until James was free of the collapsing floor.

Finally, he was through the doorway, and Meg could hear Brian praising him and telling him that paramedics would be there shortly. Then he and the dogs were back in the doorway.

"Now you," Brian said. "Get up slowly, then it's only about four steps."

"Easier said than done. Here, take this first." Meg tossed Brian her SAR pack.

He caught it and set it down in the corridor. Then he hooked his hand over the edge of the door frame, made sure his feet were safely planted in the hallway, and then leaned out to her, right hand extended. "Come on."

"Brian, if it—"

"Nope." He ruthlessly cut her off. "Not happening. We can do this."

Meg sucked in a deep breath and then slowly started to rise to her feet. She could feel the oncoming collapse the moment her weight shifted; it started as a terrifying vibration that built into a scream of shattering wood and drywall. The floor started to give way under her feet as the roof trusses above finally lost their fight with gravity.

Every ounce of fear Brian felt shone in his eyes. "No time! Jump!"

Meg put everything she had into pushing off with her still bent legs, launching herself toward Brian even as the room tilted around her, the floor and ceiling becoming vertical walls as the structure crashed to the ground. Meg kept her eyes locked on Brian's hand. There was life. Scraps of debris rained down on her as she hung suspended for a moment and then her hand slapped against Brian's wrist as her body crashed against what was left of the hallway wall, her body spinning free in open air. Tearing agony ripped through her right shoulder and she couldn't hold back a scream.

"I've got you." The words ground from between Brian's gritted teeth as he held on for dear life to both the door frame and Meg's flailing body.

Meg scrabbled with her free hand, trying to catch ahold of anything, her fingers reaching to grip the edge of the doorway, but slipping off as her body rotated away. Then her arm was caught in a viselike grip and she dangled from both arms, the pain in her shoulder dulling slightly as her body slowly rocked to a halt. Looking up, she met Hawk's eyes above bared teeth where they clamped onto her sleeve.

"Good boy, Hawk," Brian wheezed. "Now *pull!*"

Together they hauled her up, dragging her body upward until they could yank her into the hallway, falling to the floor in a tangled pile with her.

Hawk jumped on her, licking her face ecstatically. "It's okay, boy, I'm okay. And you're amazing." She looked over to where Brian pulled himself up to slump against the stairwell railing. "Thank you."

"Hey, anytime." The words puffed out between panting breaths. "But if the spirit moves you, you can always return the favor in the form of a bottle of wine."

Meg chuckled. "I can get you to do anything for a nice bottle of wine."

Meg pushed to her hands and knees and then shifted back to sit on her haunches. She rotated her shoulder, rubbing it with her left hand as the pain eased. She'd be okay, but for a moment, she thought she'd dislocated it again, now only a few months healed from the last time she took down a killer.

She looked over at their victim, lying still on the quilt, but with open and alert eyes. In the distance, a siren sounded. Craig had come through for them.

They would beat death again today.

CHAPTER 7

Debrief: A period of time when rescuers rest, share information, and plan future operations.

Saturday, July 22, 8:57 PM
Williams Farm Recreation Center
Virginia Beach, Virginia

Meg stopped in the doorway of the gymnasium, taking in the noise and chaos inside the packed room. Families were crowded together in groups, some parents clutching their children, terrified to let go, some watching from a distance as their sons and daughters played with their new best friends, children they'd met only minutes before. Pets were scattered through the gymnasium, cats in carriers, and dogs in crates or on leashes. Long lines of beds were set up against the far wall, made up with blankets and pillows, many already claimed by children overwhelmed by stress and exhaustion. A number of people milled around a food station at the other end of the room with snacks and drinks.

"Please keep your dog on his leash."

Meg pulled her gaze from the room at the sound of a female voice. Just inside the door, an older woman in a white T-shirt stood holding a clipboard.

"Sorry?" Meg asked.

"Please keep your dog on his leash. We have a lot of animals with us and not all of them are trained and we don't want any fight—" The woman cut off as Hawk stepped forward a pace from beside Meg, revealing his work vest with FBI splashed in capital letters over navy blue. "Oh. I guess I don't need to give you any advice." A smile curved her lips and she squatted down to get on Hawk's level. He enthusiastically wagged his tail at her attention. "Hi, you. You're a pretty boy. Girl?"

"Boy. His name is Hawk. We're search-and-rescue."

The woman slowly pushed to her feet. "You've had a day then, haven't you? Successful?" Her guarded eyes spoke of experience and lives lost.

"We rescued a number of live victims." Meg left it at that, leaving the dead to memory, not out of disrespect, but a need to manage the grief so she'd be fit to start it all again tomorrow.

"God bless you both." The volunteer extended the clipboard. "Would you mind signing in? It's not really needed for search teams and first responders, but we track the family members seeking shelter in case anyone is looking for them, so it's only fair to record everyone."

"No problem." Meg juggled her bags enough to free a hand and jotted down her name along with the date and her time of arrival.

"There are a few more of you down there." The woman pointed to a cluster of people at the far end of the room. "We kept a corner clear for out-of-town responders, figuring you'd need to get together to compare notes and prep for tomorrow. If you need medical attention, we have doctors and nurses on hand to take care of any concerns, and we have a temporary pharmacy set up for basic prescription needs. We served dinner a few hours ago, but are keeping what's left over hot, for our late arrivals. It's just down the hall, so please help yourself. We also have some dog food available."

"Thank you, that's very generous, but I packed for Hawk. We'll leave your food for the other dogs here who need it." Meg summoned Hawk, who heeled obediently at her side as she crossed the gymnasium, totally ignoring the shrieks of children, and barely blinking at the large red rubber ball that bounced across his path.

Meg spotted Lauren first and waved in greeting. Rocco recognized Hawk and barked happily. Meg smiled as Lauren rolled her eyes and laid a hand on Rocco's head, quieting him. Brian, Scott, and Craig looked up from conversation as Meg approached. Meg lifted a brown paper bag held in one hand.

Brian's gaze locked on the bag, instantly sizing it up. "You didn't."

"You deserve it in spades today. So, yes. I certainly did."

"How? Where? It's not like you could make a run to the corner store."

"After we got James off to the hospital with the paramedics and split up for the last of our searches for the day, Hawk and I ran into some guy who'd gone back to his house to find his cat. The whole family had left, as ordered, but the cat was spooked and went into hiding and they had to abandon her or risk getting caught by the storm. He said his entire family was a wreck over this cat, so he ignored the existing evac order to come back and search once he thought it was safe. Hawk found the cat, wet and miserable but alive, on top of a wardrobe on the second floor where it must have managed to stay mostly dry until the water receded. The man was beyond grateful to get his cat back. Said it would make him a hero in the eyes of his wife and kids, but personally, I think he's just as attached as they are. Apparently, he's a wine aficionado. He insisted I take one of his best bottles as a thank-you."

"I'll drink to that!" Brian caught her up in a hug, bags and all, trapping her full arms against her body. "You're a miracle. Thank God we're off the clock tonight." He pulled back but kept his hands on her shoulders. "You okay?"

"We've had better days, but we've also had worse." She searched his face, looking for signs of strain or pain from an injury. "How about you? You didn't hurt yourself saving me today, did you?"

"No, I'm fine. It's been a hell of a day, but at the end of it I got five minutes with Ryan on the phone." Brian's husband was a Smithsonian archivist back home in D.C. "That helped."

"I'm sure he was also relieved to hear from you."

"Yeah, he worries too much when I'm out on a rescue like this."

"Not unfounded worry, as today proved. Now, go find us some cups. We've only got one bottle, so we're going to all get about two tablespoons. Totally worth it though."

"You got that right." Brian looked over her shoulder and dropped his hands. "And now we have to split it one more way." At her look of confusion, Brian clarified. "Your sexy firefighter just walked in. He looks like he's probably also had a day that deserves alcohol."

"Sexy, huh?"

Brian flashed her a killer grin. "I'm happily married, not dead. I can still recognize his obvious assets. And don't you dare tell him that."

Meg thrust the wine bottle into his hands, and used her now free hand to mime zipping and locking her lips and then tossing the key over her shoulder. She turned to find Webb striding toward her. He looked exhausted, but gave her a smile that spoke of a successful day.

"Hi."

"Hi. Thanks again for your help with that young mother

earlier today. I didn't want to bother you because you were busy, but I knew you could help in a matter of minutes."

"It was no bother. There's always time to save another life. How's she doing?"

"I'll ask Craig to get us an update, but the paramedics were dosing her with tPA before they were on their way, and were confident she'd make a full recovery."

"Good. Here, let me help you with that." He lifted the bags from her arms. His brows snapped together when she winced and swallowed a small grunt of pain when her wrist caught in a strap, giving her right arm a small tug. "You're hurt?"

"Stand down, Mr. Paramedic. I may have tweaked my shoulder a bit, but it's okay."

His gaze dropped to her shoulder as she gave it a subtle roll. "What happened?"

"Short version, it was me and Brian in a house that partially collapsed while we were still inside. The floor dropped out from under my feet but he caught me, holding on to me by one hand. Shoulder got a bit strained but otherwise it's okay." She met his concerned eyes. "Really. If you want to take a look at it later, that's fine, but if I had concerns I'd tell you. I know I need to be at one hundred percent for tomorrow."

"I will look at it later. And I've got some anti-inflammatories you should take. Just to make sure you're in top shape."

"Works for me." She studied his face, taking in the smudges under his eyes and the fine lines radiating from the corners. "You look exhausted."

"It was a very physical day. No elevators, so we carried patients down the stairs, practically in the dark. It was . . . a challenge."

"Did everyone make it?"

One side of his mouth tipped up, answering her question. "Every one of them. Things were a little touch and go for a while. We had to stop mid-transfer to bring a couple of patients back. The worst was a preemie who went into cardiac arrest and I had to do CPR." He mimed wrapping his fingers around a tiny torso and doing minute compressions with his two thumbs. "Worked though, and we got him back. Twenty-eight weeks and scrappy as hell." He grinned, and the exhaustion melted from his face. "I have a good feeling about him. Some preemies, it's like the body is there, but the spirit hasn't arrived yet. They're passive. He's already a fighter. He's going to make it."

"That calls for wine!"

Meg and Webb turned to find Brian beside them, holding a stack of disposable paper cups in one hand and the open bottle in the other.

"Wine?" Webb asked.

"I . . . um . . . received some as a gift today as a thank-you." Brian's gaze shifted briefly toward Meg. "We're all going to share it. I'll be your sommelier this evening."

"I'm more of a beer guy myself, but this isn't the time to be picky." He pinned Meg with a stern look. "You shouldn't be drinking and taking anti-inflammatories."

"Don't worry, I'll likely only get about four sips' worth by the time we all split that bottle."

"In that case, bottoms up." Webb hoisted the bags a little higher. "Where are we?"

"Over here." Brian led the way over to the rest of the group.

Webb set Meg's bags down against the wall and then the next few minutes were spent in greetings. Brian poured and passed out cups of red wine, making a comical sad-clown face when his glass, the final one, took the last drops from the upended bottle.

Meg tapped the rim of her glass against his. "No complaining. You wanted wine, I got you wine."

"Sister, you can get me wine anytime!" He sipped from his cup. "Wow, this guy *is* an aficionado. This is spectacular. I'm sure it would be better with some breathing time and in a proper goblet, but, somehow, today, it's perfect anyway."

"I couldn't agree more." Meg stifled a yawn behind one hand. "It's going to be the perfect nightcap before I lose consciousness."

"You guys have worked damned hard today, and I'm sure you're beat." Craig paused and took a sip of his wine. "Just a quick update then before you hit the rack. We've been requested in Norfolk and Portsmouth tomorrow. Because of the combination of large areas of low-lying land, the Hampton Roads harbor, and the Nansemond, Elizabeth, and Lafayette Rivers all running through town, flooding from the storm surge has been significant. Add in a city of two hundred and fifty thousand, the largest navy base in the world, and one of NATO's strategic command centers, and there may be some unique challenges and possibly security-clearance questions. I'll have more detailed orders first thing in the morning when local organizers draw up new search plans based on today's searches." Craig looked over his shoulder. "I know this won't be the most peaceful place to bed down for the night, but we don't have many options. The locals are doing the best they can."

"It's more than enough," Scott said, his gaze fixed over Craig's shoulder at the milling crowd beyond. "They have lots to worry about and too many displaced and traumatized people to take care of. We can manage ourselves." He glanced over at the rows of cots. "Can we just bed down anywhere?"

"That's what we were told. The volunteer who signed us in told me that if we wanted to move some of the cots over here for a little privacy, they'd be fine with that."

"I brought camping equipment," Webb said. "I'll bed down there and save the space for families that need it. People are still arriving, so who knows how many they'll have by lights-out."

"Your equipment is all still out in my SUV," Meg said. "Let me give you a hand with it."

They managed in a single trip to bring in the gear, but by the time they were done, the others had lined up cots at the end of the room, leaving a clear space for them at the end.

Brian flagged them down as they came closer. "I . . . uh . . . didn't know how many cots we'd need. Do we need one for you?" he asked Meg.

Meg sized up the bags Webb balanced. "Do I need one?"

"Double air mattress. Probably more comfortable than one of those portable cots. Lots of room if you'd care to join me." One eyebrow arched in invitation.

Meg turned to Brian. "Looks like I have an offer I can't refuse."

"Good choice." Brian cocked his head toward the empty space. "Let me give you a hand setting up."

"Appreciate it. I have to admit I'm pretty bushed at this point. We've been up since two thirty."

"Us too. I think it will be an early night all around." Brian took one of the bags and led the way across the floor.

Meg's cell phone rang and she glanced at the screen. "It's Mom and Dad. I'll be with you in a minute." She answered the call, trailing slowly after the men. "Hi, how are you guys?"

"Hi, honey." Jake Jennings's affectionate voice came down the line with the slightly tinny sound that told her he had the call on speaker. "Your mom is here with me. We're tired and we've had some discouraging moments today, but I bet you've had the same experience."

Meg dropped onto the edge of one of the cots while Brian and Webb unfolded a large air mattress. She didn't try to hide any of the pain of the day; she was safe with her parents and the friends around her. "Yeah, it's been pretty bleak at times. A lot of people missing. A lot of people dead. Unspeakable destruction. But even with all that . . . hope."

"You saved lives today?"

"More than I'd have thought." She gave them a quick recap of a couple of their recoveries. "You would have been proud of us. Hawk even tracked down a family's lost cat who was hiding in their house and survived the storm. It's a little thing—"

"It's an important thing, as you well know." Meg's mother, Eda Jennings, cut her off. "Possessions can be replaced, but family can't and pets are family."

"This one sure was. By now that cat is safely back with her family and may be terrified from the experience and the changes, but she'll be okay and so will they, because they're together. How about you guys? And *where* are you?"

"We're at the Chesapeake Animal Rescue," Jake said. "It's far enough inland that it only took some external damage, so it's got lights and water and we've been able to house every animal brought in. Right now we're working with microchip registries, trying to reach families who had their pets chipped. We've reunited quite a few recovered animals but have a lot more where we can't reach anyone, and even more that aren't chipped."

"What about wildlife?"

"We have our fair share of that too. That's where we'll likely step in. They want to keep the domestic pets close in case anyone claims them in the next few weeks, but they have a few animals they've asked us to take back to the rescue, including a mother and a litter of endangered Southeastern shrews, a Belted Kingfisher with a broken wing, a pig with an injured shoulder, and a wood turtle with a badly damaged shell. There will likely be more. Your mother and I will be hauling everything back to the rescue in a few days once things lighten up here. Anyway, we're going to let you go because I can hear how tired you are and you need to get some rest. And we need to call Cara and let her know we're okay."

"Could you tell her I'm okay too? I haven't had a chance to touch base with her yet. It was on my list of things to do tonight, but if you're already calling . . ."

"We'll take care of it." It was Eda this time. "When you get clear of this assignment, you give us a call. We want to hear more about your searches, but not now while they're still fresh. And not when you have to turn around and do it all again tomorrow."

It never failed to amaze Meg how much her parents understood her. "Appreciate that. I'll talk to you soon."

"Yes, you will. Stay safe, Meg, and take care of our boy," Eda said.

Meg's gaze dropped to Hawk, where he and Lacey pushed in between Webb and Brian, curious about what they were doing. "I will. Good night, Mom. Good night, Dad."

"Good night, honey," said her father. "Sleep tight and stay safe." The line went dead.

Meg sighed and let the phone drop into her lap.

Webb looked up from the floor. "Everything okay?"

She nodded. "They're worried and trying not to let it show. And they have their own hands full. Everyone is doing what they can. I think I'm just tired and need to call it a night. It's been a long day on very little sleep."

Brian pushed to his feet, looking down at the wide air

mattress and the puffy sleeping bags draped over it. "I think you'll get a good night's sleep here." He glanced at the cots. "Probably better than us. Come on Lacey, Hawk, let's go out one more time tonight and then we're calling it quits too."

"You're sure you don't mind?" Meg asked, almost afraid to protest because the thought of taking her dog outside seemed a bit much right now.

"I'm going anyway, why not take both?" He scooped up Hawk's leash from the top of Meg's bag and then went in search of Lacey's. Finding it, he ambled out with both dogs.

Webb turned to her. "Let me take a quick look at that shoulder."

"I'm telling you it's okay." But she turned so that he could probe her shoulder with quick fingers and do a few trial movements rotating her arm. "Does that hurt?"

"No. I was lucky. It could have been worse."

"Sure could have. Seems fine, but I want you to take these just to make sure you don't have any issues tomorrow when you need to depend on being full strength." He dug in a bag and pulled out a pharmacy bottle. He opened it and tapped two pills into her outstretched palm, watching as she dry swallowed them. "Why don't you go get changed into whatever you want to sleep in?" Webb extended her overnight bag. "You must want out of those clothes."

Meg looked down at her filthy search gear. "Yeah, I do. I'll be back in a few."

The community center had a pool, so it had multiple spacious changing rooms with showers. Meg was tempted to grab a quick shower, but found she simply didn't have the energy for it. She changed and brushed her teeth, and then returned to the gymnasium wearing sleep pants and a

T-shirt. The lights had been dimmed and parents were busy getting their overtired children to bed so they could find their own rest.

Meg found Webb already tucked between the sleeping bags and gratefully slipped in with him. He pulled her in, settling her against his chest. She let out a deep sigh of contentment as she finally allowed herself to let go of the day. There would be more tomorrow, but she couldn't meet it head-on if she was exhausted.

A weight settled near her feet and she cracked open one eye to find Hawk sprawled against her legs. She reached down and ran a hand over his back, smiling as she heard his overexaggerated exhalation.

Everyone was safe for now.

Sleep claimed her, quickly spinning her into the dark.

CHAPTER 8

Nose to the Ground: The method used by a tracking dog to follow a specific scent.

Sunday, July 23, 6:27 AM
I-64
Chesapeake, Virginia

Webb whistled along with the radio while he stared out the window as the countryside flashed by. When they drove away from the coast, they left the worst of the devastation behind them, so while this inland portion of the county showed the lashings of a powerful storm, it had suffered significantly less flooding. Now the eerily denuded trees gave glimpses of the white statuary of the Roosevelt Memorial Park cemetery through Webb's window.

Meg slid him a dark, sideways glance. "You seem pretty chipper."

"It's a beautiful day. I enjoyed a cozy night with a beautiful woman in my . . . uh . . . bed"—Webb playfully waggled his eyebrows at her, cheerfully exaggerating a too short interlude that involved nothing more than unconsciousness—"and I'm headed out to do some good in the world. Why not be chipper?"

Meg reached for her coffee cup, took a silent sip, and

then threw him a venomous glare. "You're a morning person, aren't you?" The words "morning person" dripped acid.

They drove onto the high-level bridge crossing the Elizabeth River. Below them, the river sparkled in the morning sunlight. Beneath the glints of light, the water held an unhealthy brown hue, saturated with unsettled silt and flood debris.

"When you're a first responder you learn to wake up at any time of the day at a moment's notice and be ready for anything," Webb said. "I'm the type who hits the ground running."

"I may have to break up with you. I'm the type who takes a full hour and three cups of coffee to be coherent enough in the morning to form actual sentences. Luckily Cara is the same, so we can stand each other in the morning. We get up and do what we have to do and only talk to the dogs."

"You seemed okay yesterday morning at three thirty."

"That's because I hadn't had enough time in bed yet. That wasn't morning. That was still night." Another sip of coffee. "I may have to kill you if you're always like this in the mornings."

"I can make coffee." His grin was full of sly enticement. "I also can make breakfast and bring it to you in bed."

She took a long, considering sip, and a few more beats of silence passed as she carefully set her cup back down in the holder. "I may keep you then. You sound . . . useful."

"In more ways than one. You just haven't had the chance yet to enjoy that aspect of—*STOP THE CAR!*"

"What?"

"Pull off the road!"

Meg didn't ask for more explanation. She simply shoulder checked rapidly and pulled off onto the emergency stopping lane that was bordered by a guardrail, braking as quickly as she dared without knocking Hawk off his feet in the back, and turned on her four-way flashers. They stopped with a jerk, wrenching forward and then back into their seats. She did a quick visual check into the back to check on Hawk. "What happened?" She looked out the passenger window but all she could see were flooded marshlands.

Webb already had his seat belt undone and his door open. "There's a van submerged in the far side of the Elizabeth River. That section of marsh we just crossed. That last twenty or thirty feet probably turned into the low-water crossing from hell during the storm surge. If someone tried to cross it while the river was peaking . . ."

"They'd have been washed away. We need to check and see if anyone survived."

"Yeah."

Meg watched the cars speeding by, the SUV shuddering with the wind draft from each one. When a break appeared, she quickly got out of the SUV and ran around the back. She popped open the hatch and grabbed her SAR pack and Hawk's leash, and then slammed the hatch shut. Hawk was already in his work vest, so when she opened the door on the passenger side to let him out, she quickly leashed him as soon as he hit the ground at her feet. "We're going to have to get across this highway."

"We'll be fast and careful. There'll also be less traffic on the roads today than usual, since it's early on a Sunday after a major storm. We can make it." He looked down at Hawk. "He'll stick with you?"

"Like glue."

Standing at the back of the SUV, they watched several cars zoom by.

Webb took her hand, gripped it tight. "There, right after the black sedan. That's our chance."

Meg looked down at her dog, but needn't have worried; his head was high and he was bright-eyed, alert, and ready for anything. "Hawk, ready, boy. Stay . . . stay . . . now, come!"

Together they sprinted across one-half of the divided highway, stopping at the far side to size up the vehicles coming from the other direction. There was more traffic driving toward the coast as first responders and volunteers arrived to start the day's search, rescue, and recovery operations. They had to wait a full ninety seconds before they could cross, but then they were on the far side, looking out at the Elizabeth River, bounded by flooded marshland on both sides.

Meg tipped a hand over her eyes, shading them from the sun's glare. "Where is it?"

He turned her head to the right and pointed over her shoulder, toward the water. "Down there, way down there. Look for the splash of white. It's mostly submerged, in that marshy area."

"I see it. It's going to be tricky to get to."

"We can do it."

"We sure can. But first . . ." Meg dug out her cell phone, checked for a signal, and speed-dialed Craig. "Craig, I'm going to be late joining you. I was on the way to drop Todd off and then get to the Norfolk meet site when he spotted a van washed away down the Elizabeth River. We have to check it out in case there are survivors, so we've pulled off the road and are going in."

"Do you need me to arrange any assistance?" Craig asked.

"Not yet. I don't want to waste resources if the van is empty and I don't know what we're looking at yet. We're at a low-water crossing that was likely a raging torrent during the storm, so there were likely occupants in the vehicle. I'll let you know."

"Keep me in the loop." Craig ended the call.

"Craig will send help if we need it." Meg looked out

through a single line of scraggly pines and out over the flooded marshlands. The normally six-foot-tall grasses were flattened and caked with mud, with many of the long stems completely submerged in the still-flooded river. Sturdier bulrushes stood at a drunken angle, their tops shredded into fluffy white puffs. "We can see the van from here, but it's going to be a tough slog through that marsh, and possibly dangerous, especially for Hawk's shorter legs. I suggest we go down the highway a bit and cut across where we can stick to solid ground as long as possible. It looks like the forest goes out partially from there, so that's our best chance for speed."

"Agreed. We won't be on solid ground the whole way, but the longer we can stay on it, the better."

They set out at a light jog down the highway, ignoring the perplexed looks of drivers as they flashed by.

"There." Meg pointed to a small break in the trees lining the highway that led into deeper forest. She loosened up on the leash and pointed. "Hawk, jump."

Hawk took the guardrail in a single leap, cleanly sailing over the metal boundary. Meg planted one hand on the sun-warmed metal and vaulted over the guardrail, Webb hurdling over behind her. They pulled up in the shade of the trees.

"Damn," Webb murmured.

It was like a tornado had spun by, sheering off treetops and dropping razor-sharp branches randomly all over the forest floor. Many small and medium-sized trees were entirely uprooted, toppling over until their progress was halted by the remaining forest. Green leaves coated the undergrowth, ripped from their branches months before autumn's color would have spiraled them to carpet the forest floor.

Meg unclipped Hawk's leash and tucked it into her pack. "Better for him to run free at this point, now that we're away from the cars. We're going to have to pick our way through here."

"Keep your eyes open, some of these trees don't look stable. A bigger one falling could be a killer."

"Agreed. Hawk, come."

They entered the forest, going deeper into the stand of trees. It was a surreal experience, being so deep inside the forest and yet being in full sunlight with little foliage to block the sun's rays. They clambered over fallen trunks and broken limbs, and circled around any tree that looked unstable, giving each a wide berth. Soon, the flash of sunlight on water grew brighter.

They broke from the trees, and there, thirty feet into the marsh, a large white cargo van lay on its side, half-submerged in the swampy water.

Meg eyed the muddy ground beneath her boots. "Let's see how close we can get with Hawk. I don't want him getting stuck in the mud. It's going to be hard enough for us."

"He's lighter than us. That will play in his favor."

"It may. Hawk, heel."

They tromped into the marshlands, pushing partly flattened grasses farther down to use the thick stems as a carpet to stay out of the mud. Still, the saturated ground sagged beneath their weight and water flooded up over their boot tops. They left depressions in their wake, each one filling with boggy water, marking their trail in a series of silvery boot prints.

The force of the river's flow had spun the van so it lay with its roof facing them, the rising sun a bright, fractured ball reflected in the half of the cracked windshield still above water. It was a white panel van with no windows on the sides, what Meg and Cara would have called a "pedo van" as teenagers.

Meg scanned their surroundings, and found a small section of flattened marsh grass that was mostly above water.

"Hawk, come here. Sit. Stay." She slipped out of her bulky pack and set it down beside him.

"We need to wade into the river at this point," Webb said. "No other way to get in."

"I know, that's why I'm leaving Hawk behind. Lord knows he swims like a fish, but we don't need his special skills here. It's safer for him to stay back. Ready?"

Webb nodded and waded into the river, headed for the front of the van and their only easily accessible window into the inside. Meg followed, her stomach knotting in anticipation of what they might find.

The river came to mid-thigh on Webb, upper thigh on Meg, and was a hard slog. The water was opaque and dense with silt, the bottom uneven and stirred into an inches-deep soft, sucking sludge. Cold water poured into Meg's boots, freezing her feet and making each step harder with the added weight.

Webb got to the van first and cupped two hands around his eyes as he leaned into the windshield. "I was afraid of that. I see someone. We need to get in there. Give me a hand for a second, then stand back."

He slipped out of his DCFEMS jacket and Meg helped him wind it over his laced hands. Then Meg took three steps back while Webb swung with all his might at the section of the windshield with the heaviest cracking. The window gave beneath the blow, the laminated glass shattering into tiny shards as the window bowed but didn't break.

Shaking his hands free of his jacket, he turned back to her. "It's not going to give easily." He slipped his jacket back on, and then linked his hands and bent toward her. "Up you go. See if you can get in through the passenger door or window."

Bracing a hand on his shoulder, she set her boot into his cupped hands and pushed upward, his strength lifting her the rest of the way to scramble onto the van.

Webb backed off a few paces, shading his eyes from the early morning sunlight. "Can you open the door?"

"Not a chance. It's bashed in from when the van rolled. But the window has a big shattered hole. It's almost big enough for me already, so I can knock it in further, enlarge it, and get in that way."

"I'm going to see if I can get the back doors open, but if they're not open by the time you're into the back of the van, then they're locked and you need to try from the inside."

"Will do." Using her boot, she kicked away the loose, pebbled shards of laminated glass. Then she sat on the passenger door and swung her feet into the empty space below. She peered in to make sure no occupants were beneath her. "Going in." Holding on to blunted edges of the window frame, she lowered herself into the gloomy interior. Instead of landing on the solid glass of the driver's window, her feet instead sunk into soft river muck. She caught her balance and got her first look around the inside.

She was standing in the lee of the front bucket seats, the steering wheel jutting into the backs of her knees. The back of the van was essentially an open space lined with long bench seats on either side. Seat belts dangled from a now suspended bench seat, except for the belt that caught the single woman who hung limp in midair, her high-heeled feet dangling inches from the water.

One look at the bloody head wound and the haze over her open eyes told Meg they were too late. They probably would have been too late if they'd come across the van when they arrived in the area yesterday morning. This woman had likely died the night before that, at the height of the storm.

She nearly missed the second person on a quick scan, but then a blurry smudge of red below the water drew her attention toward wispy ends of floating hair and she realized another victim was submerged beneath the water. She was long gone, but were there others? She needed to get the back doors open to let in more light. Carefully inching her way around the front seat headrest, she picked her way through the tumbled van, tripping over unseen obstacles in the dark water. Conscious of the submerged body, Meg hugged the roof of the van, trying to avoid stepping on any hidden victims.

Finally reaching the suspended woman, Meg realized her initial estimate was seriously off. While her face was made up to look mature, and the skintight strappy top she wore showcased her breasts, this was a girl, not a woman. Meg swore under her breath. She reached up and pressed two fingers over the pulse point in the girl's throat, but the skin was cold and waxy, and no heartbeat met her touch.

It was then that she realized that while the girl's legs dangled, her arms did not. Closer inspection revealed why—the girl's hands were restrained by cloth-covered buckles, binding her to the seat. The implication took her breath away.

Truly trapped.

Her head jerked as the rear doors rattled but didn't open. A fist pounded twice. "Can't get them open. They must be locked." Webb's voice was muffled through the metal doors.

"Hold on," she called. "Let me try."

She made her way to the back of the van and studied the single visible door. No handle; it must be below the waterline. Meg ran her flattened palm along the door, searching blindly beneath the water, and was rewarded with a lever handle. She pulled the handle and the doors shuddered as if released, but they stayed in place. "It's unlatched, but the doors are stuck," she called. "I'm going to kick them open."

The doors held through the first kick, but exploded outward with the second. Meg nearly lost her balance as momentum carried her sideways, but she caught herself on the side of the open door as light flooded into the enclosed space.

Webb caught her arm, steadying her as she straightened, then pushed up into the van to stand hunched in the enclosed space. "Any survivors?"

"No." The word shot out, clipped and biting.

Webb's head tilted slightly in question as he stared at her with assessing eyes. "We expected that. But something's got you riled. What don't I know?"

"She's a child. And she couldn't escape, because she was restrained."

"You mean belted in?"

"I mean restrained. Buckles and straps at her wrists."

The fury roaring to life in his eyes relaxed some of the rage building in her chest. She needed to remember that they weren't helpless and that good people would find justice for these victims.

Webb's gaze swept the van, taking in the suspended girl and then dropping to the water.

"She's long gone by now, but . . ." Meg carefully shuffled over toward the floating hair. It was fine and blond, and when she got closer she realized it had a streak of pink in it. Her throat constricted.

She put color in her hair for fun, and now she's dead.

Jaws clamped together, Meg thrust an arm into the water, searching for the victim. It only took seconds, and then her fingers brushed silky fabric. She closed her eyes and focused on identifying what was beneath her fingertips. A shoulder, small and delicate. Another child. Running her fingers to the left, she found the throat, so she ran them the other way, down the arm, over the bent elbow.

Her fingers touched cloth and cold metal wrapped around a child's slender wrist.

"The second victim is also a child, also restrained at the wrists. I don't know if she was injured in the rollover, but if she was conscious she couldn't release her seat belt and swim to safety. She drowned because she couldn't get away when the water level rose over her head."

Webb let out a low, furious curse.

She dug out her cell phone with her dry hand. "I have to call Craig. We can't move them. This is a crime scene."

Webb waited while she called Craig, gave their coordinates, and outlined for him exactly what they'd found and who they needed, trying to keep her voice as cool and impersonal as possible.

She hung up and tucked the phone into her pocket. "He's contacting local Norfolk PD. But he doesn't think the case will stay with them."

"Why not? Who should have it?"

"The FBI." Meg's voice was flat, but when she turned back and gazed down at the child beneath the water, her anger tugged at its reins again, struggling to break free.

"What makes it an FBI case?"

"Look at them. Take this girl." Meg inched closer to the girl suspended from the ceiling. "Tell me how old you think she is. Just be careful, and try not to touch anything because the crime scene techs will go over the van with a fine-tooth comb."

Webb moved over cautiously and then bent so he could look up into the girl's face. He didn't answer for the space of several seconds. "I'm not good at this. Maybe sixteen or seventeen?"

"You're looking at the surface. Take away the adult makeup and clothes. Now what do you see?"

Webb took his time looking again, his gaze sliding over her face and body more assessingly. "Now I see it."

"What?"

"The fact that this girl is way too young. I'll guess fourteen?"

"I'm pegging her at thirteen."

"Jesus Christ. Thirteen and in the sex trade?"

"That's how I read it. The makeup and clothes on a girl this age certainly suggest it, but the bindings say human trafficking to me. This child wasn't selling her body voluntarily. And I'm betting she didn't do the selling at all. And that makes it an FBI case. Craig read it the same way, but wants to start with the local PD to avoid stepping on toes until we have more established evidence. Like the second victim for instance. But I think she's just as young. She's even more slight than this first victim. She could just be petite, or she could be eleven or twelve."

"Christ," Webb repeated. He looked unsettled and Meg knew it wasn't the proximity to death. As a first responder, he dealt with it more often than he'd like. "That's it? No one in the front of the van that you could see?"

"A driver? No. But when I dropped in from the top of the flipped van, I didn't land on the driver's window as I expected, I landed in river sludge."

"The window was broken like it was on the passenger side?"

Meg considered for a moment, thinking back to the instant of impact. "I don't think so. I don't remember even broken glass under my feet. Maybe the driver put the window down and tried to climb out when the van got swept down the river."

"Abandoning the girls to a sure death. What a hero."

"If we're looking at someone who's trafficking children, I don't think this is someone who would save them to protect his investment. He'd see them as disposable, especially if it came down to him or them."

Webb stared down the river out the open doors of the

van. "If the conditions were bad enough to sweep the van away in the first place, there's a good chance he wouldn't have made it. They just may not have found his body yet."

"It's a possibility." Meg scanned the inside of the van. Now that she was looking more closely, she could see that amid the dangling seat belts were empty wrist restraints. In her first check she'd missed them, seeing only what she expected to see. "Being out on the road at that point was a death sentence. What were they thinking?"

"They likely weren't. They were just panicking."

"But they didn't evacuate when they had a chance."

"I don't know much about trafficking, but can we assume that this guy was holding these girls somewhere?"

Meg shrugged. "It's not my area of expertise either, but I would imagine he was."

"Considering what he was covering up, he probably thought the safest thing to do to avoid being caught or losing his 'inventory' would be to hole up and just wait out the storm. He may then have gotten to the point where he knew they were running into trouble and had to leave. But by then it was too late. Now his girls are dead. And he may be too."

"They never had a chance. Those restraints aren't hard to put on and take off, but you need a free hand to do it and—" She broke off, staring at the straps hanging from the suspended bench seat.

"And?"

"Damn it, it's been staring me in the face. Look at this." Meg grabbed one of the restraints, pulling it over for Webb to see. "It's torn."

Webb took the end of the strap in his fingertips and rubbed at the frayed end. "There's no cuff on this one."

"Maybe it snapped in the rollover, freeing one of the girls. And she got herself out."

"And maybe others?" Webb started counting seat belts. "Four spots on this side. Assuming the same on the other, there could have been up to eight passengers."

"And we can only account for two."

They looked at each other and then spoke in unison. "Hawk."

Meg turned toward the open doors and then stopped to look back over her shoulder as she considered options. "I need one of my knives from my bag."

Webb reached into one of the pockets of his cargo pants. "I've got a multi-blade utility knife on me." He extracted a Swiss Army knife from the pocket and quickly flipped out the sturdiest blade. "Will that do?"

"Yes, thanks." She struggled back over the suspended bench seat and considered the dangling restraint straps. "Sorry, crime scene techs. You're not going to like me much." Grabbing a strap near the top, she quickly sawed it off, and then reached for the next one. Soon she held all six straps at the cut end, the wrist restraints dangling free. "We use head-up air-scenting techniques if we don't have a dedicated scent to follow, but that makes things harder because Hawk could hit on anyone, not necessarily a victim. With a designated scent, we can use head-down tracking techniques to find that particular scent. Either way, if anyone really did escape, they've been gone for more than twenty-four hours, so it's going to be tough following an older scent trail made during a storm with powerful winds."

"You think if they were restrained, those cuffs will hold their scent."

She folded up the knife and handed it back to him. "It could hold the scent of a lot of girls, more than the ones who wore them most recently, but it's our best chance."

Holding the straps high to keep them out of the water, Meg jumped out of the back of the van and started slogging toward the bank. Hawk sat exactly where she'd left him, ears perked and eyes fixed unblinkingly on her. With her free hand, she dug quickly into her pack, pulling out a clean zippered bag. Opening it, she lowered the cuffs into the bag and sealed it for the moment. Reaching into her pack again, she pulled out the keys to her SUV and extended them to Webb. "I need you to stay here and wait for Norfolk PD. Chances of anyone coming along here to disturb the crime scene are close to nil, but . . ."

"They aren't zero. I'll stay."

"If we're not back by the time the cops show up and release you, take the SUV and go where you need and I'll arrange for a pickup."

Webb jammed the keys in a front pocket of his pants. "We'll make it work. Now go. Be safe."

"I will. I'll try to stay in touch when I can." She pulled out her phone and then swung her pack onto her shoulders. "I'll call Craig as we're getting started so he's in the loop." She opened the bag and extended it to Hawk, who took a long time to take the scent. "Okay, Hawk, let's go. Find them, Hawk. Find them."

Hawk put his nose into the air and took a full fifteen seconds to scent the breeze. Then he turned and started off at a trot toward the west. Meg raised a hand to Webb as she jogged after him.

In seconds, they'd disappeared into marsh grasses.

CHAPTER 9

Size up: A quick mental evaluation of the most critical factors influencing a situation, in order to decide on a course of action.

Sunday, July 23, 7:13 AM
Firman Street
Chesapeake, Virginia

To call it a street was being generous, Meg thought, as she and Hawk jogged down the country lane that was nothing more than twin ruts. But this was where Hawk wanted to go, and he called the shots.

They'd only been a short time in the marsh before breaking into forest again. Soon they'd stumbled onto a dirt track strewn with debris and where every low-lying area was waterlogged nearly to the point of impasse. That didn't stop Hawk, however, who simply detoured around every obstacle, diving into brush and then emerging back onto the track.

Meg was grateful for the early morning quiet with only a light breeze to stir the dew-laden grasses and the brush bordering the lane. But she wasn't sure that Hawk had a reliable scent at this point. She believed that this was the right direction—anything else would require crossing the highway or swimming the river—but any scent trail was likely faint at best.

If there is any scent at all. You're predicting there were other girls in the van, but you don't actually know that.

"Hawk, stop." He did immediately as commanded and stood waiting, staring up at her. Meg swore she could see confusion in his eyes. She pulled out the bag of restraints, opening it and offering it again. He dutifully sniffed it, and then wagged his tail and shifted impatiently from side to side as if to say *Let's get a move on.*

"Okay, Hawk, you're in charge and I trust you. Find them."

The dual dirt track expanded to a gravel road flanked by storm-battered houses lining the road with greater frequency. It was between two driveways that Hawk suddenly cut left to sniff at a flattened patch in the overlong grasses along the verge. He whined and pawed at the grass. As he pawed at it a second time, Meg spotted the dark splotch discoloring the undergrowth. "Hawk, back." She carefully parted the grass with both hands. It had been partially washed toward the soil, but there was no mistaking the dark red that clung to the blades.

Blood. And no small amount of it either.

Someone was badly hurt.

A flash of white caught her eye and she combed through the long grass, pulling out a buckled restraint with a frayed strap where it had once been attached in the van.

"Good boy, Hawk." She stroked his back, crooning to him softly. "She stopped here and rested. She didn't stay, but she took the time to ditch the restraint." She added it into the bag of straps to add to the scent pool inside. "Now it's more important than ever that we find her. Find her, Hawk."

They were off again.

Before long, they hit a bend in the road, but Hawk didn't

deviate from his straight path. He pushed on through back-yards, running parallel to the interstate, the whoosh of cars speeding by a constant accompaniment to the sound of their pounding feet and labored breathing. As they were passing a large school, complete with baseball diamond, tennis courts, and a football stadium, Hawk veered away from the highway, his pace picking up when he started his familiar back-and-forth weaving pattern as he identified and ran the contained edges of the scent cone. Meg looked past him, studying the school outbuildings. He'd bypassed the baseball diamond and the outbuildings entirely, but the bleachers for the football field loomed large in front of them. His pattern tightened, his side-to-side passes becoming even narrower.

Almost there.

They ran across the asphalt oval that circled the football field, lane lines and painted numbers for the runners clearly delineated. They jogged past the massive letters painted in the grass in front of the goal posts at one end of the field—CREEK—then over the painted yard lines of the football field to head straight for the larger of the two stretches of bleachers on the west side of the field. Hawk ran under the bleachers, but Meg had to duck beneath the supporting metal framework so close to the seats.

As soon as she straightened, Meg spotted the girl. She lay limp under the seats, as if she'd tried to tuck herself out of sight. Coming closer, Meg couldn't miss the catastrophic injury that had ended her flight. Her right leg lay at an unnatural angle, and when Meg knelt down in front of her, she had to bite back the gasp of shock at the sight of blood-smeared bone, exposed and protruding through the skin.

She touched the girl's cheek. Her skin was cool, but not with the coldness of death. A quick check of her carotid revealed a rapid, thready pulse. She gently rubbed the girl's cheek, talking to her, and was rewarded with a moan and fluttered eyelashes before she went still again.

She dug her phone out of her pocket, speed-dialed Craig, and started talking the moment he answered. "I found a girl and I need paramedics."

The noise that carried down the line sounded like a groan. "We're still stretched pretty thin and response times aren't good because of how far ambulances are having to travel to get to open ERs. What's her status?"

"She's shocky and has an open leg fracture. Probably suffering from exposure and dehydration if she's been here like this for over twenty-four hours."

"I'll get help to you as fast as possible. You still have Webb with you?"

"Close enough."

"Get him to stabilize her as much as he can. I'll get someone to you ASAP."

"I don't know exactly where we are, but these are my GPS coordinates." Meg then ended the call with Craig and dialed Webb. "Is Norfolk PD there?"

"Yes." She could hear men's voices in the background behind Webb's voice. "Showed up just a few minutes ago."

"Can you get away? I need you and your trauma kit."

"You found one." His words were sharp, clipped. "Where?"

"Not sure where I am. Under some bleachers at a football field behind a school. Letters in the end zone spell out *Creek*."

"Hold on." She could hear Webb's voice, muffled as if he held his hand over the phone before he came back. "Local PD says that's Deep Creek Middle School. What's going on?"

"The girl is shocky and has a compound fracture in her lower right leg. Craig's sending help, but he's worried about arrival times because services are still stretched thin. You'll get here faster than the ambulance and can at least get her stable."

"Hang on." More muffled voices, then, "One of the cops is coming with me. He'll get me there faster than using the GPS. He says we can be there in less than ten minutes."

"See you then."

It was a long ten minutes, but it gave Meg time to really examine the unconscious girl. She looked young, about the same age as the dead girl suspended in the van. She wore a tight black skirt that came down to just past crotch level, intentionally short to show a flash of cherry-red panties beneath. The blouse she wore was practically transparent, with no bra underneath. Anger flooded Meg all over again. Girls this age shouldn't have anything weightier resting on their shoulders than homework. This one had been in a struggle for her life.

But her spunk showed through. Her heavy red lipstick was smeared across her left cheek, with a matching smudge across the back of her right hand. *Tried to wipe it off on her own.* She also wore no shoes, having kicked off what were likely high heels in the attempt to escape. Her bloody and torn left foot attested to the desperation of her flight.

How did she possibly get this far on her own? She wouldn't have been able to support her own weight on that leg.

A thought struck her like the force of a slap. *What if she wasn't on her own? What if we're tracking more than one victim?*

As they waited, Meg talked to the girl quietly, even though she remained unresponsive. Hawk paced back and forth behind her, occasionally coming up to sniff at the girl's face, then continued his pacing. Soon, a siren wailed in the distance, growing louder before fading again.

Passing us on the highway, then exiting.

The siren grew louder again, coming closer from behind her, then circling around, the sound ever increasing. With a squeal of tires, a police cruiser stopped just in her field of vision outside the bleachers. Her own SUV pulled up beside it, then Webb jumped out and popped the hatch.

"I'm here!" she called. "Under the bleachers."

Webb grabbed his bulky trauma bag from the back of the SUV and ran toward her, ducking under steel support beams. She scurried out of his way as he dropped to his knees beside the girl, tugged on latex gloves, and started his assessment.

A Norfolk PD officer, wearing a navy uniform with a heavy utility belt followed more slowly. He tipped his uniform cap to Meg. "Ma'am."

A quick glance at his nameplate provided his name. "Officer Berkeley, thank you. We appreciate the help."

"Always happy to lend a hand. And who's this?" Hawk had wandered over to give his ankles a sniff.

"That's my search-and-rescue dog, Hawk. Hawk, sit." She waited while he sat. "Now say hi to Officer Berkeley."

Hawk promptly raised his right paw and looked up at the officer, his tail waving back and forth over the gravel beneath the bleachers.

Berkeley smiled and shook the dog's paw. "Well, aren't you a smart boy."

"The smartest."

"He's definitely the bright spot in my day so far." Berkeley stared at the unconscious girl. "How's she doin'?"

"She's shocky, and dehydrated," Webb said. "It's a nasty tibial break. I'll stabilize it now, as is, because this long after the injury, there will be significant swelling and they may want to image before reducing it. It's also going to need major irrigation, and possibly debridement of dead tissue. All that needs to be done in the ER. Best thing I can do for her is get her ready to move the moment the ambo gets here."

"I don't think it's possible she got all the way here from the marsh on that leg by herself," Meg said.

Webb's gaze flicked up to her quickly. "I agree. My money is that Hawk will tell you she had help. And that help dropped her off and kept going."

Meg stood and scanned the area. "Assuming it's another girl, she'd be long gone by now."

"Long gone may be relative. They may have sheltered here from the wind and driving rain for hours. And then, by the time it cleared, this one would have already been going into shock and couldn't go any farther."

"The other girl would have had to leave her here."

"That's one way it could have played out." Webb unzipped one of the many pockets of his pack and pulled out a small shrink-wrapped silver rectangle. He passed it to Meg. "Open this and shake it out. It's a space blanket. Tuck it around her, leaving that leg and her left arm uncovered."

Meg did as directed, unfolding what turned out to be a large blanket made of paper-thin silver plastic sheeting. She snapped it in the air, unfurling its full length, and then carefully tucked it around the girl. "What's next?"

"We need to get fluids into her, then I'll work on the leg." Bending over the girl, he flipped over her left arm, quickly palpated for a vein, then pulled out alcohol swabs and a wrapped, sterile IV needle. "Here, hold this." He handed Meg a clear bag of saline. "Once I get it set up, you can hold the bag over her and give it a gentle squeeze to let gravity and a little pressure get the flow going faster." He cleaned the insertion site, opened the needle, pulled the sturdy plastic cover off with his teeth, and deftly inserted it. "Bingo," he muttered under his breath around the needle cap. He tossed the needle cap and wrapper back in the bag and pulled out a short length of IV tubing. He attached the tubing to the bag, carefully cleared any air in the tube, and then connected it to the IV needle. "Okay, give the bag a gentle squeeze. Easy . . . that's it. Now, this girl needs some morphine. I don't want her coming to with no painkillers while we're wrapping and splinting that leg." He dug into the bag and pulled out a cartridge and a clear plastic syringe shell. He snapped the cartridge into the shell, made a few quick adjustments of the plunger, and then injected the entire contents into an IV port on the tubing. "That will make her more comfortable. Now, the leg. Officer Berkeley, I could use your hands."

"Just Berk will do. And anything you need, just say the word," Berkeley responded, kneeling down beside Webb.

Webb pulled supplies from his bag—a wide, folded length of stiff foam that was orange on one side and blue on the other and stamped with the logo SAM SPLINT, a roll of navy self-adhering wrap bandage, and a sterile, sealed roll of gauze. "I'm glad she's still out for this because it will hurt like hell even with the morphine. Okay, Berk, before I stabilize the leg, I want to cover this open wound. We're not going to clean it here because they'll just do it all over again in the hospital and we don't want to wash anything into the open wound when we've only got limited irrigation fluids. Better to let the ER docs do the real job. We'll cover it to keep anything else out. Here." He pulled out another pair of gloves and passed them over to the officer. "Put these on. Risk of blood-borne viruses may be higher in this girl than in other vics her age."

Webb waited while Berkeley donned the gloves, and then showed him where he wanted him to put his hands. "We need to lift the leg just enough that I can get the gauze under it to wrap it. Put your hands here, and here, under her leg but on either side of the break to stabilize while you lift. It will only need to be for about thirty seconds, but you need to hold steady during that time. Up for it?"

"You bet." Berkeley slid his hands under the leg. "You say when."

"Just about there." Webb unfolded the stiff foam until it was about three feet long and five inches wide. He quickly bent it into a trough with a slightly wider scoop at one end. He caught Berkeley's curious look and said, "Foam-covered aluminum. You can make it into a custom splint on the fly." He laid the shaped splint across his thighs and then broke the wrapping on the gauze and loosened off the free end. "Go."

Berkeley lifted and carefully balanced the leg as Webb wrapped the open wound in several rotations around the calf to cover the protruding bone. Blood quickly soaked into the gauze, saturating it with each subsequent layer. Satisfied the wound would stay as clean as possible during transport, Webb dropped the remaining gauze back into the bag and slipped the splint under the leg. "Okay, now lower the leg into the splint and carefully pull your hands out. I've got it from below."

Together, they transferred the wrapped leg into the splint, then Berkeley held it while Webb secured the splinted leg with the self-adhesive bandage. They lowered the leg to the gravel, and Webb shaped the metal around her heel before he flipped the space blanket over her leg.

Webb checked the draining bag of saline. "That looks good." He took the girl's pulse and her blood pressure again. "Everything's looking better. I'd like to see her wake up though."

"Wouldn't it be better to stay unconscious? She still needs to be transported to the ER and then properly treated."

Webb looked up at Meg. "If she wakes up, she may be able to tell you who you're looking for. How many you're looking for. I wish we knew what her name is, but we'll give it a try anyway. Sometimes they just need a little coaxing to come back." He bent over the girl. "Honey, can you hear me? My name's Todd and I'm here to help you. You don't have to run anymore, you're safe now. You can wake up now."

He was rewarded by a whimper and the girl shifted slightly to turn her face away.

Meg clapped a hand down on Webb's shoulder. "Hold on, move back." When he looked at her, confusion streaking across his face, she clarified. "Think of what she's been through. I'd bet that was all orchestrated by men. You could be a threat to her simply because you have a Y chromosome. Let me in there."

Webb shifted away to kneel by the girl's splinted leg, and Meg moved in and bent over to brush hair away from the girl's forehead. "Hey, there. I'm Meg. My dog and I found you and we're going to make sure you're safe from now on. Can you talk to us? Tell me your name? We'd really like to get you home to your family."

The girl's eyelids fluttered a few times and then finally stayed open. Meg smiled down into eyes that blinked with confusion and pain. "Hi, honey. Can you tell me your name? Your real name, what you call yourself, not any name someone else called you."

"Mary."

Meg smiled down at the girl. *Progress.* "Mary, I have some friends with me. They're both men"—Mary flinched, but Meg kept right on talking—"but they're both very kind and they won't hurt you." She laid a hand on Webb's shoulder. "This is Todd and he's a paramedic. He fixed up your hurt leg and will stay with you until the ambulance gets here." She held out a hand to the officer. "And this is Berk. Berk is with the police."

At the word "police" Mary started to scurry backward, whimpering in pain as she dragged her shattered leg over gravel. Webb lunged forward, catching Mary's hips while Meg grasped her shoulders. As soon as Meg had a hold on her, Webb pulled back, both hands raised in the air so it was clear he wasn't touching her.

"Mary. Mary, stop struggling. It's just me. It's just Meg." The girl quieted under Meg's hands and she loosened her grip. "You're not in trouble and Berk isn't going to arrest you."

The girl spoke so quietly that Meg missed what she said.

"Mary, honey, I couldn't hear you. Say it again." Meg bent down and put her ear to Mary's lips as she spoke again. Then she straightened and looked up at Berk. "She says John told her that if the cops catch them, they'll go straight to jail and won't get out ever again."

Berkeley gave a tiny shake of his head. Meg opened her eyes wide and tipped her head toward the girl lying before them. *Tell her that.*

Berkeley crouched down so he wasn't so tall and forbidding and pulled off his uniform cap to reveal bleached-blond hair that made him suddenly look ten years younger. "Mary, the police are here to help you, not to lock you up."

"But John said—"

"John was wrong. Did you do something to break the law?"

The girl colored and pulled in on herself, her shoulders hunching up to her ears.

"No, wait, I wasn't clear," Berk continued. "Did you do something of your own free will to break the law?"

Mary silently shook her head.

"Then you're not in trouble. We just want to help you, okay?"

A siren wailed in the distance.

"Here they come," Webb said under his breath. "Get any information you need now. They're going to take her and run."

Meg turned back to the girl. "Mary, we found the van, and we know about the rollover in the river."

Mary's eyes filled, and a single tear overflowed to run slowly down one pale cheek. "Celia. And Leah." Her voice was getting clearer with each word.

"Are those the girls who died?"

Her lips clamped together, Mary just nodded.

"Was John driving the van?"

A nod.

"Do you know what happened to John?"

"He was there, then he was gone. We were rolling over and over and everything was flying. I don't know where he went."

"Mary, besides John, were you the only one to get out alive?"

The girl's gaze flicked to Berkeley, and then back to Meg.

"The other girl or girls aren't in trouble either," Meg reassured her. "We want to help them too."

Mary simply stared up at Meg, her lips trembling, her breathing shallow and rapid. Then, "Emma. Emma helped me out of the van and got me this far. When I couldn't go on, she left."

"Emma . . . that's good, honey. Do you know her last name?"

Mary shook her head. "She was the oldest of us and had been there longest. She was always trying to find a way out. Now she's free."

"But she needs help and we want to give it to her. Hawk and I will find her. Wait, I didn't introduce you. This is my search-and-rescue dog, Hawk. Come, Hawk. Sit." Hawk came close to the girl and sat down close enough for her to touch.

A smile tugged at the corners of the girl's lips for the first time since she regained consciousness.

"Hawk found you and Hawk will find Emma. Was that it though? Just you and Emma?"

"Yeah."

The siren wailed closer.

"The ambulance is almost here, honey. And they're going to take you to the hospital." Meg looked up at Berkeley, a question in her eyes. He answered with a single nod. "And Berk is going to stay with you. To keep you safe."

"What about you?" Mary asked, a tremor in her voice.

"Hawk and I are going to find Emma. And after we do, we'll come visit you in the hospital."

The ambulance pulled up, parking beside the police cruiser. Meg was relieved when two women got out, pulled a gurney from the back, and started to weave their way through the support beams.

Meg and Berkeley moved out of the way while Webb updated them on her status, what he'd done to stabilize her, and the drugs he'd provided.

Meg dug a card out of her SAR bag and handed it to Berkeley. "My cell is on there. Can you call me and update me as to her status?"

"Sure can."

"Depending on where this search goes, I may be out of touch for a while, but leave a message. I'll get it when I'm back in range."

"Will do."

Meg and Webb stood aside as Mary was loaded into the back of the ambulance, and then the ambulance drove away with lights and sirens running and Berkeley following close behind. He waved as he pulled out.

"She's in good hands," Webb said. "They're taking her to the nearest trauma center that's accepting patients, and Berk will stay with her. So, don't worry about her, just concentrate on what you have to do now."

"Which is feed and water Hawk, and down an energy bar myself because this other kid has a pretty long head start on us. I'm afraid that if this Emma knows the area, she's heading for the most remote place possible. I did my homework before we came and I've lived in Virginia all my life."

"You think you know where she's gone?"

"I know where she might have. The Great Dismal Swamp is only a couple of miles west of here."

"The Great Dismal Swamp? Seriously?"

"Seriously. It's something like one hundred thousand acres of swampland, basically unpopulated, and filled with countless places for a young girl to hide. But she could also get into serious trouble. She might think it's just a giant state park, but it's a designated nature refuge with untamed swamplands and all the normal predatory wildlife that live in that kind of habitat. They would consider her easy prey. I need to find her ASAP." She looked out over the football field and into the houses and trees that bordered it. She knew what lay beyond. "This could be a hell of a chase."

CHAPTER 10

Scent Article: an object touched only by the subject of the search, which can then be used by a tracking or trailing dog.

Sunday, July 23, 9:24 AM
Deep Creek Bridge
Edge of the Great Dismal Swamp, Chesapeake, Virginia

They jogged through backyards, open fields, and church parking lots, and then followed the George Washington Highway North for a short span over an offshoot of the Elizabeth River. Once over the bridge, the scent trail left the road and cut behind Deep Creek United Methodist church. From that point on, their path hugged the Dismal Swamp Canal.

Meg remembered her high school history lessons about the Dismal Swamp. Originally occupying more than a million acres, it was currently only a tenth of that size. Drained and logged by George Washington starting in the 1760s, millions of Atlantic white cedars, some up to two hundred years old, were cut down to be used for barrel staves for the booming whaling industry, ship masts, and cedar shingles. The area continued to be logged for over two centuries, devastating local ecosystems. An incredibly dangerous place, the swamp was inhabited by bears, bobcats, wolves, cougars, rattlesnakes, copperheads, and cottonmouths. But it was the perfect hideaway for runaway African-American slaves through the eighteenth and nineteenth centuries, and whole communities sprang up inside the swamp on the many islands hidden away from slave owners. It was more a matter of surviving than thriving, and life was brutally hard, but at least it was on their own terms. During the Civil War, the Great Dismal Swamp became part of the Underground Railroad, but during Reconstruction, as free blacks integrated back into society, the swamp slowly emptied of its human inhabitants.

Now a state park and designated national wildlife refuge, nature was reclaiming her own, but many of the original drainage ditches still existed. The Dismal Swamp Canal, hand dug through the eastern edge of the swamp by slaves, killing untold numbers in the process, opened in 1805 as part of what was now the Atlantic Intracoastal Waterway.

Only thirty-six hours after Hurricane Cole slammed through, the waterway was again in use and the lift bridge was up, allowing a schooner passage north toward the locks, the Elizabeth River and, finally, open ocean.

Meg gave the lift bridge a cursory glance, but Hawk didn't even blink in its direction. He ran ahead of her on his leash—while they were still inside of the populated area of Chesapeake, she needed to keep him close—his head up and tail high. He had the scent.

Meg wished she had Scott and Theo with her. Hawk's nose was good, but nowhere near as sensitive as the bloodhound's. Of course, Hawk more than made up for that slight shortcoming with stamina, exuberance, and pure willingness to search to the ends of the earth. But now, with a day-old trail, Theo would be an asset. Meg was tempted to call for him, but then brushed the thought aside; Scott and Theo were needed elsewhere, and possibly more than a single life rested in their hands.

They'd handle this search alone.

The trail led them south, with neighborhoods of single-family homes on their right, and the open water of the Dismal Swamp Canal to the left. Meg watched Hawk carefully. Their morning had already been full, but she had the feeling it would have nothing on the rest of the day. Emma probably had a day's lead on them, but they had endurance and training on their side. If Emma had fled to the swamp for safety, trying to stay away from populated areas, she would have had to hole up for the night as soon as she lost the light.

It would have been a terrifying night, alone in the dark, with only the sounds of wild animals for company. Meg hoped the sounds were the only company she'd experienced. Predators in the swamp would see her as easy pickings. Meg knew that if Hawk led her in the right direction—and she was sure he did—there was a chance that they wouldn't find the girl alive.

"Hawk, stop." The dog immediately halted, looking up at her, breathing hard. "Take a minute, buddy. I need a sec." She shrugged out of her SAR pack and quickly searched through it for the weapons she carried: a folding, spring-loaded tactical knife, which she tucked into a zippered pocket in her yoga pants, and her SAR knife, nestled in a wrist sheath, which she quickly strapped onto her left forearm. For a brief moment, she regretted leaving her service revolver back home in the gun safe, but shrugged it off. She would have never known she'd need it for a hurricane search, and there would have been no safe place to store the gun last night at the community center.

She'd make do with the tools at hand. And if she was lucky, she wouldn't even need them.

Hawk pushed at her knee and she looked down at him. "I need to remember I have you with me, don't I? You can be pretty damned ferocious when you need to be." As if to contradict her, Hawk looked up at her, his pink tongue dangling out one side of his mouth as he grinned up at her. But that face couldn't erase the memory of Hawk leaping through the air, fangs bared, an instant before he clamped viciously onto Daniel Mannew's wrist, sending his gunshot wide, saving Meg's life. She purposely pushed the memory of the two of them toppling off a cliff from her mind.

She ran a hand down glossy fur, so warm and full of life.

Unbidden, the memory of another dog sprang to life, fur soaked with rain as his body cooled with death, in her arms. She touched the pendant that hung around her neck, a glass creation of electric blue and black, twined with the delicate gray ashes of her first heart dog, the canine equivalent of a soul mate. "Miss you, Deuce," she whispered. "Every damn day."

Memories of Deuce, her K-9 patrol dog when she was still with the Richmond PD, shot and killed in the line of duty, still popped into her head at odd moments. When you lost a heart dog, you didn't just put that love away. It stayed with you, and pain from that loss, though blunted, could still cut deeply.

Meg took a deep breath and pushed away the unexpected melancholy as she looked down at the dog she was lucky enough to find at a terrifyingly low point in her life. Finding one heart dog in life was rare. Finding a second was even more unlikely. But Meg had been blessed by two such animals.

She ruffled his ears. "Okay, goofball. Back to work." She pulled out the sample bag and offered the restraints again to refresh him. "Find her, Hawk. Find Emma."

They jogged down the trail at a steady pace for several more minutes. Then the path ended where a water-filled ditch drained into the canal. The Great Dismal Swamp was full of these centuries-old, hand-dug drainage ditches that lowered the overall water level and allowed loggers hundreds of years ago to work on dry land instead of constantly wading through swamp water.

Across the canal was one of the last vestiges of the swamp's commercial history. A faded and battered two-story clapboard house stood facing the canal, its windows boarded, the front porch on the verge of collapse, and the redbrick chimney crumbling. The white-on-brown state park sign proclaimed it to be the SUPERINTENDENT'S HOUSE—DISMAL SWAMP CANAL COMPANY, 1810. Given its age, disuse, and the fact that it had just come through a hurricane, Meg was impressed it was still standing at all. Granted, Cole certainly wasn't the first hurricane that house had endured.

Hawk didn't even seem to consider any other option, but simply plunged into the ditch, wading through water that came up to his upper chest, his nose high, still following the scent trail. Meg suspected this would be only the first of many times she was about to get soaked, and gamely jogged into the muddy ditch in his wake. The shallow water wasn't as numbingly cold as the Elizabeth River, and only came up to just below her knees, but the unseen rocks and branches sunk into its opaque depths made for a difficult crossing, and more than once she risked turning an ankle or losing her balance and falling face-first into the muck.

"Hawk, stop." Meg struggled out of the ditch after him, a dark muddy stain marking the water level on her yoga pants. "Come here." She unhooked the leash and then unsnapped and removed his vest. "I have a bad feeling that this place will be full of brambles and thorns and the vest will not only make you hot, but will get caught on everything as you go by." She coiled the leash and slipped it into her SAR pack, and then rolled up the vest and slid it into one of the external pockets of the bag.

On this side of the ditch, a clear path cut west, following the drainage channel. A sign, with the Army Corps of Engineers logo and the words GREAT DISMAL SWAMP NATIONAL WILDLIFE REFUGE marked it as the Big Entry Ditch trail, with a warning for hikers to use it at their own risk. But except for debris left from the storm, the trail looked well maintained.

"Good boy, Hawk. Find Emma."

Hawk took a moment to sample the air, then he took the path running west, leaping gracefully over a small downed tree across the trail. Meg planted a foot on the trunk and pushed off it with a little jump, following her dog.

He lost the scent five hundred feet down the trail and Meg's heart sank. She knew this was going to be hard, this task of looking for shed skin cells and the scent they carried a day after winds and passing wildlife could have scattered them far and wide. She gave Hawk a moment to cast about, his nose down to the dirt track. He wandered about for a minute, circling back the way they'd come, trying to pick up the scent again, when he suddenly lunged to his right, darting into the underbrush. Meg dove in after him, struggling through the thick bushes and vines. She bit back a curse as the hooked thorns of a climbing greenbrier vine caught in her hair and her top, and scratched at her cheeks. She threw her forearms up in front of her face and pushed on, breaking into a stand of trees that flanked a small drainage ditch. She glanced back toward the Big Entry Ditch trail and realized the path went over a small culvert built to drain this smaller ditch. She'd missed it altogether, but Emma hadn't. She'd cut away from the main path in a bid to escape.

Did she know John was still alive, or did she just fear it? Either way, getting lost appears to be her main goal. And this is the place to do it.

Getting lost from Hawk would take more than teenage gumption.

"Come on, Hawk, let's keep going. Find Emma."

He had the scent again, she could tell from the sureness of his steps and the speed with which he trotted along the side of the ditch, always right on the edge and at risk of falling in. Somehow, he remained sure-footed on dry land. Which was better than Meg could say, as she slid off the rain-softened dirt into the ditch more than once, pausing as her boot stuck in the sucking mud. Once she even had to grab the trunk of a nearby tree to use as leverage to pull free.

But the soft mud gave Meg a significant advantage— ahead of Hawk, she could occasionally see the imprint of a shoe marking the path they followed. Someone had been through this area after the hurricane. And Hawk knew it was Emma.

Had it been a hike on a lovely spring day she would have been better able to appreciate the beauty around her. The swamp was farther inland and the punishing winds were losing some of their punch and were unable to penetrate the dense foliage. A life lived in Virginia told her the names of many of the trees: apart from the Atlantic white cedar there were stands of oak, beech, and ash trees as well as holly and sassafras. Small wildlife scurried out of sight in the underbrush, and birdsong filtered through the leaves, accompanied by the occasional streak of yellow or blue as birds took flight when they drew near. Frogs called to each other from the surrounding wetlands and insects buzzed nonstop. A dragonfly landed on a branch near her in an iridescent rainbow swirl, resting for only a moment before buzzing away again. Sunlight shone through the leaves, dappling the greenery below and a gentle breeze rustled the treetops above.

Meg slapped at a mosquito feasting on the side of her neck, remembering that the swamp's beauty came at a certain cost. That cost could also come in the form of four-legged predators. She made a fist with her left hand, just to feel the sheath around her forearm pull tight.

The ditch ran straight for what Meg estimated must have been about a mile before it cut to the southwest. It was hard slogging for another two or three miles after that, Meg estimated, admitting to herself that she was simply guessing at the distance. She knew how fast she and Hawk could cover distances at a jog, but this slow push through the foliage made distance hard to guesstimate.

They broke out into sunlight and a two-lane track wide enough for a vehicle, which hugged a more substantial drainage ditch full of sluggish water covered with light green algae.

Open space. Will be harder to catch the scent than when it was trapped in the foliage.

Meg looked up at the sky overhead, the sun coming close to cresting in the sky. She pulled out her phone to check the time: 11:17. Also, she noted, she had no signal. Not really a surprise this deep into no-man's-land.

"Hawk, time to stop for a drink."

They took ten minutes, sitting in the grass in the shade of the forest to rehydrate and have some high energy snacks to fuel the next part of the search. Then Meg took out the bag, gave Hawk the scent, and they were on the run again.

In less than half a mile they came to a short fence partially blocking the way, and another Army Corp of Engineers sign marking the end of the Portsmouth Ditch trail.

"Well, buddy, the trail ends here. Where do we go?"

Hawk looked up at her, tongue lolling, and immediately

stepped around the wooden barrier meant to keep the public out but which meant nothing to him.

"Okay, that answers my question. Portsmouth Ditch, lead the way."

Shortly after entering the canopy again, the path veered away from the ditch. Twenty feet later, Meg stepped into swamp water. Hawk stopped, the water halfway up his front legs, his nose in the air, scenting.

Meg scanned the area. All around was water, and those trees that could survive the watery root bed went on for as far as she could see, mostly bald cypress trees, some with Spanish moss dangling nearly to the water. Old cypress stumps studded water thick with algae, and a fallen tree lay in front of them, half submerged, the top half coated with bright green moss.

She couldn't see anything that betrayed which direction Emma might have gone, but judging from the distance into the swamp, her gut told her the girl had stumbled off the path the previous night as darkness fell. She lost the less traveled part of Portsmouth Ditch as her guide and had wandered away from it, deeper into the murkier areas of the swamp. And once in the swamp proper, and not the flanking forest land, she was in real trouble.

"Hawk, we have to find her. Find Emma."

She could only hope the girl was still above water. If Hawk lost the scent while in this part of the swamp, Meg would certainly fear the worst.

Together they slogged through the dense, silty water, thick with organic matter smelling of decay. It was especially hard going for Hawk, whose shorter stature put him at a decided disadvantage. Meg often had to help him scramble to stay above water because the swamp was too densely packed with rotting tree limbs, trunks, and disintegrating plant life to allow him to swim most of the time. Biting flies swooped in, looking for their piece of flesh—and often taking it—and the call of a raptor, too close for comfort, made Meg stick even closer to Hawk.

Finally, after a half hour, solid ground rose under her boots, and then they were scrambling up onto an island in the swamp. They both collapsed onto dry land, breathing hard. Shrugging her SAR pack from her shoulders, Meg let herself lie back, staring up through the flat, pinelike boughs of an ancient, massive bald cypress that towered half in and half out of the swamp waters. Sunlight filtered through the shifting branches overhead as her heart still pounded with the effort to get this far through the swamp. It was hard work for them, a team that trained nearly daily and was at peak physical condition. She couldn't imagine how hard it would have been for Emma, who also wouldn't have been dressed for this kind of physical workout. When the girl had gotten into that van, she would never have had any idea that her life was about to turn upside down and her freedom and very existence were about to be on the line.

Meg rolled her head to the right to find herself only inches from Hawk's brown eyes. "You okay, bud?"

The muffled sound of his tail thumping the dirt was her response. He was wet and muddy and had likely lost a few chunks of flesh to black-, horse-, and deer flies, but he was on the trail, in his element, and couldn't be happier.

With a groan she pushed herself up and rooted through her bag. She pulled out a collapsible bowl and several bottles of water. She poured the first into Hawk's bowl; only once he was lapping thirstily did she unscrew the cap of her own bottle to quench her thirst. Next, she gave him a proper meal and then opened her supplies. They ate in silence for a while, just listening to the sounds of the swamp around them.

"Can you imagine this place at night, in the dark?" Hawk gazed at her with his ears perked, listening intently. "It must be *so* dark in here. Enough canopy to block the moon, too far from any big city for ambient light. And the swamp full of predators looking for their next meal. She must have been terrified." Meg looked around with a sliver of the foreboding Emma must have felt. Assuming she was still alive at that point. "We have to find her, Hawk."

At the sound of his name, Hawk's ears perked. She gave him a thumping pat on the back and he returned the favor with a long, slobbery kiss. Meg laughed and wiped her cheek. "Gotta teach you to kiss with less tongue." He just grinned at her with more tail thumping. Meg pushed to her feet and shouldered her pack. "Okay, you look ready to get started again. I wonder how far this island goes?" Hands on her hips, she turned in a slow circle, assessing the land and the swamp surrounding it. "This must be the kind of island the runaway slaves hid on during the Civil War. Chances of anyone risking their lives to find them here would be small. And . . . where are you going?"

Hawk had wandered about forty feet ahead, but instead of coming back, he sat down and turned his head to look at her.

He's alerting?

The bottom dropped out of Meg's stomach as she ran over. Instead of a body out of sight, all Hawk had found was a little hollow of grasses and dead leaves. On closer inspection, Meg realized the grass in the hollow was flattened. She dropped to her knees, examining the soil around the hollow.

Tread marks. The same ones that had marked the hidden ditch.

Meg threw an arm around Hawk and gave him a squeeze. "You brilliant boy! She was here. In fact, I bet this is where she spent last night. Smart boy, Hawk!" She gave him a smacking kiss on the top of the head. "Okay, you know what you're looking for. She's not here now, so she's moved on. Hawk, this is Emma. Find her. Find Emma."

They waded through the swamp for about another twenty minutes before stepping out onto dry land again. It wasn't an island, but rather the solid ground surrounding another drainage ditch that ran nearly north-south. For a moment, Hawk cast about for the scent, and Meg was just about to pull the restraints out again to offer to him when his head and tail shot up simultaneously and he trotted south, following the ditch. Meg stuffed the bag back into her SAR pack and jogged after him.

Occasionally, Meg found a broken branch or a shoe print in the soft soil, reassuring her they were on the right path. She noted that the steps looked like they shuffled and dragged.

"We need to find Emma, Hawk. She's got to be tired. And that's going to make her a target."

Hawk's ears twitched at her voice, but he kept up the same steady trot.

We need to find her soon, or we'll be tired and could also be a target.

Soon, up ahead, came the glimmer of sunlight flashing off water. And not a trickle in a ditch. A lot of water. They slipped from the trees and stopped, facing the Great Dismal Swamp's Lake Drummond.

Meg gaped at the unearthly beauty of the lake. Light clouds scudded across the sky, perfectly reflected in the smooth, unruffled surface of the lake. Giant bald cypress trees skirted the edge of the lake and grew out into its depths, some so mammoth, Meg bet they must have been close to seven- or eight-hundred years old.

Centuries before the first pilgrim set foot on Plymouth Rock. Hard to wrap your mind around a living tree that old.

A huge cypress's massive boughs spread wide over the water, reflected back to look even taller than its one hundred feet. Nearby, a great blue heron stood motionless, his head tipped down toward the glasslike surface of the lake.

Catching sight of Hawk, he spread his wings and launched gracefully into the air, sailing over a black willow, looking for more peaceful waters to fish. A rustling to their left drew Meg's gaze, and she had just enough time to see a painted turtle splash from a flat rock into the shallow edge of the lake.

Meg pulled her attention from the lake itself to scan the shoreline, but it seemed deserted. She pulled her binoculars from her pack and took a second look. The edge of the lake was a continual line of trees and underbrush. Farther down the lake, a wooden promontory, likely the outlook at the end of one of the park's designated hiking trails, projected out into the water. Even it was deserted.

People are cleaning up after the storm, not out for an afternoon's hike.

That suited Meg, as it made their job easier with fewer conflicting odors.

"Okay, Hawk, you got us this far, now where did she go? Find Emma, Hawk." She offered the scent again to refresh him and he set off to their right, down the edge of the lake. They didn't stay by the lake for long, heading into the brush, even if only to stay thirty or forty feet in. "I bet she found the lake too exposed. Stay with her, buddy."

A scream ripped through the still air. A girl's scream.

Emma.

"Hawk, go, find Emma! Go!"

Hawk bolted in the direction of the scream, Meg sprinting behind him.

Another scream, one filled with pure terror and desperation.

Then, deadly silence.

CHAPTER 11

Hug-A-Tree and Survive: An educational program developed by a Border Patrol agent after the death of a lost child from hypothermia. The program is aimed at children ages seven through eleven and emphasizes, "If you are lost, stay put—hug a tree—until help arrives." Rights to the program were donated to the National Association for Search and Rescue in 2005.

Sunday, July 23, 12:58 PM
Dismal Swamp National Wildlife Refuge
Chesapeake, Virginia

Side by side, Meg and Hawk crashed through the dense trees, jerking to a halt as the ground disappeared beneath their feet to slope down into swamp water again.

Meg frantically searched the swamp looking for any signs of life.

"NO!"

The shriek jerked her head to the right, toward a sight that froze her blood—a girl was crab walking backward, partway up a felled tree, slick with lichen and draped with Spanish moss that dangled into the water below. But Meg couldn't spare any attention for the girl, not when the biggest alligator she'd ever seen was crawling up the trunk after her.

The girl screamed and kicked out, but the alligator just snapped lazily at her.

No matter what the girl did, she was going to lose. If she kept climbing, she'd run out of tree and the reptile would catch up. If she lost her grip and fell into the water below, the alligator would simply go in after her to its preferred killing ground. One vicious clamp of those teeth and it would pull her under in a death roll, and that would be the end. And from the look of terror on the girl's face, she knew it.

Not if Meg had anything to do with it.

"Hawk, with me!" Meg sprinted along the edge of the swamp water, yelling and waving her arms in the air to distract the reptile. The alligator paused only briefly to swing its heavy, flat head to fix her with a slitted green eye. "Get away from her." Her fingers found the handle of her knife by touch alone and she yanked it from the sheath. Now she just had to get close enough to use it. She was handy with a knife in hand-to-hand combat with a human, but she had serious doubts about her ability to successfully throw the knife with the precision and strength required to pierce the alligator's hide. And if the blade just skittered off and fell into the water, she'd be down a knife, at a time when three lives could depend on every weapon she carried.

Coming within five feet of the reptile, Meg quickly assessed the situation. She needed to lure it off the trunk, so Emma could get down. But tackling it and trying to knock it down into the water would most likely be a death sentence. That meant she needed to force it to turn on her and follow her onto dry land. She remembered from Southern search-and-rescue training that the average human could outrun an alligator's top land speed of ten miles per hour for short periods of time, but for that to happen, Emma would need to be down off the trunk. If she'd only known to run.

Meg picked up a small rock from the dirt and hurled it at the alligator with all her strength. The rock bounced off its shoulder and the alligator paused in its upward climb. Meg picked up another rock, took another step closer and whipped it at him. "Hawk, speak!"

Hawk joined the fray, teeth bared, growling and barking, his front feet splayed wide and his head dropped between his shoulders. That caught the alligator's attention, likely because of the wolves that inhabited the area. The alligator immediately slithered back down the trunk and slid onto the ground below to deal with the more relevant threat. His meal could wait.

Meg kept her eyes locked on the dog versus alligator standoff forming in front of her and took a step closer, her knife clutched in her hand. "Emma? Emma, you need to listen to me. I need you to get down off that tree trunk. We're search-and-rescue and we're here to help. Get down. Get behind me. I don't know how long we can hold him."

In her peripheral vision, the girl slid down the tree and hopped to the ground. The alligator saw the movement too, and the moment Emma's feet hit the ground, it lunged for her, its jaws opening just before the long, jagged teeth clamped over her calf.

Emma screamed in agony as the alligator gave her a jerk that yanked her off her feet. Then it started to drag her toward the water. Once in the water, it would be game over.

"Talon, back!" Meg's use of Hawk's "don't mess with me" name, the one she only used when instant compliance was absolutely required, had Hawk backing off, albeit reluctantly.

Now that her dog was out of the way, Meg took two running steps and launched herself through the air. She landed on the animal's scaly back, digging into its shoulder with the fingers of her left hand and using the leverage of her body to drive her knife into the right side of its thick neck. The alligator roared, whipping its head abruptly to one side, yanking another haggard scream from Emma, but it didn't let go.

In the back of her mind, Meg heard Hawk going crazy just to her right, but tuned him out to focus. She had to make the alligator let Emma go. Otherwise, she was dead.

Meg had one idea, but didn't know if it would work. Pulling back with her right arm, she slammed the knife back into the gator's neck, using the hilt of the knife as a makeshift handgrip to pull her body up and over the top of its head. With her left hand, she slammed down repeatedly with all her strength on the flat snout, directly on its nostrils.

To her amazement, the tactic worked, and the viselike jaws popped open, freeing Emma, who scrambled away as fast as she could. "Talon, go! Emma, with him. Go!"

Meg couldn't look to ensure he complied; she had to trust her dog.

Now it was just her and the gator. A very pissed off gator, who was trying to reach around to rip her off its back.

One chance to get away. She didn't have to kill him; she just needed to get in front of him at a sprint.

If this didn't work, there was no one to help her.

She ripped the knife from the gator's neck and, clamping her knees around its torso like it was a bucking bronco, she clutched the hilt in both hands. Leaning forward, she drove the knife into its right eye, deep enough to feel the knife scrape bone. Just as quickly, she yanked the knife out and rolled off the screaming animal—agony or death throes, she wasn't sure, and couldn't afford the time to check—hit the ground running, and tore straight for the trees where she imagined Hawk would have led Emma. She pushed through the cloying undergrowth, using the blood-smeared knife to hack away the vines in her path. Meg ran for a full two minutes before she took the time to stop, pressing her fists to her knees as she bent over, breathing hard, her knife still clutched tightly in her hand. She tried to slow her breathing as much as possible, listening for any sign of pursuit, but there was only quiet.

She gave herself twenty seconds to get some of her breath back. Realizing she still held the bloody blade, she wiped it clean on a moss-covered rock, then slid it home in the sheath. Straightening, she looked around, but she was surrounded by vines and trees. "Hawk?" she called.

A bark to her left gave her their direction. "Hawk, stay. I'm coming."

A few minutes of wandering through the forest and two more commands for Hawk to speak, and she found them. They'd come upon yet another ditch, but this one was wider and flanked by a double dirt track with grass growing between the ruts. Hawk sat on that grass, Emma collapsed beside him, one arm thrown over his back, her face buried in his fur. Her position gave Meg the chance to get a better look without making the girl self-conscious. In the swamp, all Meg had was a vague impression of long, blond hair and a short skirt, but now she could see the short skirt was actually a black V-neck sheath dress paired with ballerina flats over bare feet, and the loose hair was matted, filthy, and full of brambles and bits of twigs.

Meg knelt down beside the girl. Before they did anything else, Meg needed to treat her bite with the first aid supplies in her SAR pack as a temporary fix until Emma got real medical treatment.

Meg laid a hand on the girl's shoulder, rubbing gently. "Emma, you're safe now."

The girl raised her head, but where Meg was expecting to see tears and terror, there was only defiant exhaustion. Her makeup was skillfully applied, but had mostly worn off at this point, and her face was smudged with dirt. "You can't promise that."

"Actually, I can." Meg slid her pack off her shoulders and dragged it beside her. Opening the front pocket, she pulled out her FBI identification and flipped open the case.

Emma looked in confusion from Meg to Hawk and back again. "You're FBI?"

"We are. Search-and-rescue, and before that I was with the Richmond PD." She met the girl's eyes. "Emma, I know what happened to you."

The eyes that fixed on her were full of suspicion. "How do you know my name?"

"I was driving down I-64 this morning with a paramedic firefighter when he spotted the van in the river. We pulled off and checked it out. Evidence in the van told us there were occupants missing, and Hawk led us to Mary." A mixture of hope and fear sprung into Emma's eyes, so Meg answered the question before she could voice it. "Mary's at the hospital now. She was in shock and her leg is in bad shape, but they'll look after her. She's safe and she's going to make it. She's also not in trouble with law enforcement."

Emma's defiant posture deflated and she sank a little further into Hawk. "Thank God."

"Mary told us about you, including your name. Now, I need you to let me take a look at that leg. It will need real treatment or you'll risk serious infection, but I can at least clean and cover it for now. You're sure it's not broken?"

"Don't think I could run on it if it was."

Meg pulled out the small first aid kit she kept at the bottom of her SAR pack. She opened it and took out a handful of alcohol wipes, some gauze, and a roll of medical tape. "Okay, I need you to extend your leg so I can see it."

Momentary indecision flashed over Emma's face, but then she shifted enough to extend her leg.

Meg swallowed the gasp that threatened to break free at the sight of the bruised flesh, pierced in a perfect imprint of the gator's U-shaped bite. Blood ran from each puncture wound, down her leg and over her foot to pool in her shoe, and smeared over her calf from her flight through the forest with Hawk. Meg opened several of the alcohol swabs. "Take a breath; this is going to really hurt." She started to clean the wounds, feeling Emma's calf tighten reflexively under her hand at the sting of alcohol. She glanced up; the girl had gone sheet white, her lips pressed in a tight, bloodless line, but she hadn't made a single murmur of pain. *Gutsy girl. Get her talking. Keep her distracted.* "All Mary told us was your name. We figured out the rest."

"The rest?" Emma's words were strangled.

"We know you're a victim of human trafficking and that you've been trapped in the sex trade for a while."

Other girls might have blushed and averted their eyes, but Emma met her gaze head-on. "What makes you think that?"

"As I said, I was Richmond PD. I've seen it all. The girls in the van, Celia and Leah, they were too young to look the way they did. The makeup, the clothes, that's not the way preteen girls dress, even when they push the boundaries to look older. I was a preteen girl once. I remember. But the big red flag was the restraints." Meg's gaze shifted to Emma's slender wrists, each of which was circled with abrasions. "Did you pull the strap free, or did it break on you during the rollover?"

For a moment, Emma just stared at her, wide-eyed. "A little of both. I was yanking on it as hard as I could, but the force of the crash probably helped."

"With one hand free, you could free the other. And then Mary."

"Everyone else was gone." The words came out on a

hoarse croak. "Mary, she was hurt so bad. I almost had to carry her."

Meg tossed down a bloody wipe, opened a fresh one, and continued working on the bite. "You got her out of danger and away from the water. You got her to shelter in a terrible storm, didn't you?"

Emma simply stared, but didn't disagree.

"Then you couldn't take her any farther. That was a really bad break. You had to leave her, but why didn't you get her any help?"

Silence rode heavy for several heartbeats and Emma's internal battle played out on her face. After years of being indoctrinated into not trusting law enforcement, Meg could see the battle between those rules and a young woman's yearning for freedom.

Meg stopped cleaning and laid a hand on Emma's knee. Making contact. Trying to make a connection. "I know you've been taught that cops are the enemy. Yes, I'm an ex-cop. But I'm search-and-rescue now. Saving lives, finding the lost, that's what Hawk and I do." Hawk looked up at the sound of his name and she smiled at him and stroked a hand down his fur. Watching Emma's eyes follow the gesture almost longingly, she tried a change in tack. She went back to working on the wound, but asked, "You like animals?"

Emma made a noise in her throat that Meg took as an affirmative response.

"Do you think animals have an intuition, a kind of sixth sense that tells them something about a person? If someone is to be trusted, or feared?"

"Yes."

"So, what does Hawk say to you?"

Emma sat up a little straighter against Hawk, and ran a hand over his neck and shoulder. "He trusts you. In the swamp, he followed your commands even though it meant leaving you. He . . . he led me away to safety, got me away from that gator, but he left you behind."

"Hawk and I have been a team for over two years now. We trust each other implicitly with our lives. He's saved me. I've saved him. He trusts me to make the right call because it's what we need to do to save a victim. Do you think he'd trust me like that if I was the kind of person who would mess you up somehow?"

The girl shrugged and tipped her head down to rest on Hawk's shoulder.

"I'm asking you these questions because I want to help. It's what Hawk and I do. There's nothing in it for us personally except the satisfaction of burying some son-of-a-bitch who totally deserves it." Meg let venom saturate her tone, leaning on memories of burned, shattered bodies, and fingertips scraped down to bone in an attempt to escape being buried alive.

Emma's gaze slid upward to stare at Meg, a new understanding dawning.

Meg took a breath and forced away the anger that rose up at the memories. "When I ask you these questions, it's because I can help you. But to help you, I need you to tell me everything you can. Can you give trusting us a try?"

Emma gave her a long, unblinking stare. "Screw with me once, and I'm gone."

"Totally fair. I'm just telling you, it's not going to happen. Now, back to Mary. Why didn't you call for help?"

"She made me promise not to. She was terrified that the cops would lock her away forever."

"You could have made the promise to her, gotten away, and told someone about her."

Emma shook her head fast enough that her long hair rippled. "No. We . . . us girls . . . we had a pact. Everyone else lied, everyone else broke promises. Not us. Never us."

A shred of decency and honesty in a world where none seemed to exist. Meg could understand why the girls would value that. "Would you like to see her?"

"Mary?"

"She's in the hospital. We can take you to her." Meg grabbed the third wipe, thinking one more cleaning would finish the job, then she'd wrap the wound. She'd leave the deep cleaning and the antibiotic pills and ointments to the ER.

"What if she's not there?"

"She'll be there. I could be wrong, but I suspect that leg is going to need surgery. If not, she's going to need rehydrating and a cast. She's only been there for a few hours. She'll still be there." Meg reached for the roll of gauze, tore open the plastic and started to wrap Emma's calf.

"Okay."

"We'll get you treated at the same time. Emma, is there any family I can call for you?"

The wall went up so fast that if Meg hadn't seen Emma's expression go blank, her eyes flat and dead, she might not have believed the other girl had ever existed. "No."

"Are you sure? I—"

"I said no." Emma cut her off, swiftly. Viciously.

Back off, Jennings. You were making progress, don't blow it all now. "Okay," Meg said lightly. "We'll just get you treated." She taped the gauze securely, repacked her bag, and pushed to her feet. She held out a hand to Emma. The girl slapped her palm into Meg's and let herself be hauled to her feet.

Meg pulled out her phone and checked for a signal—still nothing. She gauged the sun up above and the direction of shadows in the forest flanking the twin tracks. She pointed to the northwest. "That way. We may be closer to civilization straight through the swamp that way"—she pointed due west—"but I think we've all had enough of the swamp and its inhabitants for now. Hawk, come."

Hawk stood and all three of them started down the rough road beside the ditch. Meg didn't say anything, but she noted that Hawk heeled beside Emma, who gamely limped along, setting their pace.

Emma had gone about fifteen feet when she suddenly stopped, Hawk halting with her. "What happened to the gator? Did you kill it?"

"Without getting graphic, I'm pretty sure he couldn't survive what I had to do to get away from him."

"What did you do?"

Meg hesitated for a second, but then decided that with everything else that had happened to this girl, it was only fair for her to know that this particular nightmare wasn't going to come after her. "I jammed my knife through its right eye and into its brain. I didn't stick around to make sure he died, but I can't see how that particular injury could be survived."

"Good." It was the only word Emma spoke, but when she started to walk again, her head was a little higher with the news that one enemy was vanquished.

It looked like hope.

CHAPTER 12

Incident Commander: The person responsible for managing emergency personnel committed to the rescue operation.

Sunday, July 23, 5:28 PM
Children's Hospital of the King's Daughters
Norfolk, Virginia

Meg and Hawk met Craig in the corridor outside Mary's hospital room. "What's the word on jurisdiction?"

"It's ours." Craig stopped as laughter burst from inside the room. "They're both in there?"

Meg nodded. "They disinfected and wrapped Emma's leg, and got her cleaned up and lent her some nurses' greens because her own clothes were filthy. Not that she'd ever want to wear them again. Mary's surgery is set for tomorrow. Her fracture was worse than I thought, with a few smaller pieces of bone also broken off, so they need to do surgery to stabilize it." She glanced in the open doorway, toward the couple who sat in chairs against the wall, looking scared and ecstatic at the same time. "Mary's parents are here," she said quietly. "Mary's only fourteen. They had a falling out about a year ago over a new, older 'boyfriend' the parents were uncomfortable with. Turns out they were right because when Mary ran away from home to be with the guy, he sucked her into the sex trade and then she couldn't get out."

"She could have called her parents."

"You and I know that as adults, but Mary honestly thought her parents wouldn't take her back, that with all that had happened they'd blame her and consider her damaged goods. They don't. They know there's a long road to travel now, but they don't care because they have her back. Emma, on the other hand, is not that lucky. She says she's on her own. She also says she's eighteen and no longer a minor. We don't have any official ID for her, or even a last name, so we have to believe her unless we learn otherwise. So we won't be handing her over to juvie or calling in Child Protective Services."

"Would she help with an investigation?"

"I haven't outright asked her, but I think so. Mary's parents though, they don't want their daughter involved."

Craig's brows snapped together and his tone rose. "Don't want her to help find the man who did this to her?"

Meg grabbed his arm and dragged him a few more feet down the hallway and away from the open door. She gave Hawk the hand signals to follow and then sit at her feet. "See it from their point of view. She's young, physically injured, has been physically and mentally abused, and they just got her back. There are also symptoms of drug abuse, so there may be a lot more to her recovery than they think. They just want to leave this life behind entirely to work on getting her better and back into some kind of normalcy. It would help us to have her testimony, but honestly, if I was in their shoes, I'm not sure I wouldn't do the same thing. Even if we catch the guy tomorrow, there will be a court case and potentially an appeal. It could go on for years. They don't want to keep dragging her back into that life. They want her to heal and move on."

"It's all about Emma then."

"You don't sound impressed."

"I think we need all the help we can get. Anyway, the Norfolk field office has sent out SAC Walter Van Cleave to talk to her while we still know her location."

Meg had been staring off down the hall, watching a nurse deftly steer a wheelchair around an empty gurney and a forest of unused IV poles lining the overcrowded corridor, but now her head snapped back sharply. "You're afraid she's going to rabbit on us."

"I think there's a good chance. We can't charge her and hold her. She's free to just walk out the door. And then where does she go? You said she has no family. Back to the streets, then? Out to find another pimp who will help her find johns? Do you know what the statistics are on getting someone out of this lifestyle alive?"

Meg simply stared at him for a moment, surprised at the bite in his words. "I don't. But it sounds like you do. Has this case hit a nerve?"

Craig ran a hand through his hair and turned away to pace several steps down the corridor and back again. "Sorry. I didn't mean to go off on you. I do have some experience with this stuff. Earlier in my career, when I was still a special agent, I worked on one of the human trafficking task forces. We were in California dealing with the masses of immigrants getting into the state and trading their freedom for forced labor and captivity on the farms there. Or in the hotels. Or on estates. The terrible conditions and the disregard for human life, all to save a buck and turn around and make a buck on their backs . . . it still pisses me off."

"Was the task force successful?"

"Some of the time. We definitely broke up a few trafficking rings during the six months I was there. But I always felt that one ring disappearing just opened up a vacuum to be filled by another. We could never get ahead of it. At least the groups I was working on never involved the sex trade. Well, not as the main focus. Women got caught in these rings, a few in the fields, more in domestic work, working up to eighteen hours a day, earning pennies that were then taken to pay for the debt of their entry into the U.S. Many of those women were sexually abused by both the men who ran the trafficking rings and the men who hired their services. They considered it a bonus."

"That's awful. Considering the geographic location, it must be rampant down there."

"It is. But there's more of it here than you might imagine. North Carolina and Virginia both have serious trafficking problems. And it looks like we stumbled into it."

"I'm sorry about that. I know you needed me today."

"We did okay. But already, only two days out, it's becoming more of a recovery than a rescue. Almost anyone who survived the storm has come out from where they sheltered or has been discovered. Now we're finding those who can't call for help because they didn't survive."

"What was Norfolk like?"

"Less direct wind damage, but because of the way the storm was moving and the way the storm surge wrapped around the peninsula, the flooding has been catastrophic. The surge pushed up the Elizabeth River and into all its tributaries. We were helping with civilian searches, but were asked to steer clear of Naval Station Norfolk."

"They'll have their own search dogs if they're needed, with proper clearance already in place. But they must have had all their carriers and destroyers out to sea before the storm hit."

"They did. It's a massive base, right at sea level where the mouth of the Elizabeth River meets Hampton Roads, and they apparently already have a serious issue with flooding due to rising ocean levels. They took a direct hit from Hurricane Cole. We offered our assistance, but they declined. Which was fine, because we had more than enough to do without worrying about the base."

"I'll be back to help tomorrow. How many more days here, do you think?"

"Two or three at most. Soon, we're going to be the wrong K-9 teams for them and they're going to need Victim Recovery. I've already given SAC Randolph the heads-up, and he says he can have his people here within eight hours as soon as they are given the go. Maybe in a day or two . . ." Craig's voice trailed off as his gaze fixed over Meg's shoulder.

She swiveled to see what he was looking at. Twenty feet down the hallway a tall, lean man with dark hair cut almost military short stood at the nurses' station, his identification flip case open and extended as he talked to a nurse. "That must be SAC Van Cleave."

"That's what I was thinking."

Meg turned her back to the nurses' station. "Know anything about him?"

"Not personally. When I heard who we were going to be handing this off to, I looked him up. Ex–air force, flew Tomcats in Operation Desert Storm. Been with the Bureau for nearly twenty years. Going by his record he seems like a good man with a lot of experience. Also sounds like a straight shooter with no bullshit tolerated."

"Sounds perfect."

"Better still, he hasn't burned out. My six months working human trafficking as a junior agent was enough to show me that wasn't my niche. It looks like he's been doing this in the Norfolk office for close to a decade."

"Can't beat that kind of experience," Meg said. "Does he work in conjunction with local law enforcement?"

"That's what I've been told, so he'll have some useful contacts. Here he comes."

Meg turned around to face the man coming down the hallway in the standard FBI uniform of white dress shirt paired with a dark suit and tie. Craig stepped up to stand beside her, holding out his hand. "SAC Van Cleave. I'm SAC Craig Beaumont from the Forensic Canine Unit out of D.C."

"Beaumont, nice to meet you." The special agent in charge shook hands with him, then turned to Meg. "Walter Van Cleave."

Meg shook hands. "Meg Jennings. Canine handler for the Human Scent Evidence Team."

Van Cleave's head tilted slightly as he considered her. "You're the one who tracked the girls."

"Yes." Standing so close to Van Cleave, a faint scent caught at Meg, tugging at a long-buried memory. Not cigarette smoke, nothing so acidic, something mellower, almost carrying a trace of cherries. Then it hit her—pipe smoke, and from a similar blend of tobacco as the one her Irish grandfather used. She blinked at him in surprise. In this day and age, a man who smoked a pipe. He was a throwback to the classic 1950s G-man. Walter Van Cleave was a rarity in more ways than one apparently.

"That your search dog?" Pointing down at Hawk, Van Cleave interrupted her thoughts.

"Yes. One of the nurses was kind enough to let me get him into one of the shower stalls for a quick wash off, so he's clean now." She indicated the muddy waterline clearly distinct on her yoga pants. "Cleaner than me." She sniffed at her right sleeve and wrinkled her nose in disgust. "Sorry, I didn't realize I still smell so much like swamp."

"It was for a good cause." Van Cleave pointed to the open door. "Emma is in there?"

Meg nodded. "With the second victim, Mary, but Mary's parents don't want her involved in this. Local PD took down her story, so you'll have their details, but at this point, they don't want her involved anymore. She's a minor, so we have to respect that."

"The older girl is willing to talk?"

"I hope so. I haven't said anything to her yet because I didn't want her changing her mind before you got here."

"I can talk to the nurses to see if they can find us a meeting room," Craig offered. "To get the ball rolling. Unless you want to take her back to the field office."

"No, that's not usually a good idea," Van Cleave said. "These kids have been through hell and they're taught that law enforcement is the enemy. A neutral location is better, so let's see if there's anything available here." He turned to Meg. "Do you have a rapport with her?"

"I think so. I found her in the swamp and rescued her from an alligator, so we have the threads of trust starting."

Van Cleave's eyebrows lifted at the mention of the reptile. "It sounds like there's an interesting story there. You'll have to share it sometime." He turned to Craig. "Beaumont, if you can get us a room, that would be great. Then leave it to us. One strange man in the mix is going to be bad enough. Two may make her clam up."

"Sure. Give me a few minutes to get you set up." Craig headed for the nurses' station.

"What's your strategy in a situation like this?" Meg asked.

"I've handled a lot of these cases. There are a few risks.

One, these girls are convinced we're the bad guys and can't be trusted, and they'll often do anything to get away. Two, in conjunction with that, you have to be as non-threatening as possible. You can't build trust if they're terrified of you. Three, a lot of them are compulsive liars, so you have to read the person, not necessarily the story, especially at the beginning."

"What you're saying is you're actually part profiler."

"You have to be. But I think we have an advantage here that she's already got something of a connection with you."

"And with Hawk."

"Interesting." Van Cleave's eyes narrowed in calculation as he stared down at Hawk. "Is it okay if we use that?"

"Sure. As long as she's no threat to him, he can be used as a therapy dog."

"I like it. Also, when we're in there, only refer to me as 'Van,' and never by my rank. I need to make a connection with her and I need to step back from a law enforcement persona. You already don't have that."

"I kind of do. I told her I was an ex-cop out of the Richmond PD. But mostly I think she just associates me with Hawk."

"That's good." His gaze shot over her shoulder. "Here comes Beaumont."

Craig joined them. "I found you a room. One of the rooms they use for doctors' meetings down a floor. Room 314."

"Excellent, thanks. I'll have your handler back to you in a few hours."

"Sounds good," Craig said. "Meg, let me know how it goes. And I'll text you where we're bunking down tonight. Does Webb still have your SUV?"

"And all my stuff, yeah. I'll let him know where to meet you guys, if that's okay with you."

"Sure. He's practically one of the team now." He turned to Van Cleave and held out his hand. "Good to meet you. I worked trafficking for six months, so I have an idea of what you're up against. Good luck."

Van Cleave took his hand. "Thanks." He looked over at Meg. "I suspect we're going to need it."

CHAPTER 13

Aiming Off: A cross-country navigational technique to locate an unseen destination, such as a shelter or stream crossing, by navigating along a visible landscape feature.

Sunday, July 23, 6:37 PM
Children's Hospital of the King's Daughters
Norfolk, Virginia

"Emma, come on in here." Her arms cradling a large pizza box that balanced a tray of drinks, Meg led the way into a meeting room that consisted of an oblong table surrounded by eight chairs and a white board on one long wall. "I hope fully loaded works for you. You said you weren't a vegetarian, and I wasn't sure what you liked, so I figured you could just pick off what you don't want." She set the box down on the table. "Hawk, don't get under my feet." She shot a glance at Emma. "This dog. Honestly, any time he smells meat, he's all over me."

What she didn't let on was that Hawk's terrible manners were in response to her hand signals for him to come closer.

"Can you call him over, just until I get this all set out?" Meg looked down at her dog with a look of irritated impatience. "You already had your dinner. You don't need ours too."

"Come here, Hawk." Emma sat down in a chair on the long side of the table and patted her thighs.

Meg surreptitiously gave him the hand signal to go, before looking up at Emma. "Thanks. He's great, but you know dogs sometimes—they think with their stomachs, kind of like most men." She knew she'd said the wrong thing when Emma's expression closed over, and she wanted to kick herself. Most of the men Emma had likely known concentrated on more brazen appetites. She went for a different spin. *She doesn't know you don't have a brother.* "When we were growing up, my brother Jake was a stomach with legs. When he was thirteen, two things ruled his life—a killer case of acne and a bottomless pit for a stomach. My mother used to lament filling the fridge one day and coming home to an empty fridge two days later. Once she baked a cake as a surprise for my dad, and when she came home Jake had eaten the whole thing. All by himself. I didn't even get a crumb. I honestly thought she was going to kill him that day. I can still hear him making excuses, his voice breaking because it was in the middle of changing. *Sorry, Mom, I didn't know you made it for anyone in particular.*" She did the quote like she imagined a teenage boy would do, the words full of exaggerated vocal dips and whine. The corner of Emma's lips twitched and Meg decided it was time to stop while she was ahead. "You wanted a Coke, right?"

"Yes."

Meg slid a fountain cup toward her, then flipped open the pizza box and pushed it and a stack of napkins toward Emma. "Help yourself. Take as much as you like."

Emma didn't move. "When is that agent coming?"

"You mean Van? He's going to eat with us, so he'll be along anytime. Now, come on, you get first dibs."

The girl had to be starving, but she only selected two pieces, taking a moment to remove all the onions and peppers before picking up the first slice and taking a bite. Her eyes closed in pleasure, and Meg wondered how long it had been since she'd gotten to experience something as simple as a favorite food. *Withholding luxuries is just another method of control. Providing luxuries trains them as well as Pavlov's dogs, even when it's something as basic as pizza.*

Meg was just reaching for her own slice when Van Cleave came through the door. His suit jacket was tossed over his arm, his tie was missing, and the top two buttons of his dress shirt were undone. *Going for the casual, friendly look.*

Van gave them both a sheepish smile. "Sorry I'm late." He held out a hand to Emma. "Walter Van Cleave."

"Agent Van Cleave?"

"Special Agent in Charge if you want to split hairs, but I don't think we need to be that formal. Please call me Van. I don't like to stand on ceremony. All right! Pizza!"

Meg rolled her eyes in Emma's direction, who actually smiled.

"Help yourself," Meg said. "Hawk staying out of trouble?"

Emma reached down to stroke the dog, who gazed up at her . . . and her pizza.

Meg bent to look under the table, giving Hawk the hand signal to stay. When she straightened, she threw an apologetic glance at Emma. "I hope you don't mind. He's a total mooch. Just don't give him anything. He'd love to eat an entire meat lover's pizza, but it would make him sick."

"I don't mind. Really. He's a sweetheart."

Van Cleave sat down with a stack of pizza and reached for the drink Meg pushed at him. "Emma, Meg says you're willing to talk to us today. We appreciate that. Thank you."

Emma put the pizza back down. "I don't think I can help." Her voice was flat.

Meg wondered if she was fighting for control.

"You'd be surprised what you know and how that can help. Can we start with the basics? What's your full birth name?"

"Emma."

Van Cleave waited a few beats. "Your last name?"

"I don't have one of those anymore. I'm just Emma."

Van Cleave considered her for a moment, blinked and continued. "Maybe that's something you'll share with us later on, once you know us a bit better. We know from the scene of the accident that you were in the van with three other girls. Can you tell me how you all got there?"

Emma's eyes stayed downcast and she picked at her pizza, taking toppings off, piling them on a napkin, putting them back on.

Meg reached over and put a hand on Emma's arm. The girl's muscles tightened at the contact, but Meg took a chance and left it there. "I know this makes you uncomfortable, but Van is here to help. And he can't do that until he knows more about you and the others."

To Meg's surprise, the girl yanked her arm away and turned on Van Cleave, fire blazing in her eyes and voice. "How can you help? Law enforcement's useless. They pretend not to see and they never help. Nobody cares about us."

Meg was about to cut in, in an attempt to smooth over a rocky start, but Van beat her to it. "I can only speak for myself and the agents I know, but you couldn't be more wrong. Do you know how many kids I've pulled off the streets and out of hotel rooms?" He didn't wait for her to even attempt a guess, but simply barreled on. "Eighty-six. Do you know how many men and boys I've taken out of the fields? One hundred and seventy-two. Maybe that's just a drop in the bucket, but, for me, it's personal. That's lives saved. If I wanted to, I could work a nine-to-five job where I push papers. Truthfully, it would make my life a lot easier, and would give me a lot less angst to drag around. But that's not what I do, it's not who I am. Instead, each of those people means so much to me that I carry them around in my head."

"You expect me to believe you? That you rescued that many people?" Scorn laced Emma's tone.

Meg thought it was the sound of someone who'd been burned by the adults in her life so many times she'd stopped counting.

"If you want proof, I could put you in contact with Vicki Sterling, who at fourteen was addicted to heroin, which is how her pimp kept farming her out to clients through storefront properties. Vicki went through rehab and is now taking classes in social work, so she can work with underage kids who are trying to get out of the sex trade. Or Miguel Perez, only twenty and fresh off the bus, trying to make a life for himself, but who ended up indebted for his travel to Virginia and slaving on a soy farm for pennies a day, most of which he didn't get to keep. Or how about Ji-Hoon Kim, who only wanted to earn enough money to bring her family over from South Korea, but instead ended up working in an illicit massage parlor." He paused, letting silence lie heavy for a few seconds. "Do you need more names?" He pulled out his cell phone. "Should I call one of them now so you can find out about me firsthand?"

Emma shook her head, her eyes downcast as her shoulders drooped. "What's the point? There's too many of them. You can't win." The fight in her dissolved, and now her voice was quiet, laden with the defeat of years of fruitless struggles.

"It seems like it only makes a tiny dent in a huge tangled mess," Meg said, "but everything helps. Look at Mary. We went after her. Should we not have bothered? Of course we should have, because every life counts. But it's not a single life. We not only saved Mary; we saved her parents. They'd lost their daughter and were just going through the motions. Now they have their child back." Emma's eyes rose to hers and Meg could see she'd scored a point. "Saving a single life has consequences, just like ending a life does. It's a center point and everything radiates out from it. If you help us get to the center of the ring, we'll save more than just a single life. So . . . will you help?"

Emma glanced from Meg to Van Cleave and back again. "You're on this case?"

"Me?" Meg glanced down at Hawk. "We're FBI, but not in the classic agent sense. We work cases as we're needed and don't usually stay on until the end. That's the job of investigative agents."

Emma hunched in on herself, curling in as if for self-protection. "Then I'm out."

"You're out if Meg and Hawk are off the case?" Van Cleave clarified.

"Yeah."

"And if I get approval for her to stay on?" Meg's head whipped toward Van Cleave, but he held up an index finger, staying her protest. "Emma?"

"I'll stay if she and Hawk stay."

"Do you need my word on that before we start?"

"Yeah."

"Done. Meg, a moment outside?"

Meg stood, giving the signal for Hawk to stay with Emma for comfort; she'd be able to keep an eye on him through the window in the door. She followed Van Cleave out into the hallway, closing the door behind her. Then she turned on him. "You can't promise that," she hissed in a stage whisper. "My SAC expects me to be back with the search teams tomorrow. Lives could depend on it."

"I read the reports coming in. The rescue is a recovery by this point. They need cadaver dogs, not search-and-rescue. And the lives you'd save here could far outnumber any you'd save on the coast."

"That's not your call to make."

"I can make it my call. Do you have any idea what these people go through? How long they last out there under these men? Farmhands are literally worked to death. Kids are hooked on drugs to keep them under the control of their pimps. More of them die from overdoses than ever get out. Immigrants are lured with the hope of a better life and find themselves in a cycle of killing debt, degradation, and abuse. Look, I'm sorry she made a connection with you and your dog, and I know you have specific skills that are better used elsewhere, but do you know how rare she is?"

When Meg simply stared up at him, her anger muted in the face of his passion for his calling, he continued. "*Extremely*. A kid who is gutsy enough to escape a certain death, not only escape but to save another victim with her? A kid who somehow seems to have avoided the clutches of drug addiction and has a clear head, so she'll be able to recall people and places? A young woman who has reached the age of majority, so we don't have walls thrown up by parents or have to trip over CPS to get the job done? One who is most certainly carrying around significant baggage but who has the potential to get out of that life to make something of herself? Yes, she can be of help to us. We, in turn, can give her her life back, as well as those of everyone else we free. Isn't that worth taking yourself out of your own comfort zone for a while?"

Meg pushed down irritation that he thought she didn't want to work the case because it made her squeamish. "That's not it at all. I was Richmond PD; I know about cases like this. My concern is my commitment to my team and our own caseload. Having me is one thing, but it takes

Hawk away from the team. And no, before you ask, I can't hand him off to someone else. We're a team and one doesn't go without the other. You get me for this case, you get my dog too." Meg forced herself to take a breath and to roll some of the tension out of her shoulders. "How about this? I'll call Craig and see if he agrees to my staying on for a short period of time. If he green-lights it, I'm in for as long as he can manage without me. If not, I'm out and I'll be sorry that I couldn't help you."

"I can call my assistant director to speak on my behalf, if that would help."

"Let me deal with this first. Craig may need to take it up to Executive Assistant Director Adam Peters for final approval. What?" she asked when Van Cleave winced.

"I hear Peters is a hard-ass."

"He can be, but he and I have recently come to an understanding. He may be a bigger asset to your cause than you think. I'm going to call now, so give me a few minutes. Go eat pizza and discuss the merits of Snapchat versus Instagram with her."

"Snapchat?"

Meg rolled her eyes. "Find something—anything—not case-related to chat about."

Five minutes later she was back in the room, her cell phone still in her hand. She gave a subtle nod to Van Cleave and then sat back in her chair, picked up her pizza and took a bite, as if she'd never left.

Emma glanced at her cautiously. "Are you and Hawk staying?"

"We are. For as long as you need us."

Emma's torso sagged, her hands falling limply into her lap. "Okay."

Meg reached over and gripped her hand. "You can do this. We're both here to help and to keep you safe. That's a promise."

"Okay, let's get into it then," Van Cleave said. "Let start with who ran you. Do you know his name?"

"He called himself John, but I never thought that was his real name. Why would he tell us that?"

"Smart girl. He probably didn't. No last name given?"

Emma shook her head.

"Did he keep you in a house?"

"Yes. I can take you there."

Van Cleave froze, his body absolutely still except for the sharpening of his gaze. "You can?"

"If you want. You won't find anyone there though. We left because of the storm."

"Even if we can't find anyone, we'll find evidence and maybe, just maybe, he'll come back at some point for his stuff and we'll nail him. Even if he doesn't, finding a holding house as opposed to a temporary storefront is a huge break. That gives us a chance to connect other perps with the ring as well as other victims. So, the storm was moving in . . ."

"John didn't want to leave. He wanted to hole up and wait for it to pass. Safer and easier to lie low that way. A few of the girls were out working already, but there were four of us still there. It got to a point where it wasn't safe to stay, so he loaded us all into the van. Normally he moved us one at a time to a job by car, but had the van for when there was a 'party' requiring more than one of us." The corners of her lips tipped down. "Or all of us."

Meg winced and couldn't help but remember what she'd been doing at this age. Finishing high school, planning for college, and deciding what to spend her birthday money on—clothes, shoes, or a new MP3 player.

"How did he get you all in without one of you trying to make a break for it?"

"He took us out one at a time. He kept us locked in one of the upstairs rooms until then. And we knew he was armed. He never failed to show us his gun or his knife and remind us that we were disposable. Like garbage, he always used to say. If he killed one of us, he'd just put us out with the weekly trash. He put us in the van, buckled us in, and bound our wrists so we were trapped in our seat belts. We could hardly get to the van because of how bad the storm was. Never seen wind like that—the rain was blowing sideways. When we were all in the van, he tried to outrun the storm. I could see the crash coming before we even got there . . ." Her eyes went unfocused, hazy with memory.

"At the low-water crossing?"

"Yeah. I could sorta see out the front windshield, but it was hard with the rain. Even with the wipers going full speed, it wasn't clear. Up ahead, I could just barely see the road kind of disappear. It went wavy, even through all that rain. I realized it was underwater. I screamed at John to stop, that we could turn around and go home, but he said we couldn't and we had no choice but to go through. He floored it and tried to ram through the flood. But it wasn't like a deep puddle; there was a current there. It hit the front of the van and spun us. The other girls were screaming and crying. Except for Mary; she was dead quiet. Never made a sound. Then the van rolled and everything was crashing and being thrown around. John opened his window . . . and then he was gone."

"He got sucked out into the storm, or he jumped?" Meg asked.

Emma shrugged, the carelessness of the action telling Meg more about her opinion of John than words could. "Not sure. I think he jumped. It would be like him to save his own skin and leave us to die alone."

"But you didn't die." Not wanting her to get sucked into bad memories, Meg tugged her along. "You got out. Tell us how you did that."

"I managed to pull one hand free at some point during

the roll, so once we finally came to a stop, I was able to get the other hand loose." She blinked furiously, as if holding back tears. "I wasn't fast enough. Celia was in the seat beside me and we ended up hanging in midair, but something had hit her in the head. It grazed me as it went by. Something big and heavy. Maybe the metal toolbox. By the time we stopped rolling, she was already gone. Mary and Leah were on the other side of the van, underwater. I couldn't get to them both in time." Her voice broke. "I tried, but I couldn't do it."

"You got Mary out." Van Cleave's voice was calm, the tone of someone who had soothed the distraught before. "Most people would have just saved themselves."

Emma sniffed and rubbed the back of her hand over her nose. "We had no one else. We had to stick together."

"And you did. You got Mary out. And then got her away from the river."

"That was hard. Her leg was really bad and the storm kept knocking us down. She couldn't go too far in the end. At least I got her to shelter. I don't know if she fell asleep or lost consciousness, but she was out for a while. I waited until the storm died down, then I had to go. She knew she was slowing me down and made me leave."

"That's what friends do," Meg said. "She wanted you to make it, so she let you go. And in the end, you both made it."

"Can you tell us how long you've been with John?" Van Cleave asked.

"About three years? I don't even know what date it is now, but we could track the seasons changing, and we knew when the big holidays happened."

"We can at least help with that." Meg told her the current date. "So, how did you hook up with John?"

Emma worried a loose thread on the hem of her scrub top. She opened her mouth to speak, closed it, and sat back in her chair, silent.

Meg and Van Cleave exchanged glances.

"You're not in trouble," Meg clarified. "We're not trying to find a way to burn you."

Emma took a long sip from her cup, then set it down, spinning it a few times before she spoke. "I was young, and very stupid. I never would have fallen for it now."

"Emma . . ." Van Cleave waited until the girl looked up at him. "We're not judging you. If you think that both of us didn't do stupid things when we were younger, you're dead wrong, let me tell you. We all lived, and most certainly learned."

Emma stared at him skeptically, but remained silent.

"How about I trade my really stupid story for yours?" he offered.

"You'd share that?"

"Sure. Why should you have to feel stupid by yourself?"

Emma stared at him, her slack face reflecting pure bafflement. "Has anyone ever told you that you don't act like a cop?"

"That's because I'm not a cop. I'm a federal agent on a task force to stop human trafficking." He aimed an index finger at her. "You're not my target." He angled a thumb over his shoulder, pointed toward the door. "They're out there somewhere." He paused to take a quick sip of his drink. "I could tell you about the time I faked a rejection letter from an Ivy League school so a girl I had a massive crush on would feel sorry for me and go to the prom with me—"

"You did not," Meg interrupted.

"I sure did." He flashed a grin full of teeth. "Worked too." He raised his left hand, wiggling his fingers to highlight his wedding ring. "Been married to her for nearly thirty years. Granted, she was a little put out when she found out that I'd faked it. Didn't speak to me for a whole week. Of course, we were about two months away from our wedding day, so she had to seriously consider giving me a second chance. But that was just a stupid prank that led to a good outcome. Let's take my penchant for 2:00 AM street racing when I was sixteen. Lost control of my car one day, rolled it and nearly killed myself and my best friend. I broke my arm, he ended up in the ICU. In the end, the cops chalked it up to reckless driving and speeding. I did community service for it, and my friend was rewarded with his life. Luckily for me, that record got expunged when I reached the age of majority or I'd never have made it into the air force and then into the FBI. So . . ." He leaned back and propped his arm on the top of the chair beside him. "Did your stupidity nearly kill someone?"

"No."

"Then you were smarter than me. How did you meet John?"

Emma locked gazes with him for a moment. It was clear the moment she decided it was safe to tell her story, simply from the way her body relaxed and opened up as her chin rose. "I ran away from home. It wasn't a good situation and I was sure I'd be safer and happier on the streets. But the streets weren't safe at all. All my stuff got stolen and I was begging for food or money. Then I got arrested for shoplifting." She looked up to meet Van Cleave's eyes. "I was so hungry. I just wanted food. I got away with it twice. Got caught the third time."

"What happened?" he asked gently.

"I did some time in juvie. Then I was transferred to a private reentry facility. That's where I met John."

Meg was familiar with both reentry facilities and the private prison system. She was not a fan of the latter. At all. Powerful, publicly-traded companies building and running private incarceration facilities where profit was the end goal. And profit meant they needed the facilities to be full. Mandatory minimum sentencing was a boon to the private prison system, which happily took the overflow from the state-run systems. They'd also branched out into reentry facilities—places where those who'd served their time went to "learn" how to reenter society as useful and contributing members. Ideally, the facilities would give convicts the best chance at starting a new life, and hopefully never darkening the door of another prison. In concept, these facilities had merit. Where it got sticky was when they were also run by private companies that had a vested interest in increased recidivism, because convicts who fell back on old ways and re-offended would return to prison, once again increasing their profits.

"He was nice to me," Emma continued. "He was friendly and told me I was pretty, and actually listened when I talked. We were leaving at the same time and he knew I was going back to the streets, so he offered me a room in his house, no strings attached. Winter was coming and it was getting cold, so I took him up on it. At first everything went great. The only thing he did I didn't like was he kept offering me drugs. Heroin mostly. The reason I left home was because my mom was an addict, and that sure as hell wasn't something I was going to try after seeing how it ruined her life. Then he asked me to do some favors, dropping some packages off to his 'buddies.' I found out later they contained crack and heroin. Sometimes meth. When I told him I didn't want to do that anymore, he hit me for the first time and told me I didn't have a choice. I was an accomplice, and the mandatory minimums for drug running when I already had a criminal record would have me behind bars for most of my adult life. He'd hate to have that information slip to the police. Then he used that as leverage for me to start doing sexual 'favors' for his friends. At first, just the odd one. Then a few more. Soon it was every night, a different hotel room, a different guy or guys. By that time, he'd moved me into a house with six other girls and I was trapped. I thought . . ." Her hand dropped to her belly. "I thought he'd let me go when I got pregnant. No man would want me with a big belly. Instead, he took that away from me too, before it hurt his business. He took everything away." She started rocking back and forth in her chair.

"I think I missed it," Meg said softly. "All I hear in your story is a young woman doing whatever she needed to do to survive. What was so stupid that you didn't want to tell us?"

The eyes that turned on her held the devastated disappointment of years of being beaten down. "That I fell for his offer. That I might be worthy of his love and would do anything for it and for attention. In the end, I wasn't."

"Emma, I want you to listen to me." Van Cleave leaned across the table, both palms pressed flat to the surface. "You are worthy of affection and attention. Clearly, you were too worthy for his. And you're going to be the strong person who shows him that, when we track him down and put him away. You have my word on it. Will you help us get started on it tonight? Will you show us the house?"

The rocking stopped. "You want to start now?"

"Why not? You have something better to do?"

"I thought you would—you know, go home to your wife or something."

"This is something better to do. My wife understands what I need to do and fully supports it. You need me tonight more than she does." He glanced at Meg. "Can you and Hawk come?"

"Sure. I hope you can drive because my SUV is somewhere across town."

"Sure." Van Cleave pushed back from his desk. "We have a few hours of daylight left. It's more than enough time to bring this son of a bitch down."

CHAPTER 14

Catching Feature: A visible, obvious landmark which can be used to navigate to another remote, unseen location.

Sunday, July 23, 7:49 PM
West 48th Street
Norfolk, Virginia

Meg had no words. Van Cleave did, most of them blue.

They stood on what was left of West 48th Street, having had to park Van Cleave's sedan four blocks away and hike in to the site through what was left of the Larchmont-Edgewater neighborhood. Situated behind the Norfolk Southern Lambert's Point Docks and a cluster of apartment buildings, this was an older neighborhood. The house Emma led them to was at the end of the street, a redbrick bungalow, sheltered on three sides by overgrown oak, ash, and pine trees. The other side of the property opened onto the waters of Hampton Roads Harbor.

At least that's what Meg's phone showed them through Google Street View. Now, the trees were felled, splintered, or washed away. The house itself was simply gone.

"It got swept out to sea?" Emma's voice was full of shock. "All of it?"

"Looks like it." Meg stepped onto the property, wading through sand layered over the grass a full six inches deep. "Hawk, with me." She still had him on his leash, but she scanned the area to see if there was cause to let him off lead to search, if there was any hint of life remaining. Hawk had his nose in the air, scenting the winds, but he looked up at her and whined.

Nothing.

She turned to Van Cleave. "This would have been a bad area for the storm tide. We're at the mouth of the Elizabeth River here. The water would have come in like a wall, stories high, pulverizing anything in its path, and then either driving it inland, or, more likely, washing it back out to sea. There's nothing. And Hawk is telling me there are no survivors."

Van Cleave had left his suit jacket in his car, so he paced over the sand in his shirtsleeves, his hands jammed deep in his pockets. "I really hoped we'd have a good chance at finding something." He turned to Emma, who stood staring at the footprint of the house's foundation, scoured practically clean. "You okay?"

"It's like it never existed. Like the storm just came in and wiped it clean away." A smile unevenly tilted one side of her lips. "It seems right somehow. It was an evil place."

Meg walked to her, Hawk at her side, to rub a hand over her back. "I'm sorry you lost your things."

Emma's shrug was pure indifference. "They were just things. Now I have nothing from my years here. Nothing to take with me."

"Maybe it's easier to make a fresh start that way?"

"Maybe." She turned to Van Cleave. "Now you don't have anything. Sorry."

"Hardly your fault." Van Cleave picked his way over the sand and around debris to her. "And I do have something. I have you. There's a lot more you know we haven't gone over. Locations, men, other girls in the house. And more about John. He's my focus to start. He leads back to everything else."

"You think he's a connection to the wider circle?" Meg asked as Emma dropped to her knees to pet Hawk, something Meg suspected was more for her comfort than the dog's.

"I do. These small groups rarely function in isolation. They're often part of a larger organization. So 'John,' or whatever his name might be, is the key to our going deeper. To pulling down the whole house of cards." He stopped, his gaze locked on Emma, who was stifling a huge yawn behind her hand. "But not tonight. We've done enough for today. Let's regroup in the morning."

Emma looked up, suddenly unsure. "Where will I go until then?"

"Don't worry, I have the perfect place. It's a shelter run by a friend of mine." When Emma shot to her feet, her eyes wide, he held up a hand. "Not that kind of shelter. You won't have to go to classes or attend Bible lessons. This is a place for runaways who are just looking for a safe roof over their heads. My friend Lily runs it and takes in anyone I bring to her. She's kind and she won't ask any questions. You'll have food and clean sheets and privacy for maybe the first time in a long time. Meg and Hawk and I will take you there tonight and make sure you're safely settled, then I'll come get you tomorrow. Okay?"

"Okay." She sank down next to Hawk again, running her hands over his fur.

Van Cleave turned to Meg. "Can you meet us tomorrow at the Norfolk field office? I want to work with Emma to do a profile on John, and then I want her to look at mug shots. He went through reentry, so he has to be in the system. If on the slim chance we can't find his photo, I have a really talented sketch artist on hand who can take a vague recollection from a witness and turn it into an amazingly realistic sketch. If we need to, we'll go wide on network TV with it. But I bet we'll track him down from a profile and mug shot."

"I'll have my vehicle back by then, so that will work fine. What time do you want to start?"

"Nine too early for you?"

"Not at all. My team will already be out searching by then." She crouched down next to Emma. "By the time you get to the field office, I'll be there and so will Hawk, okay? You can hang out with Hawk the whole time you're there. Will that make it easier?"

Emma nodded, but seemed too overwhelmed to speak.

"You've taken a huge step today. Tomorrow, we're going to start the search for that man who hurt you. And then we'll make him pay."

CHAPTER 15

Last Known Position: The last known location of a subject, based upon physical evidence.

Monday, July 24, 8:55 AM
FBI Field Office
Norfolk, Virginia

Meg walked into an office as familiar as any of the handful of other field offices she'd visited over the years—the cluttered corridors, clusters of desks, forests of monitors all bearing a desktop image of the FBI logo, and the surrounding glass-fronted offices that lined the perimeter. It gave her an instant feeling of comfort.

It clearly had the opposite effect on the young woman at her side. Emma walked stiffly, her movements jerky and her eyes shifting from side to side, as if expecting an attack to come from any direction. A fish out of water in the worst possible way.

In a late-night phone call to Van Cleave, Meg had offered to pick Emma up on her way into the field office. She had her SUV back from Webb, and thought picking Emma up would get the girl back with Hawk sooner, and it would save Van Cleave a trip. He'd been happy to oblige.

She'd spent the night with the team and Webb again, at

the same community center, so she'd been able to hear about what she'd missed. When she'd apologized for being sidetracked, Brian, Lauren, and Scott had been unanimous in their opinion that she needed to be on the human trafficking case.

"To tell you the truth," Lauren said. "I'm a little jealous. I'm getting worried about Rocco. He's not taking the lack of live rescues well, and hiding live volunteers gets less and less convincing when you keep doing it day in and day out." She turned to Craig. "What's our time line on this?"

"Tomorrow is our last day." Craig put his mug of lethal black coffee down on the dog crate they were using as a table in the middle of their circle of chairs. "Randolph and his team of cadaver dogs are coming in on Tuesday, so we'll head back to D.C. tomorrow night. Except for you," he said to Meg.

"And I have no idea how long I'll be," she said. She turned to Webb, beside her nursing his own coffee. "What about you?"

"I've been asked to stay on for a few more days. They don't really need me as a paramedic anymore, but they have requested that a few of us from DCFEMS hang around for a few more days in the role of firefighter to help with recovery operations, and admin cleared it for the lot of us. They offered to put me up at one of the firehouses, but I told them I had a place for tonight anyway." He raised his mug, toasting the team. "I'll head there tomorrow with the rest of my guys. And maybe we'll end up going home together in a few days."

"You're awfully optimistic about my case. Granted, Emma will need me for only so long, so we'll see."

Now looking at Emma, Meg was again unsure how long she'd be needed here, and it gnawed at her. She knew this was important, but in the back of her mind, she couldn't help but feel that it was a waste of Hawk's talents.

Let's get the show on the road and see how fast we move along.

Meg extended Hawk's leash to Emma. "Hey, can you hold on to Hawk for a minute while I find out where Van is?" Without waiting, she pushed the leash into Emma's hands and then wove through the maze of desks to a young man at a computer. She glanced back; as she hoped, Emma was too busy talking to Hawk to concentrate on her surroundings.

She stood by the young man's desk, and when he didn't look up, she cleared her throat to get his attention. "Excuse me, I'm looking for SAC Van Cleave."

The young agent didn't even look away from his screen. "Far end of the office, second door from the left. His nameplate is on his window."

"Thanks." Meg made her way back to Emma and took Hawk's leash. "Follow me." They wound through the maze of desks to the far end of the room. Van Cleave sat behind his glass office wall, his name and rank on a brass plaque affixed next to the door. Meg rapped her knuckles on the open door. "Good morning."

Van Cleave raised his head from the document he was reading and put it and his pen down. He stood, smiling warmly at them. "Good morning. How was your night?"

"I was at a community center, so it was loud and bright, but I was with my team, so it was all good," Meg said.

"Your friend is nice," Emma said. She brushed a hand over the T-shirt and jeans she wore. "She gave me these clothes and a place to sleep and made sure I got breakfast this morning."

"And if I know Lily, she didn't ask any questions. She's a firm believer in letting kids talk when they're ready and that pushing only makes them clam up. If you ever want to talk to someone, she'd be a good ear and could offer some sage, nonjudgmental advice. She was an addict once, and out on the streets herself. If anyone understands the pressures a lot of kids are under, it's Lily." He indicated the two chairs opposite his desk. "Have a seat." He closed his office door and then sat behind his desk again. "Emma, you're still willing to help us?"

"Sure."

"Okay, we're going to start with the basics. To find John, we need to identify him. You met him in reentry. My money is on the fact that someone who traffics in young girls is not a sterling model citizen, so he'll likely have multiple hits in the system. Do you know what a mug shot is?"

"You mean the pictures taken of a person when they get arrested?"

Van Cleave jabbed an index finger at her. "Right on. Now, we don't use those big books anymore that you used to see in crime shows. All photos are digitized. As you can imagine, there are a lot of them, but we can enter search parameters to narrow down the number of pictures. Let's look at some basic details." He pushed back from his desk and stood. "Was he taller or shorter than me? How about his weight? Fatter? Skinnier?" He flexed his biceps. "Remember, I spend my day behind a desk, so he's probably more muscular?"

Emma studied him for a second, then stood, stepped over Hawk, who lay at her feet, and circled the desk to stand in front of Van Cleave. She looked up at him. "A little shorter. Maybe an inch or two, but no more. Bigger than you, but not fat, definitely more muscular. John liked to work out with weights." Her lips tightened. "He once knocked one of the girls unconscious with a single punch."

"Good information." Van Cleave sat back down again while Emma returned to her chair. "I'll make the height range a little wider to make sure we don't miss him, so I'll say my six-foot-one down to five-foot-ten. Weight range . . . let's say one-ninety to two-twenty." He two-finger typed details into some of the search fields on his computer. "Age?"

Emma flopped back in her chair, her hand dropping to find Hawk below. "That's harder."

"Don't say 'old,' because at your age that's everything thirty and up." He looked at Meg and gave an exaggerated wince. "That makes you old too."

"And you, ancient," Meg retorted, trying to match his attempt to keep things light for Emma.

"Don't I know it. Some mornings it's hard to drag these dusty old bones out of bed. Emma, anything besides old?"

"I'm probably going to be off. He looked worn. Tired out. I bet he's younger than he looks."

"Take that in account and do your best to compensate for it. How old do you think he might have been? Twenty? Forty?"

"Definitely not forty. Not twenty either." She gave Van Cleave a wobbly half-smile. "Maybe twenty-five to thirty?"

"That works for me." He entered more data. "Skin color?"

"White."

"Eye color?"

"Blue."

"Hair?"

"Sort of a sandy blond. Kind of messy, like he always needed a haircut."

"Good. Good. Any distinguishing marks?"

Emma cocked her head to one side. "Like a mole or a scar?"

"Sure. Or a tattoo."

Emma sat up straighter, looking energized for the first time since entering the field office. "He has a tattoo on his left forearm. It's kind of tribal and the guy who did it made it look 3-D, like it's actually carved into his skin. John's an asshole, but his tattoo is super cool."

"And you said you didn't know much." Van Cleave's

grin was pure triumph. "An individual mark like that is gold for making an identification. You said it's a tribal mark. Could you draw it?" He rummaged in his desk and pulled out a yellow legal pad and a pencil and offered them to Emma.

Emma laid the pad in her lap and tentatively started to sketch. "I'm not a great artist, but I'll do my best."

"I can't draw stick people," Meg said. "You're already doing way better than I ever could."

For a few minutes, there was only the scratch of pencil on paper as she drew, with the occasional mumbled curse accompanied by mad erasing. Finally, she put the pencil down, stared at the sketch, her head bobbing as if satisfied. "This is as close as I can make it." She turned around the pad of paper so Meg and Van Cleave could see her work.

The drawing showed a number of swirling lines crossing and curling over each other, each one ending in curving thorny points. Each line was shaded as if three dimensional, the background dark, as if the flesh was excised from those spots.

"That's fantastic." Van Cleave took the pad of paper. "As long as he had that tattoo when he was arrested, I think you just nailed him to the wall. And if he didn't, it's still going to be the single identifying factor that brings him in. Well done. Can you think of any other distinguishing physical traits?"

"No."

"Good enough. I'll run the physical characteristics and we'll leave the tattoo as confirmation, as he might not have had it at the time of booking." Van Cleave hit the enter key with a flourish and then leaned back in his chair. "We'll leave that to think for a few minutes." He laughed at his own joke. "We may want to get lunch, it can sometimes take so long. Or how about just a coffee? Or a soda?"

"How bad is the coffee here?" Meg asked. "Remember? Ex-cop? I know all about cop coffee, even when it's at the Bureau. It's *all* cop coffee."

"Aha! Got you there. I splurged last year and bought one of those pod coffeemakers for the office. Everyone chips in ten bucks a month, and one of the admin assistants keeps the pods stocked. She's also a rabid recycler, so if she finds one of those plastic pods in the trash, she'll hunt down whoever did it. So, we get decent coffee and we save the environment. Emma, would you like something? I can also make you a hot chocolate."

"I'd like that, thanks."

"Meg?"

"Coffee. And since you've likely got a million kinds, surprise me. I like it with both cream and sugar, regular."

"Done." Van Cleave practically jogged out of the office.

Baffled, Emma looked at Meg. "Is he for real?"

"Meaning, is he really that nice a guy that he gets pleasure from doing good in both the big and small sense of the word? Yeah, he really is. He's a classic G-man."

"G-man?"

"A government man. It's a slang term for an FBI agent, straight out of the nineteen-thirties and Al Capone. Basically, he's an old-fashioned good guy. His only focus is on solving crime. Kind of refreshing actually. I know too many agents who just want to climb the ladder, or have some other kind of agenda. He just wants to put the bad guys away."

The G-man was back in just a few minutes, balancing three covered paper cups. He handed them out and then sat back down. He gave his monitor a cursory glance—the program was still running the search parameters—and pulled a small, leather-bound notebook out of his desk drawer and uncapped a fancy silver pen. "Okay, while it's searching, let's run over some details. I've already got some notes going for this case, but there are lots of blank spaces that still need to be filled in."

Emma studied the notebook. "You're going to write it down by hand?"

"Absolutely. I'll add it to the electronic case file later, but the notebook travels with me. If I need to refer to something, I can; all the info is right there."

Emma and Meg exchanged a glance that reflected their shared thought—*G-man*.

"Okay," Van Cleave said, scanning down the scratchy blue handwriting already in the notebook. "You said you met John in reentry and then met up with him again when you were both out. What happened after that? Tell me as much as you can remember in as much detail as possible."

Van Cleave patiently helped Emma through every detail she could recall—men, especially repeat customers, hookup locations, payments, other girls in the house, and when drugs were involved.

Emma flopped back in her chair, one hand dropping down to stroke Hawk, looking exhausted from the telling.

"Anything else you can think of?"

"No." Her head drooped forward, but then shot back up almost immediately. "Wait!"

"What?"

"The book. John's little book."

"Back up. What book?"

"He had one of those little spiral-ring notebooks with a black plastic cover that he carried everywhere with him. He kept all his business details in it. Contact names, appointments in the calendar, details about customers. When you find him, you need to get the book. Don't let him destroy it."

Van Cleave and Meg exchanged a glance. "Sounds like that could be a good portion of the case against him."

"He'd have to have that information somewhere," Meg

said. "Most people would use a phone, but he's kicking it old school. And paper never runs out of battery power or glitches on you. And you can burn it, if you need to. Phones can be harder to destroy."

"They can be, to my great joy and happiness. Emma, did you ever overhear John talking about the trafficking operation?"

"They tried to keep us in the dark and out of earshot as much as possible. But John did a lot of his business by phone, and I once heard a bit of a conversation when his phone rang while we were in the car going to a location. He didn't say much, but he mentioned a vineyard, something about 'upping the supplies,' and mentioned the name Maverick."

Van Cleave stopped writing. "Do you remember when this was? What time of year?"

Emma closed her eyes, concentrating. "I'm not sure, but if I had to guess, late summer or maybe early fall?"

Van Cleave exchanged a look with Meg. "That's the kind of connection I'm looking for. Not just running girls for the sex trade, but a connection into one of the other organizational arms. Virginia has a lot of vineyards. In the late summer and right through the fall, they need hands. A *lot* of hands. The kind of hands you don't keep on all year."

"The kind you don't report on your taxes as employees because then you'd have to provide real wages and some form of benefits?" Meg asked.

"Exactly that kind. Some of them bring in migrant workers, pay them practically nothing, work them from dawn until dusk, and then cut them loose when the season is over with no responsibility for where they might find shelter or their next paycheck. I wanted to find this guy before, but now I *really* want to find him."

As if on cue, his computer gave a quiet *ding* and a list of names with small thumbnail photos scrolled down the screen. Van Cleave closed his notebook, set his pen on the cover, and rolled back his chair. He stepped aside and held out a hand toward it. "Emma, have a seat." He waited until she circled the desk and settled in his chair before showing her how to open each entry for a better look at the photo and some limited details. "Remember, some of these photos might not be that recent, so anyone that rings any bells, no matter how faint, let me know." He picked up his coffee and settled in the chair Emma had vacated to watch as she made her way through the list.

Fifteen minutes later, she froze, staring unblinkingly at the face on the screen. "Van?"

"Got something?" Van Cleave had been watching her intently, even as he and Meg had been chatting about common Bureau pet peeves. Now, while his voice was smoothly casual, his body tensed, as if ready to spring from the chair.

"This was years ago and he looks super young, but I'm pretty sure this is him. I don't see a tattoo though."

Van Cleave got up and came around the desk to brace one hand on its surface as he leaned in for a better look. "You're not seeing all the information. This is just the interface for witnesses. I can access additional information, including any distinguishing physical markings. If he had a tattoo at the time of his arrest, we'll be able to match it to what you've drawn." A few clicks and keystrokes and a much larger file was displayed on screen. He clicked on a thumbnail and a photo of an intricate three-dimensional tribal tattoo filled the screen. Picking up the yellow legal pad with Emma's sketch of John's tattoo, he held it next to the photographic image of an actual tattoo. "That is damned good, young lady. Not exact, but you nailed the tone and the basic design."

Meg moved to prop her hip on the corner of the desk

for a better view and whistled at the two images side by side. "I'll say. Who is our mystery man?"

"Emma, can I get my chair back, please? Thanks." He sat back down behind his desk and started exploring the file. "According to this, his real name is Luke Reed. Now, let's see what he was up to. Ah, here we are. Mr. Reed had a little problem with assault. Convicted three times of assault and battery. Accused of sexual assault but the victim recanted her story. They must have gotten to her. Might have paid her off to change her story. More likely, they threatened her. Happens way too often. He was found guilty and incarcerated all three times, twice for six months, and the third time for nine months. Once inside, he was supposedly a model citizen. Each time he went through the same residential custody reentry program. Chesapeake Community Corrections Service Center." He looked up from his monitor. "Apparently this program isn't working for him. He's re-offended each time anyway."

"Is it odd that he'd be in the same program three times? I didn't think they were used that often. Most offenders are just released from prison and go out into the world."

Van Cleave shrugged in Meg's direction. "Maybe it's just the new thing these days? We're more concerned with arresting them as opposed to reforming them, so maybe we're not up on all the new trends in offender rehabilitation."

"I'm even mostly out of the loop on arresting them." She glanced at Van Cleave, then at Emma, and then back again. She jerked her head subtly toward the door.

Van Cleave's answering nod said he understood. "Emma, we need to make a couple of phone calls, so why don't you wait where you'll be more comfortable in those cushy chairs out there." He pointed to two overstuffed armchairs that made up a small waiting area outside his glass wall.

"Why don't you take Hawk with you for company," Meg offered. "Oh wait, you should take these." She dug in her bag and pulled out three jerky treats that she passed surreptitiously to Emma. Hawk, of course, wasn't remotely fooled, following the movement of her hand with bright eyes and a thumping tail. "He's trained not to beg and not to take a treat until it's held out for him. Then say 'take it,' along with his name."

Emma and Hawk left Van Cleave's office and Meg watched as they went over to the chairs. Emma flopped down in one, one knee hooked over the arm, and told Hawk to sit. Then she held out a treat to him. Hawk held absolutely still, even his tail was motionless. Then she told him to take it, and the treat was gone and the tail was back in motion. Emma laughed and gave him a big hug.

Van Cleave quietly closed his office door. "That is one well-behaved dog."

"Thanks. He's a smart boy. There pretty much isn't anything I can't teach him."

Van Cleave sat back down and propped his elbows on the chair arms, steepling his fingers. "You got rid of her so we can talk. What's on your mind?"

"I didn't want to get into case particulars with her in the room. What if Reed's using reentry to feed his organization, taking advantage of his time through the reentry program to make contact with vulnerable girls? Targeting kids who don't have family or anyone else waiting for them on the other side. He makes friends with them, convincing them he's a nice guy, possibly even boyfriend material, getting them to trust him. Then he'd get them into a situation they couldn't escape. Some kids he probably hooked on drugs so once they were addicted they'd do whatever he wanted, just to get that next hit. He tried that with Emma, but when she didn't take that bait, he had to find another leverage point—the mandatory minimums and the threat of going back to jail."

"You're thinking that we might be able to cross-reference girls who were at the reentry facility at the same time to see if he dragged them into the ring as well." Van Cleave bent back over his keyboard. "That's a good connection."

"Thanks. I'm wondering how many other girls might still be out there. Emma said three girls were already out working when the storm hit. We can get specific details on them from her, and maybe you can track them down if they made it through the storm?"

"Sure can," Van Cleave agreed. "I'm not sure if the storm was a blessing or a curse for those girls. Yes, they got away from Reed, but who knows if they escaped to somewhere safe—"

"Or if they fell into a worse situation," Meg finished for him. "For all of Reed's threats to the girls themselves, they were still an investment to him. He didn't want them getting battered and bruised, because his customers might object."

"But someone with no investment might see them as instantly disposable. They could be in real danger now, with the risk growing each day they're out there on their own. You know how situations like this work—the first few days are critical. After that, they may be dragged into the city's underbelly and our chances of successfully pulling them out shrink exponentially. Not to mention that if we can track any of them down, they might also be able to strengthen our case. Before Emma leaves, I'll get as much information on each of them as I can so I can get bulletins out to the Norfolk and Virginia Beach PDs." He started to say something and then stopped, staring at Meg. "What? You have a funny look on your face."

"I'm just thinking . . ."

Van Cleave crossed his arms over his chest and waited her out.

"I have a contact that might be useful to us."

"Like a confidential informant?"

"More like the guy who has the confidential informants in his pocket. A lot of them. Ever heard of Clay McCord?"

"The hotshot *Washington Post* reporter who covered the war in Iraq? Wasn't he also the one that bomber was sending messages to?"

"That's him. What would you say if I called him in on this? He can ferret out information like nobody's business because he has the kind of contacts law enforcement doesn't."

Skepticism radiated from Van Cleave as his fingers tapped a repetitive rhythm on his crossed arm. "Can we trust him?"

"Absolutely. He's worked two cases with me behind the scenes, trading his help and silence for the scoop on the story once he's given the green light from the Bureau. He's also dating my sister. And, he's currently nearby because he was covering Hurricane Cole, so he's likely somewhere on the coast of North Carolina still. Why don't I call him? You've got your hands full, but I could fill him in and let him know what kinds of information we're looking for. Then if anything hits, I'll loop you back in." When Van Cleave nodded his assent, she pulled out her cell phone, speed-dialed McCord, put the phone on speaker, and placed it on Van Cleave's desk.

"McCord."

Meg couldn't help smiling at the sound of his voice. Even though Cara had passed along that he had come through Hurricane Cole in one piece, it was good to hear his voice. "Hey, McCord."

"Meg! How are you?"

"Good. I have a question for you. First, I want you to know you're on speaker and I'm here with Special Agent in Charge Walter Van Cleave from the Norfolk FBI field office."

"Sure. What's up?"

"Are you nearly done in North Carolina?"

"I can be. Does the Bureau have something my editor would find meatier than a hurricane that's already blown itself out?"

"Depends on what you can contribute. How are your ties to the Virginia crime world?"

McCord laughed. "Not bad, if I do say so myself. Looking for something in particular?"

"Connections in human trafficking. Specifically, the sex trade with little girls."

There was dead silence for a moment before McCord spoke. "There's no snappy comeback for that. That's despicable."

"No question. And now you understand why we're looking for some undercover information that your kind of CIs might be able to deliver. Can you meet me so I can run through what we're looking for?"

"Why don't I drive up tonight? You and I could have dinner and you can run me through what you know."

Meg glanced at Van Cleave, who mouthed, *As long as you're sure you can trust him.* She nodded back. "That works. McCord, standard agreement for silence until you're released. Then you'll have the exclusive."

"Deal, as always. I'll see you tonight then."

"Todd is here too, so you'll see him as well."

"All right! Getting the band back together."

"We're in Norfolk, but I'll text you an address where to meet us. Drive safe." She ended the call and looked up at Van Cleave.

"You're sure he can be trusted?" Van Cleave asked.

"I'd trust him with my life. I literally trusted him with my sister's and never regretted it. He's solid. Worst-case scenario, he won't be able to dig anything up and he'll have nothing to report. But he won't go public with anything until we say so. He's been reliable on that several times, and Executive Assistant Director Peters and Director Clarkson are both good with him. Let's give him a chance. In the meantime, what do you want to do?"

"I'm going to put a BOLO out on Reed. Then let's get Emma back to the shelter. After that, you and I will pay a visit to the Chesapeake Community Corrections Service Center. Let's find out more about Mr. Reed and who he might have crossed paths with."

"What if they won't cooperate without a warrant?"

"Then we'll get one of those." Van Cleave's sunny smile was backed by steel. "But you know how that would look. It usually seems that it's those with something to hide who make you come back with a warrant." The smile dropped as if it had never been there. "And if they have something to hide, they'll regret making me wait. It doesn't pay to get in my way during an investigation."

CHAPTER 16

Critique: A formal review of a search-and-rescue incident or a training exercise designed to identify operational errors and lessons learned.

Monday, July 24, 10:47 AM
Chesapeake Community Corrections Service Center
Chesapeake, Virginia

Meg and Van Cleave stood at the front security desk of the reentry facility, waiting to be cleared through the locked double doors. Both FBI identifications lay flat on the counter inside the booth as the security guard took down their information from behind a bulletproof glass window.

"I'll need you to leave any firearms with me," the guard said. "No weapons are allowed inside the facility."

"Understandable." Van Cleave opened his suit jacket to show that he wore neither shoulder nor belt holster. "I left my gun at the field office for that reason."

"I'm unarmed," Meg said. "But my dog is a trained law enforcement K-9 and will be accompanying me."

The guard braced both hands on the counter and leaned forward to look down over the edge of the window to where Hawk sat still at Meg's knee, the leash in her hand attached to his FBI vest. "Working dog?"

"He is. Is there a problem with that?"

The guard shrugged. "I guess not. But if there's any problems with him, you're both out of here."

"There won't be any problems with him." Meg's voice carried a hard edge, leaving no room for discussion.

The guard gave her a sideways look and pushed their IDs back out through the small cutout at the bottom of the window. "Through the double doors, down the hallway, second door on the right. Ask for Mason Pate. You're lucky. Mr. Pate isn't always in the office, but he arrived about an hour ago and he'd be the best person to talk to."

Van Cleave picked up his flip case and slipped it back into his inside breast pocket. "Thank you. We appreciate the help." He held out a hand for Meg and Hawk to precede him and then followed. As they approached the double doors, a loud buzz vibrated the metal, accompanied by the sharp metallic snap of the locks releasing. Meg opened the door and walked through with Hawk, and Van Cleave pulled the door closed behind them.

The facility looked like any standard industrial building—cinder-block walls, dull, light gray paint, no adornments, and not a single splash of color.

"This place is depressing," Meg said under her breath.

"It's essentially a prison," Van Cleave countered. "One meant for inmates nearing the end of their confinement, so you'd assume therefore on their best behavior to get the hell out of here. But still a prison."

The second doorway on their right was open; they passed through it into a small office and walked into an explosion of color. A petite woman with hair a shade of red that had to come from a bottle, wearing a dress of brilliant electric blue, sat behind a desk covered with multicolored file folders, a vibrant vase of wildflowers, and a selection of mismatched framed photos. Bright knickknacks and tiny flags cluttered the tops of filing cabinets surrounding her, and burgundy curtains waved gently in the breeze coming in the open window. The resulting clash of tones was nearly migraine-inducing. Meg could only assume that the occupant of the office did it in self-defense to ward off daily depression.

The woman looked up as they entered, her eyes instantly dropping down to Hawk, a bright smile curving her hot-pink lips at the sight of the dog. "Well, hello there. And who is this fine representative of the FBI?"

"This is Hawk. Hawk, say hi."

Hawk immediately sat down and politely raised a paw in greeting.

The woman behind the desk let out a squeal that nearly went ultrasonic as she jumped out of the chair to shake his paw. "Well, haven't you just made my day." She took a moment to stroke his head and murmur to him, and was rewarded by the thump of his tail. She reluctantly straightened. "I'm sure you didn't come in today to treat me to a visit. How can I help you?"

Van Cleave pulled out his ID again, flipping it open and extending it. "FBI Special Agent in Charge Walter Van Cleave and FBI handler Meg Jennings. We don't have an appointment, but we'd like to see Mr. Pate, please."

"Let me see if Mr. Pate is available." She took her seat and picked up her phone, her long, blood-red nails clacking on the buttons as she keyed in an extension. "Mr. Pate, I have two FBI agents in the office here to see you. No, they don't have an appointment, but they're asking if you're available to meet with them. Of course, sir." She placed the handset back in the cradle and pushed her rolling chair back from her desk. "Mr. Pate can make a few minutes for you now." She led them over to a door on the far side of her tiny office and opened it for them.

Van Cleave went through and Meg and Hawk followed, the door closing behind them with a soft click. They found themselves back in mind-numbing industrial neutral tones again, right down to the beige suit and brown tie worn by the man with mouse-brown hair behind the desk.

Van Cleave extended his ID and held out his hand. "Special Agent in Charge Walter Van Cleave." The two men shook.

Meg stepped forward, Hawk heeling at her knee. "FBI K-9 handler Meg Jennings and my partner, Hawk."

Mason Pate was a tall, portly man, slightly balding, his rounded stomach giving him an air of joviality matched by a sunny smile and a vigorous handshake. "Come in, please, sit down." He indicated two chairs in front of his desk and then took his own tall-backed leather desk chair.

Meg sat and gave Hawk a hand signal—*down*—while Van Cleave took the second chair.

"This is rather unexpected," said Pate. "Is there a problem with one of our residents?"

Residents, not inmates.

"Not any of your current residents," Van Cleave answered. He reached into his pocket and pulled out a folded piece of paper. He unfolded it and passed it across to Pate. "This is Luke Reed. Do you recognize him?"

Pate took a long moment to consider the mug shot Van Cleave had printed back in his office. "He doesn't look familiar to me." He laid the photo down on his desk and continued to study it. "While I manage this facility, it's only one of several I'm responsible for, and I'm only rarely in contact with our residents. We have competent staff doing that job, and I leave them to do it without the boss staring over their shoulder and micromanaging."

Meg settled back in her chair, comfortably crossing her legs. "Mr. Pate, can you give us an outline of the role of this facility? Many inmates are simply released at the end of their sentence and return to society. What does this center do that's different?"

"That's a good question, Ms. Jennings. We're a facility dedicated to ensuring that our residents have the best chance of success once they leave incarceration. It's a relatively new process—forty years ago, a facility like this didn't exist. Recidivism rates are often high, so sociologists, lawmakers, law enforcement, and prison management put their heads together to find a way to decrease the chances of re-offending. Reentry programs were what they came up with, starting about a decade ago. There are a number of levels of reentry. Some reentry programs are done in custody, but by and large those facilities are already maximally stressed simply caring for often violent inmates, let alone preparing some of them to reenter society. At the Harper Group, we run facilities that accept inmates from both the state-run and private prison systems. We have facilities like this one that are residential facilities. We also run day reporting centers for men and women out on probation who are trying to rebuild their lives but need additional support. Many of them are unemployed, and the lack of structure in their lives often drives them to re-offend. Our programs give structure and purpose and teach them life skills that many never learned at home, often because of stressful family environments when they were younger."

Pate swiveled in his chair and reached for a framed photograph that sat on the wide windowsill behind him. He passed it across to Van Cleave, who tilted it so Meg could see. The photograph showed a dozen young men and a few women, all of them under twenty years of age, most of whom were African American or Hispanic, lined up in two neat rows. They all wore blue graduation gowns and caps, held black folders, and all were smiling. "That's one of our graduation classes."

"You have actual graduation ceremonies?" Meg asked.

Pate chuckled. "You probably think it's silly, but we believe these ceremonies are important, especially for our juvenile residents. Most of them have never been to a graduation ceremony because they dropped out of high school. And many of these kids are multiple re-offenders already, which is why they were referred to us in the first place."

Van Cleave handed the framed photo back to Pate. "Who refers the kids to you?"

"A variety of people. Sometimes a judge makes it part of the sentencing. In that case, it's often a judge who has seen the same kid more than once in his courtroom, or sometimes he's read their full record and sees the pattern and knows they need a little boost to get started in the right direction. Sometimes a prison social worker will recommend an inmate for reentry. Sometimes it's the inmate himself who knows he's not ready to be on his own yet and has heard about the program and will request entry. As long as the warden approves, the inmate can move to a residential service like this one. If the warden does not approve, sometimes that same inmate can attend a day reporting center once he or she is released."

"Who pays for that?"

"It's covered by the Virginia Department of Social Services. They have some of their own programs as well, but not enough to meet the need. The VDSS knows that in the long run, it's cheaper to help inmates integrate into society than it is to house them for years or even for life, depending on the crime. When you're looking at approximately twelve thousand adults and five hundred juveniles released from prisons in the state every single year, services like this are essentially prevention. The end goals are keeping costs down and increasing public safety. Reentry programs do both."

"What specifically do you do to help inmates reintegrate successfully into society?" Meg asked.

"We have a variety of programs and services in both the residential and day reporting centers. You need to remember that some of these behaviors are so ingrained, it can take significant effort to turn them around. We offer one-on-one cognitive behavioral therapy to change both the base criminal mind-set and the thinking patterns that come from it, as well as group therapy where residents see that others have the same hopes and fears they do. This also helps them make connections and friendships based on common bonds they can then take out into the world. We teach life skills to promote independence once they are outside these walls. We help those who need assistance with the immigration process, as many are illegal immigrants. A facility like this is essentially a minimum security, dual-service facility that in the end costs the state less money because the reentry program overlaps with the end of inmate sentencing. But the day reporting centers are important too, and serve a different function. We do daily check-ins, can assist with drug and alcohol testing, and help make sure parolees make regular contact with their parole officers. Individual inmates and parolees have different needs, so we cover all the bases to fill those gaps. However, they all want to repair their relationships with their children and the rest of their families, get clean and sober and stay that way, and find employment. If we've done our job right, we hope to never see them again." Pate sat back in his chair with a rolling laugh. "And I sound like I'm pitching to a room full of investors."

"But isn't catering to your investors really your end goal?" Meg asked. "This is, after all, a business, so isn't your job to ensure profits for the investors? Doesn't hoping to never see them again go against that? If that happens, you lose your chance to make a profit from them."

Pate's smile dissolved as his brow furrowed and the

light in his eyes dulled. "That's a very cynical outlook, Ms. Jennings."

"It is a business outlook I'm sure some of your investors hold."

"Maybe they do, but it's not mine. We do good work here, and let me assure you, we have no lack of clients. We have a long way to go before we work ourselves out of business. And, sadly, new future criminals are being born daily. I don't think there will ever be a lack of need for us." He tapped the printed image spread open on his blotter. "Now that you have an idea of what we do, what does this gentleman have to do with us?"

"He came through this facility," Meg said, taking care to meet Pate's gaze before saying, "Twice."

Pate winced. "Sometimes we don't do the job as well the first time as we'd like. Hopefully the second time was more effective."

"Not exactly," Van Cleave said. "We've tied him to a human trafficking ring. Forcing little girls to work the sex trade is his current business acumen."

Pate started to say something, then closed his mouth. He sighed and tried again. "I'm sorry, I don't know what to say. It looks like we tried and failed twice." He turned to Meg. "Inmates aren't stupid. They know we expect to hear certain things and see a certain attitude, and some of them project that, even if they are just doing it to get out faster." He picked up the photo and stared at it. "And it's hurt others in the process. I assume you're looking for him?"

"Yes. And when we find him, we're going to be adding two counts of involuntary manslaughter to the mix. You won't have to worry about him failing out of your facility a third time." Van Cleave's tone was biting. "I'm going to make sure he's put away so tight, release from prison is never going to be something he's going to worry about."

"Manslaughter? You said he was trafficking little girls."

"That's correct. However, he also tied them up in a van and left them to drown during the hurricane, so I'll be pushing the D.A. for the full penalty for manslaughter." Van Cleave looked away and gathered himself, his fingers on the arms of the chair clenching tight, then releasing. "My apologies. Parts of this case are infuriating, but I don't have to take it out on you."

"No, no, I understand. It's a special kind of hell when children are involved. Is there any other way I can help?"

"We think he may have been making some of his victim contacts inside this facility. We'd like to know when he was here and we'd like lists of what inmates attended at the same time." He paused for a moment. "We understand if you are uncomfortable with the request. Please understand that I'll be back tomorrow with a warrant for that, and possibly more, if you are unwilling to cooperate today. He trapped twelve- and thirteen-year-old girls in the sex trade, and now they're dead. I'm certain I can get any judge in town to agree to sign a warrant for me. Your choice though."

Pate squinted as if pained. "I absolutely understand. And I can give you all the adult names. But I need you to realize that we're a mixed group of juveniles and adults here. And while the two groups only mix to a minimal extent, there is some contact."

"You let the two groups intermingle?" Meg asked. "That's unusual. Usually juveniles are kept separate."

"That's what we used to do, but we tried it as an experiment and we found that the adults would often mentor the juveniles. And that had some major advantages. You're a teenager, just about to get out of prison, and you're still pretty cocky and full of yourself. You're just unlucky that you got caught and these social workers and their life lessons are full of garbage. Then you meet a guy who's re-offended and is trying to turn his life around. Sometimes it's that guy who will get through to you when absolutely no one else will. That's the guy who will make an impression and make you stop and think that maybe you don't have all the answers. It's always fully supervised, and if any of the juveniles feel pressure of any kind, they can come to us and ask not to be involved in the mixed group settings. We've had very few of those. The overwhelming majority of kids said that they valued the insight of the adults because they look at them and realize that they could screw themselves up just as badly. Sometimes the insight that you're at a turning point in your life is priceless. And sometimes you need to look at someone else's mistakes to find that insight."

Van Cleave sat back and crossed his ankle over his opposite knee. But his white knuckles belied his casual stance. "You can give us the adults, but are refusing the juvenile names?"

"I have to." Pate spread his hands wide, fingers splayed. "My hands are tied when it comes to our underage residents. Come back tomorrow with a warrant from the judge ordering me to provide the names and I'll do exactly that. It protects all of us from a later lawsuit. You know I'm obligated to protect the underage in our care. I'd be revealing not just your potential victims, but everyone who deserves their privacy. Didn't we all screw up as kids and don't all kids deserve the chance to move past those mistakes?" He turned to his keyboard. "Now, you said his name is Luke Reed? Let me look him up and I'll give you the complete adult roster from that time period. Then can I take you for a tour of the facility? It might help to see for yourselves how any connections might have been formed."

"Sure." Van Cleave's single-word response was tight and clipped.

Pate started tapping and clicking and muttering to himself about dates and cell blocks and therapy groups.

Meg touched Van Cleave lightly on the sleeve and gave him a small smile when his head finally turned in her direction, revealing the full force of his frustration.

She tried to convey the best message she could without saying a word.

Don't beat yourself up. You're doing the best you can.

He's not wrong; he has to protect the children.

Even a small step forward is still in the right direction.

Tomorrow was going to be a big day. By then they'd have McCord on the scent and a warrant in hand.

That's when the dominoes would start to fall.

CHAPTER 17

Consequence Management: Disaster response focused on minimizing loss of life, suffering, and damage.

Monday, July 24, 6:23 PM
Greenbrier Grill House
Chesapeake, Virginia

"There he is."

At Meg's words, Webb turned around to where McCord, tall, blond, and sporting wire-rimmed glasses, stood in the doorway of the roadhouse. Raising an arm over his head, Webb waved McCord over.

Grinning, McCord wove through tables. "Great to see you guys." He clapped them both on the shoulder before taking the chair next to Webb, letting his leather laptop bag slide off his shoulder to prop against a chair leg. "I have to admit, your call caught me a little off guard. I wasn't expecting to see you until I got home."

"I wasn't expecting to get pulled into a criminal investigation," countered Meg. "This was supposed to be just a search-and-rescue mission, but we made a big left turn. Before we get into all that, how was experiencing the storm firsthand?"

"Not something I had on my bucket list, and now that

I've done it, not something I will ever feel the need to do again. You see the pictures on TV, watch the reporters get tossed around by the wind, and you just don't have a clue as to how bad it is. I mean, it looks bad, but I've never been in a storm that made me think I might die. It was scary. And I spent three years in a war zone, so that's saying something."

"Glad you made it through in one piece." Webb picked up his beer and toasted McCord.

"I could use one of those. It's been a dry few days." McCord twisted in his seat, caught the eye of a pretty red-headed waitress, and turned a one-hundred-watt smile on her. "Do you guys have Devil's Backbone?"

"What self-respecting Virginia restaurant wouldn't?"

"IPA?"

"Absolutely."

"I'll have one of those." He winked at her. "Thanks."

He turned back to find Meg's beady eye fixed on him. "What?"

"Flirting with the waitstaff?"

"I *really* want a beer. If a wink and a smile will hurry it along, I know Cara won't mind. She understands a man's need for beer. It's been a hell of a few days."

"Amen," said Webb.

Within minutes, the waitress delivered his beer in a tall pint glass. McCord took a long sip, mumbled, "There is a God," and sat back in his chair.

"Smile." Meg pulled out her phone and snapped a quick picture of him with his hands wrapped lovingly around his glass.

"What's that for?"

Meg's head was down, her thumbs flying over the virtual keyboard. "I promised proof of life to Cara."

A laugh escaped McCord. "She knows I made it through the hurricane. I've talked to her every day."

"Yeah, but it's not the same as a picture to prove you're in one piece. Date a girl, get her pain-in-the-ass sister in the bargain." She punctuated the sentence with a congenial punch in the arm. She put her phone down on top of the menu and picked up her glass of white wine. "Decide what you're having and then we can get down to business."

"As long as they have red meat, I'm good." It took McCord all of forty-five seconds to decide on his meal and close his menu. "Why don't we get the part of the conversation that's going to kill my appetite over with so by the time the food arrives, I'll be able to eat."

Meg quickly brought him up-to-date with the case.

"Son of a bitch," McCord muttered. "It takes a special kind of lowlife to take advantage of vulnerable kids just to make a buck."

"The world is a wonderful place," Webb said.

"Sometimes. A lot of the rest of the time it seriously sucks." McCord turned back to Meg. "What do you need me for?"

"We're looking for connections to the seedier side of Virginia's crime world."

"And nothing says *seedy* like Clay McCord." McCord took another sip of his beer. "But seriously, I may be able to help. Do you remember that story I did about eighteen months ago about the prison system in Virginia? The state of the system and the number of prisoners they're farming out to private institutions that are cutting back on everything from personnel to health care to safeguard their profit margins?"

"I have to admit I may have missed that one," Meg said.

"You should look it up. It's a solid article and as relevant today as it was when it went to press. The U.S. has the largest prison population in the world with nearly one in one hundred people incarcerated. It's insane. And it goes without saying that there is a racially biased skew in there that would knock your socks off."

"I know all about that. I had to fight that bias in my own department when I was on patrol. I assume in the course of this exposé that you talked to a lot of ex-cons."

"Yeah. Not that anyone came out and said they had a hand in human trafficking, but there were certainly a few who did time for pimping, so that's where I'd start. It's the most similar crime."

"You've got access to your notes from that investigation?" Webb asked. "You can track these guys down again?"

McCord reached down, dug in his bag for a second and pulled out his laptop. "Never leave home without it." He handed his menu to Meg, pushed aside his cutlery, and booted up. "I have all my notes here, as well as backed up at home and in the cloud. That includes any and all personal details on the men I interviewed. And women. It was an equal opportunity article." With a few clicks, he opened up a folder and scanned the contents. "Now, finding them might be a little harder because it's been a while since I've made contact. But I have their addresses from eighteen months ago, and phone numbers for a lot of them, so that's where I'll start once I review all their records. Assuming they aren't back inside as a guest of the state again. You want to concentrate on anyone who's come through the reentry program?"

"Preferably Chesapeake Community Corrections Service Center, but for any of the prisons or reentry facilities, I'd like to know if anyone saw it being used as a recruiting site. Keep in mind we're not just talking about young girls; we're also talking teenage boys who could work in either the sex trade or on farms."

"You're not mentioning adults. Do you think it's doubtful they're using this strategy on that age group?" Webb asked. "You'd like to think that adults are wise enough not to fall for these scenarios."

"You know and I know that's not always the case." Mc-Cord's head was down and his eyes were locked on the screen, but he reached out with his left hand and unerringly grabbed his beer, raising it to his lips without taking a second away from his work. "People can be vulnerable at any age. Also, one of the things I learned while researching this story is that often the mentally ill end up behind bars, instead of getting the help they really need. And when they're released, they can be the first to re-offend because they don't have the skills to stay out of trouble. If an offer gets made to them, they may not recognize it as too good to be true and they'll jump at it. I'll spend some time tomorrow morning trying to find some of these. I've also got some contacts in a couple of the papers down here. I can give them a buzz and see if they might have anything useful. You're not only looking for guys running the rings, but I assume you're also looking for the clients."

Meg's stomach rolled and she set down her wine. "These guys are having sex with thirteen-year-old girls. Hell, yes."

"I hate to stand up for these bastards," Webb said, "but just remember how bad my estimate was." He glanced at McCord, who looked up from his laptop in confusion. "When we found the van, Meg had me guess the age of one of the dead girls. I was off by about four years because of the clothes and the makeup. I'm not making excuses for them, I'm just saying some of them might legitimately think the girls were legal and in the trade of their own free will."

"Normally, I'd be with you on that," McCord said. "But I've done some stories with sex workers. The girls who are out on the streets are one thing. They may be run by pimps, but usually they make their own choices. They don't like the look of a guy, they don't get in his car. These kids, they don't have that kind of choice. They're delivered like a package to the paying customer, and they are supposed to put out and shut up. The guys using this service expect to get what they paid for, period. Okay, give me the name again."

"Luke Reed is the 'John' Emma described as running the show. And in a phone call, she heard the name 'Maverick' mentioned."

McCord had a fresh document open and was quickly typing notes. "I'll see what I can dig up on all this on a fairly short time line." He sat back and looked at his watch. "I should be able to get started on it tonight, as it's still early. How about . . ." He trailed off as the waitress returned to take their orders. Once she retreated, menus tucked under her arm, McCord continued. "How about some of your police contacts? Could you talk to your sergeant, the one who helped us figure out where Mannew got all his bomb materials?"

"Sergeant Archer . . . that's actually a really good idea." Meg swirled the straw-colored liquid in her glass, watching the legs run back down. "This certainly isn't his jurisdiction—that must be a good hundred miles away—but he's likely got contacts down here in the various departments that might be able to give us some good starting points. I'll call him tonight."

"If you get anything I could use, email me the info. The more parallel lines of investigation we have going on this, the better." He took a long draught of his beer. "You need to promise me something though. These guys are going to come to you as anonymous sources. The moment the Feebs want their personal info, they're going to rabbit. These are ex-cons, some of them still living right on the line of legalities, or even over it. Journalistically, they're protected sources, so their anonymity is nonnegotiable."

"No arguments from me," Meg said. "And you won't get one from the special agent in charge I'm working with, Walter Van Cleave. He's the straightest shooter I've seen in a long time in the Bureau. He wants to get the job done, and he'll give you the leeway to do it as long as it's legal, and the First Amendment says it is. He wants a clean case, but he's not going to be interested in bringing down someone who helps our success."

"Excellent."

"He's working on cross-referencing lists of adults who went through reentry with Reed, and trying to see what happened to them. So far, it's just the adults, since Pate won't budge on the kids without a warrant. Van Cleave is already arranging for one because that information is crucial. Reentry maybe have been one of Reed's main ways of bringing the vulnerable and isolated into his clutches."

McCord saved the documents and closed the lid of his laptop. "Kind of makes you want fifteen minutes in a room with him with no cameras, doesn't it? To teach him what that kind of vulnerability is like and how it feels to be on the short end of it?"

"Sure does." Webb's words were a low growl.

McCord held out a fist and Webb bumped his to it.

"That's not how the system works," Meg said, squelching the urge to roll her eyes at the manly posturing.

"Oh, we know. And we know we can't do it. Doesn't mean we don't want to." Webb lifted his beer to his lips, and the golden-brown eyes that met Meg's over the rim were deadly serious.

She shook her head at him. "You firefighters. You're always straight to the point, with no playing around."

"That's the kind of guys and gals we are. When seconds count, there's no time for BS. Get in, get the job done, and get out with your life and hopefully someone else's. We don't have time for conferences and group decision making."

McCord leaned an elbow on the table, considering Webb. "You know, you're giving me an idea for a great story. The men and women of DCFEMS—what it's really like to run into the building when everyone else is running out."

"Don't forget to ask him about this year's firefighters calendar." Meg turned a big grin on Webb. "He's Mr. June."

"Really?" McCord drew the word out, skepticism and interest intermingling.

"Hey, it was for a good cause."

"Wait a second." McCord turned on Meg. "I saw that calendar sitting on your kitchen table."

"It's on the wall now." Meg held up her hands to frame Webb's face like she was a director blocking a scene. "We're off by a month though. It's still on Mr. June."

"Bloody hell," Webb muttered.

McCord laughed so loudly heads turned. "I'm definitely including that in the article."

"Not if you want active participation, you aren't."

"Just wait until I work my magic. You'll be putty in my hands. You and all your coworkers who could probably run circles around me." He clapped a hand on Webb's shoulder. "Don't worry. I'm looking for gritty realism, not beefcake."

"That I can give you."

"Awesome. Let's think about it once we're all home again. Would be great publicity for the department." He turned back to Meg. "Anything else about this case I need to know?"

"The only other thing we did today was take a tour of the reentry facility with Pate. Basically, it's a minimal security facility with a heavy helping of social workers and psychologists. One-on-one therapy sessions, group therapy sessions, life skills classes. Most of the time, the kids are kept separated from the adults. But there are times and places within the facility where the kids and the adults mix. Some group therapy sessions, some mealtimes, some outdoor recreational periods. Any kid who is uncomfortable with mixing with the adults is removed from the situation, no questions asked, and isn't brought into contact with them again. As long as a kid doesn't complain about mixing it up with the adults, there were times when Reed could have sunk his claws into someone young, scared, lonely, and looking for positive affirmation."

"It's just a matter of getting the warrant to confirm that," Webb said. "How long will that take?"

"We should have it first thing tomorrow, or Van Cleave is going to be standing on some poor judge's doorstep looking for a signature." Meg spotted their waitress winding her way toward them, a tray balanced high on her shoulder and loaded with dishes. "Okay, here comes our food. No more shop talk that will ruin the meal for us."

"Deal," said McCord. "There will be time enough for that later tonight and tomorrow. I have a bad feeling about the hornet's nest we're about to kick over. I hope you all can run like the wind."

CHAPTER 18

Belay: A term used by high/low angle rescue teams to describe the action of one person controlling the descent of another person or object from an elevated position.

Tuesday, July 25, 8:20 AM
FBI Field Office
Norfolk, Virginia

Meg rapped her knuckles on Van Cleave's door frame. "Good morning."

Van Cleave looked up from the document he was reviewing. He looked haggard, the lines on his face deeper than usual, with his top shirt button undone and his tie slightly askew. Meg blinked and studied him more closely. Wasn't that the same striped tie and blue shirt as yesterday?

"Good morning," he said, reaching for his coffee cup and downing a big swallow.

"I'm not sure it is. You didn't go home yesterday, did you?"

"What gave me away?"

Meg came into the office and closed the door behind her. Hawk wandered over to Van Cleave, greeted him enthusiastically, but then seemed overly fascinated by his pant hems.

"What happened? Where did you go?"

Van Cleave looked down. "Am I seriously being sold out by a dog?"

"A dog with an amazing sense of smell, but yes. Hawk, come here, boy." She waited as he came to her chair. "Down, buddy." The dog flopped to the floor. "You don't have to be Sherlock Holmes to deduce it. You're wearing the same clothes as yesterday, you look exhausted, your cup has multiple rings around it, indicating you've nuked your coffee to rewarm it after it's gone cold a few times, and you've walked through something that caught Hawk's nose as worthy of examination." She pointed at the document he was reviewing. "Our warrant?"

"Just delivered by one of the junior agents. I was . . . busy."

Meg didn't ask again. She simply sat back and raised her eyebrows in expectation.

Van Cleave downed what was left of his coffee and thumped the mug down on his desk, glaring at it. "That's not working."

"Perhaps what you really need is a nap?"

"You're not kidding." He sat back in his chair, letting his body slide down a few inches, only stopping when his elbows caught on the arms of the chair. "Luke Reed is dead."

Meg bolted upright in her chair. "Really? How?"

"He never survived the storm. His body was found along Deep Creek, in a mass of downed trees, brush, and other debris in a marshy area near Deep Creek Lock Park. The park was closed for the weekend due to high water levels, but it reopened yesterday morning. Last night, just before dark, some guy found the body. Rather, his dog did. He had let the dog off the leash for a run, but the dog went straight toward the river and into the marsh, and then wouldn't stop barking at a pile of debris. The guy waded out to investigate and uncovered the body just enough to identify it as human. He called the cops, they came out and recovered the corpse. They had one of those little portable fingerprint gizmos with them, and from that they ID'd him on scene as Reed."

"And you had a BOLO out on Reed, so they called you. You went out there, didn't you? That explains the magical pant hems, at least as far as Hawk is concerned. You went through the marsh dressed like that."

"I stayed late in the office and arranged to meet a judge to lay out the case for him. I left him with the warrant to review and sign, with instructions that I'd pick it up from him on my way into the office this morning. I'd just gotten home when I got the call. Didn't even have time to change out of my suit. Kissed my wife, patted my dog, and went right back out."

"Was your wife mad?"

"No. As I said, she gets it. She knows that lives often hang in the balance in my cases and my time often isn't my own. I make it up to her in fantastically thoughtful gifts, and vacations of her choice where I don't take a cell phone with me. My staff has to go to pretty extreme measures to contact me on vacation, which means that if they do, it's pretty damned serious. It's only happened once. No, my wife is a trooper. My dog on the other hand . . . I still feel guilty from the look on his face as I went back out the door."

"You went to the site and confirmed it was Reed?"

"Did my best. After days in the water, he wasn't in good shape. But between that and the fingerprint ID, it's definitely him. Unfortunately, he wasn't carrying his book, and believe me, I looked everywhere on him. Anyway, by the time we extracted him and got him sent to the morgue, the sun was coming up, so I just came straight to the office." He picked up his mug as if to drink again, remembered it was empty and set it back down. "I need more coffee."

"No, you need two hours of downtime. It's too early to serve that warrant yet anyway. Is there a place you can crash here?"

"Amazingly enough, this isn't the first time someone in this office has been up all night. There's a supply closet with a cot in it and a Do Not Disturb sign someone swiped from a hotel to hang on the doorknob." He glanced up at the clock on his wall. "I can hit the rack for an hour, maybe two tops, but then I have to get moving."

"That seems reasonable to me. You'll be useless for the rest of the day otherwise." Meg looked down at the warrant on his desk. "With Reed gone, is that the end of the investigation once we identify our missing girls or any other victims that might have fallen into his clutches?"

"Not that we've had any luck yet with the missing girls, but Reed is not the end of the investigation. Not even close. We have too many other threads to tug. Do you really think he was working in isolation?"

Meg pulled back slightly, surprised at his condescending tone. "This isn't my area of expertise. That's why I'm asking you."

Van Cleave hung his head for a second, one hand brushing over the short ends of his buzz-cut hair. "Sorry, that was bordering on snarky. I really do need that nap." He huffed out a breath, gathered another. "These groups don't usually work on their own. Mostly they're smaller operations that are linked to a much larger one. Sort of like how the mob functions with a big boss."

"We just got one of the guppies, now we need the big fish."

"Just like that. We know about 'Maverick,' or at least his alias, but we need to find out who that really is. Is he the top of the operation or just another rung on the ladder?"

"I'm supposed to meet up with McCord this afternoon. I laid it all out for him last night and he had some solid contacts to go after. I have to give him time to work, but I want an update by this afternoon. Do you need me with you when you serve Pate with the warrant?"

"No, if you have other stuff to do, take care of it. Call me later with an update?"

"I will. And I expect to hear that you really did take that nap. Van, you won't help these kids if you're too exhausted to think straight."

"I know, I know. You're not a mother, are you?"

"Not yet. Haven't found the right partner." She paused. "Maybe."

"That sounds like there might be a possibility there after all. Well, when you get to that point, you have the mom nagging down pat." He softened his words with a wide grin. "Thanks. Apparently, I need a good mom nag, and my wife, who is a master, isn't around."

Meg stood. "Get some rest, then let's get to it again. I'll call as soon as I have an update for you."

As Meg went out the door, she glanced back, only to find Van Cleave staring at the warrant. She knew that look. It came from a feeling way down in your gut that you'd just lost the biggest lead in your case and you weren't sure you could come back from it.

Been there, done that.

He might be exhausted and discouraged, but they weren't out of the running yet.

She and McCord would make sure of it.

CHAPTER 19

Bloodhound: A breed of scent dog that is renowned for its keen sense of smell. Developed in the Middle Ages, its physical characteristics and tenaciousness make it a prized tracking/trailing canine. It has been used in the U.S. since the 1800s to track fugitives and missing slaves. It is, however, a notoriously short-lived breed.

Tuesday, July 25, 3:01 PM
Tidewater Drive
Norfolk, Virginia

Meg waited as McCord approached from down the street. She was standing on the corner of Tidewater Drive and East Charlotte Street, having parked her car along one of the side streets as he'd instructed. She scanned the area around her. Only a few blocks away from downtown Norfolk, this appeared to be an area that the city forgot long before Cole swept through. She stood across from one of Norfolk's middle schools, with its lower windows bricked in and the athletics field now simply an unattended swamp. The other side of the road held low income housing—identical two-story, plain-faced, redbrick structures with front doors every fifteen feet down their length for maximum occupancy. In front of her, Tidewater's uneven grading was evident in the half of the road underwater. The sewer system was still too backed up to handle the post-storm drainage.

Street flooding was likely a sign of the area's bigger problem, as evidenced by the state of the subsidized housing. Many of the units had belongings tossed out onto the muddy front grass, and clothing and towels dangled from upstairs windows.

Meg turned toward the south. In the distance, over the raised access of the I-264, she could see the tall floodlight towers of the baseball stadium. Beyond lay the Elizabeth River.

This neighborhood would have been hit hard on Friday night and would have been inside the evacuation zone because everything would have been underwater once the storm surge rolled in.

She turned back to watch McCord's approach. He was wearing khaki shorts with sneakers, a T-shirt emblazoned with FRIEND OF THE POD, and sunglasses to shade his eyes from the glare. He waved in greeting.

"What's with all the subterfuge?" Meg asked.

"I gave you directions on where to meet me. Where's the subterfuge?"

"You wouldn't tell me anything. Why we're here, or what you found out from your contacts."

He crouched down to greet Hawk, who enthusiastically licked his face. "Hey, buddy, how's it going?" He pushed to his feet. "I'm almost embarrassed to admit it, but I miss Cody."

Meg fixed him with a puzzled stare. "Why on earth would you be embarrassed? You're with animal people. I miss Hawk like the devil whenever we're apart. And Cody's fine. Cara takes care of him like he's one of her own."

"I know. And she Skypes me so I can see him and talk to him. It always confuses the hell out of him. He can hear my voice but he hasn't figured out I'm the picture on the screen. He's cute, but he may not be the sharpest knife in the drawer."

"He's a smart boy. He's just a little behind the curve when it comes to technology. So? What are we doing here?"

McCord scanned the area around them, then spotted a bench out in front of the YMCA on the opposite corner. "Come sit down and I'll catch you up. Then we're going to take a little walk."

"Where?"

"All in good time."

"Have you been told lately that you're a pain in the ass, McCord?"

He made her an exaggerated deep bow. "No, but it warms my heart to hear you say it."

Rolling her eyes, Meg sat down on the bench. "Okay, spill."

"Absolutely." McCord sat down and held out his hands for Hawk, who came to sit between his knees. McCord stroked him while he talked. "So, Luke Reed. He is one nasty dude."

"Oh! I haven't told you yet."

McCord's hands stilled. "Told me what?"

"Reed's dead. Apparently, his attempt to get out of the van dumped him in a raging river and he drowned, according to the prelim autopsy report Van Cleave just passed on."

"Couldn't have happened to a nicer guy." Sarcasm rolled off every word. McCord ran his hands over Hawk again, who sighed and rested his muzzle on McCord's thigh. "The late, definitely not-so-great, Luke Reed was a bad apple in every sense of the word. He was arrested three times for assault and had a rape charge dropped."

"That much I knew."

"Figured you would. What you don't know about is the

stuff he didn't get caught for. Seems this guy was well-known for his brutal takedowns and temper. Did your girl talk about that?"

"She said he knocked out one of the girls with a single right hook."

"That sounds about right for him. He was all about control and would use physical force to get it."

"He used drugs on a lot of the girls," Meg said. "Kept them high and wanting more. They'd do whatever he wanted."

"As I said, couldn't have happened to a nicer guy." Mc-Cord's words were rock hard. "I got similar info from numerous contacts. One of the girls knew about him but refused to tell me anything. Now that I know he's dead, I'll circle back to her and see if she's got anything new."

"When you talk to her, ask her if she's heard anything about any of his other girls. Three of them were out working the night of the storm, and we're trying to find them. The cops are coming up empty so far, but maybe your contacts will know more. Did any of them know Reed by his real name?"

"Most of them did. One person knew the house on West 48th you told me about and could identify him from the location. Another guy goes by the name of Razor—"

"Seriously?"

"Yeah. He goes by the name of Razor, and I got the most information out of him. Razor is still on the outside, but I got the impression from his lifestyle that the clock may be ticking on that one. Razor has his fingers in a lot of pies."

"Little girls?"

"No. He made it crystal clear he's not interested in kids. Truth to be told, I think he's all hardcore drugs, but they interact with these lowlifes keeping the kids. Want to keep the kids hooked and in line? You need a dealer who may wonder about the amount you're buying, but will keep his wondering to himself.'"

"Right. Makes sense."

"Good ol' Razor was a little loath to discuss business with me until I forked over two hundred and fifty dollars. Don't worry," he said, patting Meg's knee when she winced. "I had it on me because I expected I'd need to do a little you-scratch-my-back-I'll-scratch-yours. I have a discretionary fund at the *Post* for just this kind of thing. I'll get reimbursed later. That's sometimes the cost of doing this kind of business. Anyway, Razor got a lot chattier after that. Told me about a place where Reed liked to do business. A bar." He turned on the bench and pointed down East Charlotte. "That bar, way down there."

Meg followed his finger. "That explains why we're here."

"I bring you to the nicest places. Anyway, I want to check this place out. It was apparently where he often did business."

Meg sat up straighter. "You mean, met with potential clients and set up appointments with his girls?"

"Exactly that kind of business. You wouldn't want any of your clients to learn where your home base is. Piss one of them off, they can turn your whole operation over to the cops. Instead, you find neutral territory."

"Anything else come out of your contacts?"

"Nothing else that you didn't already know. The bar was the big piece of new info. If Reed was a regular there, I'm hoping the bartender or the waitstaff might be familiar with him."

"And his clients. Van Cleave wants to take them all down."

"No arguments here. Want to go over and pop in? We're a little early for happy hour, but if the unemployment rate is as high around here as I think it might be, they'll likely already be open."

"Works for me."

They got up from the bench and walked down the street toward a row of small shop fronts a block and a half toward downtown.

Meg studied the various squat, brick buildings with windowed fronts. "Which one is it?"

"According to Google Street View, it's the one on the corner. See the sign MILLER'S TAP HOUSE? That one."

As they approached, Meg got a better look at the outside of the building. The side wall was covered with nondescript graffiti—huge bubble-letter words, smaller scrawls in different colors, and smaller, indistinct drawings. "Great area of town, McCord."

"And this is why I wanted to meet you down the street, not at the tavern. I didn't want you there alone." When she slid him a sideways glare, he clarified, "I know you're more than capable of looking after yourself. I know what you can do, what Hawk can do. But I didn't want to put you in the position of having to defend yourself, because then there are explanations and paperwork and interviews. I just figured there was a smaller chance you'd be bothered if I was with you." He jabbed her with his elbow. "And this way, you can protect me."

"That's your reasoning, delicate flower? You who've lived in a war zone?"

"That's my story and I'm sticking with it."

She laughed and shoulder bumped him back. On this third case with him, their working together was beginning to feel completely natural. Sometimes when he wasn't around, she missed his irreverent sense of humor lightening the mood. McCord was never serious if he could be a smart-ass instead.

Unless it was a situation devoid of humor.

"I'm not liking the look of this."

Meg looked from the grim set of McCord's mouth to where his eyes were fixed. "Damn. I didn't count on that. They're closed?"

On the far side of the street, the tavern had a large hand-written sign on the door—CLOSED DUE TO FLOOD—and wooden boards crisscrossed over the windows. The rest of the street looked deserted and Meg wasn't sure if that was its normal state or this was simply post-storm desolation.

"They got hit by the storm hard. Looks like it even blew out their windows." McCord quickly looked both ways and then crossed the street, Meg and Hawk trotting to keep up with him.

"They're close enough to the river that the storm tide would have left them pretty deep in seawater. It doesn't look like an overly prosperous establishment. They may not be insured."

"Or they are and are fighting with their insurance company just like everyone else in the area. Not that you can clean up quickly from something like this." Reaching the tavern, McCord leaned in to look through the window. "Not totally blown out, but a good portion of the glass is gone." He grasped one of the boards and gave it a gentle shake. The wood rocked under his hand. "Not that these boards are going to keep looters out. Is the door locked?"

Meg stepped up onto the concrete stoop and tried the handle. "Yes. The owner is likely doing what he can to keep people out with what he has at hand. Do we know who the owner is?"

"No, but with your contacts, you can track that down pretty easily. You want to pay him a visit?"

"We have to start somewhere." Meg joined him at the window to peer into the gloom. Weak daylight trickled inside to reveal toppled tables and chairs, shattered glasses, a broken pool cue, and a mangled tin sign for Bud Light. She went back to the front door to look through the shattered glass. "Looks like we struck out. Again." She allowed herself five seconds of pique and gave the heavy wooden door a solid kick. It rattled at the force of the blow, but stayed in place. "We have the world's worst luck. Reed is dead, the best lead on him evaporated, and we're back to square one."

"I really thought we had something here. But maybe we can still get some info from the owner. His place may be closed, but unless he died in it, he's still around somewhere." They started down the sidewalk toward where she'd parked.

They were forty feet away, getting ready to cross the street, when movement caught Meg's eye. Glancing back, she caught sight of a man crossing the street, heading straight for the pub. She grabbed McCord's arm just as he was about to step off the curb. "Wait."

The man stepped up to the front door and put a key in the lock. Meg turned and started to jog back down the street toward him. The man turned at the sound of pounding feet, but his eyes weren't on her; they were fixed on Hawk, running at her side.

"Excuse me!" Meg jammed her hand in her pocket as she ran, and managed to extract her ID and flip it open. "FBI. Could I ask you a few questions?"

The man shrank back into the doorway. "Call off your dog."

Meg pulled up sharply ten feet from him. "Hawk, sit."

The dog immediately complied.

"He's not going to hurt you. He's search-and-rescue."

"Don't need rescuing."

"No, sir. Could I ask you a few questions?"

"'Bout?"

"One of your patrons. You're the owner of this establishment?"

"For what it's worth." The man's gaze shot over Meg's shoulder.

Meg turned to find McCord behind her. "Mr. . . ." Her voice trailed off as she looked back at the older man.

The man paused for a minute before saying, "Who wants to know?"

"I'm Meg Jennings with the FBI. Mr. . . ."

"Miller." The name was a reluctant grunt through clenched teeth.

"Mr. Miller, this is Mr. Clay McCord from the *Washington Post*." When the man tried to take an involuntary step back but hit the brick wall instead, Meg hurried to explain. "He's not writing a story on you or your place. He's assisting me with an FBI case that is unrelated to you directly. We're actually hoping you can provide some information about one of your patrons."

"People come to my place because I leave them alone to do their thing. Take a hike. Go talk to someone else."

He twisted the doorknob and pushed open the door, but Meg stepped up onto the stoop with him. "I'd hate to have to ask you to take this conversation out to the local field office, but I will if needed. Sir, you aren't in trouble, but we desperately need your help."

Dark eyes squinted at her. "Who you need information about?"

"Luke Reed."

Miller stiffened, his jaw tightening, but he remained silent.

"If you're worried about retribution from Reed, he's dead. Drowned in Deep Creek on Monday. We know he was into some pretty awful stuff, and that children in his care were abused. We just want to make sure there isn't anyone else involved. If there is, we need to help them."

The man continued to stare, his dark eyes flat and emotionless. "What's in it for me?"

"The FBI leaving you alone and not looking into your business venture."

Miller stepped forward, crowding Meg, who didn't budge. "That's fucking blackmail."

Hawk lurched to his feet, a low growl rumbling from the back of his throat. Meg put her hand on his head, but didn't verbally tell him to stand down. She met Miller's angry gaze without blinking. "It's hardly blackmail. If you have nothing to hide, then I have zero power over you. Think about it. Is it worth a stand to cover the tracks of a dead man?"

Miller cursed low under his breath, then he pushed open the door and stepped back. "We'll talk inside."

Meg stepped toward the door and his arm shot out. "No dogs allowed." But then he hesitated, glancing through the door at his ruined bar, his lips twisted in a frown. He wasn't going to be serving customers for a long time, if ever. "Oh, fuck it. Bring on the health department." He waved her and Hawk in.

Meg stepped into the dim space, giving her eyes a moment to adjust from daylight into the interior gloom. Eyeing the shattered glass, she kicked a section clear and signaled Hawk into it. Pulling out his search-and-rescue boots, she helped him into them. No way was her dog being put out of commission by slicing up his paws in here.

Miller pushed past her, kicking debris out of his path as he made his way behind the bar. "They say the power's back on. We'll see."

McCord stepped in behind her. "Charming fellow," he muttered in her ear.

"I'll say. I get that he's pissed because he lost his livelihood and may never be able to afford to get it back, but he's hiding something he really doesn't want us to know. I don't need to, but I'm happy to use the shadow of it as leverage."

With an ambient buzz, fluorescent lights glowed dimly overhead, gradually strengthening, giving a clearer view of the chaos inside. It looked like the bar had been put through a blender—every item was thrown about haphazardly, mostly to land on the floor in pieces.

McCord whistled.

"Yeah, it's done for. I'm done for. No way the insurance'll cover this. The bastards'll claim act of God." Nevertheless, Miller started to pick up items, sorting them into whole and still usable, shattered and garbage.

With a glance at Meg that said *This is your show, go for it*, McCord started to lend a hand.

Why not? Meg gave Hawk the hand signal to sit and stay, and then picked up a bar stool and stood it upright. Minus the torn leather seat—and she wasn't sure it wasn't like that before Cole stormed through—it was still in decent shape. "Mr. Miller, what can you tell us about Luke Reed? We understand he was a regular customer here. That he liked to do . . . business here."

Miller glanced at her sideways and, for a moment, his gaze held hers. She could see the calculation there. "What do you know about his business?"

Let's get this out of the way once and for all.

"We know about his girls. Underage girls he trafficked into the sex trade. We've been led to believe by others outside his circle that he would sometimes meet clients here to set up meets with his girls. Can you confirm that?"

Miller glanced from Meg to McCord. "He's dead. There's no mistake?"

"None," McCord said. "ID'd by fingerprints."

"Mean son of a bitch. Had it coming." When Meg

stared at him silently, he said, "Went after a couple of my girls."

"I can see why that would be upsetting." Meg found a broom under some debris behind the bar and started to sweep broken glass into a pile. "I assume you knew the nature of his business?"

"He never came out and said it, but you hear things when you're workin'. You make assumptions. I knew he was selling women, but you say they was little girls?"

"Yes. He might have had his hands in more than one pie, but this piece of it involved selling the services of underage girls to older men."

"Fucker."

The word was mumbled, but Meg still caught a wisp of it. "You thought he was prostituting women, and you never kicked him out of the bar or called the cops on him?"

Miller slammed a chair down defensively and took one step toward Meg. "Lady, I don't know where you get off, but—"

"Hey, hey!" McCord stepped in between them, holding out a hand, palm out, toward Miller. "She's just asking you some questions." He turned toward Miller, putting Meg behind him, out of sight. "You know and I know it's not that easy. That there are repercussions from doing things like going to law enforcement. You can't afford to lose business, right?"

"Fuck, no."

"And if word got out that you were a snitch, some people might not consider it a safe place to be or to meet contacts." He turned around and gave Meg a pointed look. "We get that."

She returned the pointed look and gave him a hand flick to move out of the way. His eyes clearly said *Take it easy or he'll clam up*, but he stepped back.

Meg bent down and picked up a lowball glass. She held it up to the light, looking for cracks. Miraculously, it was intact. "I'm sorry, Mr. Miller, I wasn't implying that you weren't doing your civic duty. I'm just trying to get a feel for the atmosphere in this place when it was open for business. I can't see that right now." She set the glass down on one end of the bar. "Mr. Reed was a regular customer?"

There was a pause, then a vague grumble. "Yeah."

"And how often was that to conduct business?"

"Most times."

This is like pulling teeth. He'd answer in monosyllables if he could. "Did he have regular hours or were his visits random?"

"Random. But he always sat there." Miller pointed to a booth at the back of the tavern, near the back corner and away from the kitchens and the bathrooms, but near the single emergency exit.

Meg used the broom to help clear a path to the back of the pub. The booth was tall-backed, with worn leather padding and a scarred table. She perched on the edge of one of the benches and looked toward the front door. "He could see everyone who entered the bar from here. And there was no reason for the waitstaff or customers to wander by accidentally." She stood and walked to the emergency exit. On it, a sign proclaimed EMERGENCY EXIT ONLY, DOOR ALARM WILL SOUND. Meg gave the door a push and an ear-splitting shriek blared. She quickly pulled the door shut. "No one was using this door to go out and grab a smoke or to make a deal, that's for sure."

"No."

"He would have had total privacy back here." McCord joined her and stood by the booth. "If he was doing business, he would have wanted to keep the foot traffic and associated ears down to a minimum. Did he have an understanding with the waitresses?"

Miller nodded. "They knew to keep away unless he actually waved someone over for service. Whenever any of the girls got close, there was no conversation."

"So how did you know what was going on?" Meg asked. "If no one could get close enough to hear . . ."

"Because my place is behind the bar." Miller stepped behind the long stretch of wood, standing at the end closest to the booth, where a small inset sink was located. "This was the end for cleaning up, so we didn't keep chairs this far down the bar. But I'd be down here working sometimes. I'd see things. Or hear them."

"And Reed knew that?" McCord asked.

"He probably suspected. I never said a thing. Well, not about that."

Meg crossed the room to stand at the bar and propped one foot on the dull metal boot rail four inches off the floor. "What about, then?"

"He roughed up one of my girls. He sometimes yelled or swore at 'em, but this time it got physical. When I got between them, he complained she was listening to his private conversations. She wasn't. It was a busy night; all the booths were full and she was serving the booth next to him." He slammed a whiskey bottle down on the counter. "No one roughs up my girls."

"Understandable," Meg said. "Did you throw him out?"

"Got in his face. Threatened to. Made it clear we're not interested in his business, we're just running a bar. After that, he continued to come, but most of the time it was when it wasn't so busy and tables around him were empty."

"You said you saw things," McCord said. "What kinds of things?"

Miller glanced at Meg, but then addressed his answer to McCord. "Money changing hands."

"A lot of money?"

"Looked like it to me."

"What else?"

"The kind of people he met with. Looked like they'd never been in a place like this."

"What do you mean?" Meg asked.

"They come in with their fancy suits, looking really uncomfortable. Until they became repeat customers."

"He had repeat customers?"

"Sure."

"Any you could identify?"

"I'd recognize them if I saw them, but I don't know who they were."

"That's a good start," Meg said. "You saw money changing hands, but never any product? No drugs or anything?"

"Always knew he was selling a service. Never came in with anything. Customers never left with anything."

"You say he never came in with anything. He never had a book with him? One of those spiral-bound organizers that fits in your pocket?"

"Oh, I saw that a lot. When I said he never came in with anything, I meant anything his customer left with. But he always had that book. Used to make notes after his meetings."

Meg glanced at McCord. "That book must have had all his notes about his customers and which girls he planned to send to them. It wasn't found on him, so it's probably somewhere out in the Atlantic by now." She looked back to where Miller had stopped cleaning up debris to lean against the back counter of the bar. Behind him, the remains of a mirror, now cracked and shattered to show only drywall behind, ran the length of the bar. Shelves that once held bottles now only held jagged pieces of glass. "Mr. Miller, I appreciate that you were reluctant to talk to us, but you've been a huge help. Is there anything else you can add? You've told us about his clients and his notebook. Did you leave anything out?"

"Like . . . associates?"

"People who worked with him instead of men who hired his girls?" Meg asked.

"There were a couple guys who'd come in sometimes. But mostly just one guy."

"Do you know his name?"

"This guy was too cool to use his own name. Went by Maverick."

McCord went absolutely still beside Meg. She cleared her throat before she trusted her voice to sound sufficiently casual. "Maverick?"

"Yeah."

"He never used his real name?"

"No."

"Do you know where he fit into Reed's organization?"

"I think he was his boss. Reed was always so . . ." He seemed to be searching for the right word.

"Deferential? Always bowing to his instructions?"

"Yeah, like that."

Meg stomped on the urge to fist-pump the air. They finally had their first solid hint that they were touching on the edge of a much larger organization. Reed might be dead, but there were others to take down.

"Would you recognize him if you saw him again?"

"Yeah."

"Would you be willing to work with a sketch artist to come up with a face?"

Miller shrugged. "Wouldn't it be easier to look at a picture of him?"

"It would. You have one?"

Miller tipped his head up and scanned the dark upper corners of the bar. Then he pointed into the corner at right angles to Reed's booth. "I might."

Meg spun around to follow his finger and choked back a gasp before it could break free.

A security camera.

You've been out of investigations and doing search-and-rescue too long. You're getting rusty. This wouldn't have slipped by you when you were still on the Richmond PD.

She met McCord's gaze. *The clients. This could be huge.*

"Three cameras," Miller said. "One outside, two in." He pointed to another at the far end of the room. "I got 'em installed a few years ago."

"You have footage from the cameras? It wouldn't have gotten destroyed in the hurricane?"

"Too big a risk to keep expensive equipment here. I been robbed before, so I had to do something so thieves knew they were watched and would stop after casing the bar. I got something called IP cameras and traded free booze for some college kid putting the system together and getting me online. What did he call it? The cloud? Offsite storage? All I know is no damned kids can steal my computer because it isn't here. I'll have footage from the last fourteen days that we were open and had power. May have some older bits too."

"We would appreciate that. Would you prefer we served you with a warrant for it?"

For a second Miller's eyes filled with alarm, but then calculation shone through. "That way I can say I had no choice but to give it to you?" He kicked a broken jar and it skittered across the floor, scattering green olives in a rolling spray. "In case I ever open again?"

"You're doing us a favor, I can do the same in return. That way you can bitch about the feds and no one will call you a snitch."

"I can go one better," McCord said. "You let me know who your insurance company is, and I'll give them a friendly call looking for a story about this place and their lack of support. The *Washington Post* is pretty well-known.

That may give them a good scare and they may help you just to get me off their backs."

"Why you doin' this?" Miller's words were laced with suspicion as he looked from one to the other.

"Mr. Miller, I *really* want to find out what's going on here and to find other girls we know are involved. Reed and his associates hurt children without a single thought. Anyone who does that needs to pay. You help us do that, I'm happy to help you come out of it squeaky clean." Meg looked around the bar. "You've lost a lot of glassware and bottles, but the place looks like it dried out okay. You'll be back in business in a couple of weeks. And you may even have a pretty good story to tell from behind the bar. Just keep this all on the down-low for now. When can you get the data?"

"I'll call the kid back in as soon as you come in with a warrant. He can get it right away."

"Perfect. How about noon tomorrow to give my colleague enough time to get the warrant." She turned to McCord. "And in the meantime, you have some threads to pull."

Meeting his gaze, she knew he was focused on the same thread as she.

Maverick.

CHAPTER 20

Confinement Search: A search where the objective is to confine the subject within a specified area.

Wednesday, July 26, 8:12 AM
FBI Field Office
Norfolk, Virginia

Meg propped one shoulder against the doorjamb. "Good morning."

Van Cleave looked up blearily. "Morning."

"I thought you'd be here early, but don't tell me you were here all night."

"No. Came in around six. I have your warrant." He started sifting through the pile of paperwork on his desk. "Somewhere. I swear. Ah, here it is." He pulled a white business envelope out from beneath a stacked pile of forms.

Meg entered the office with Hawk at her side, and took the proffered envelope. "Miller says he'll be back at his tavern at noon, so I'll take this to him around one o'clock just to give him some leeway. Then we'll see what the security footage gives us." She dropped into a chair and motioned for Hawk to lie down. "I'd love it if we got clients identified from it. Getting the scumbags who run the ring is only part of the process in my mind. We need the buyers as well as the sellers. Oh, by the way, I have something else for you."

"What's that?"

"McCord came through with a name for us overnight. When I woke up I found the email he sent at five this morning. His last line was 'Going to bed finally. Don't call me, I'll call you.' Looks like it took him a while to get the information he was looking for."

"A name for Maverick?"

"Yes." Meg pulled out her phone and opened McCord's email. "Tuco Ramírez."

"You're kidding."

Meg looked up. "Sorry?"

"The name. You're kidding me, right?"

"No." She turned her phone around to show it to Van Cleave. "See?"

Van Cleave took the phone, scanned the email, and handed it back. "Well, that's an alias if I ever saw one. Let's look him up with that assumption in mind."

"Why would you think it's an alias? There are lots of Mexican immigrants in this area."

"Because that's the name of one of the three main characters in *The Good, the Bad and the Ugly*."

"With Clint Eastwood?" Meg rolled her eyes and flopped back in her chair. "I'm surrounded by cowboys."

Van Cleave looked up from typing the name into his system, his fingers frozen over the keys. "How so?"

"McCord? Clay McCord? *The Deputy*?"

Van Cleave stared at her, brows drawn together in confusion. "I don't follow."

"McCord, my reporter friend from the *Washington Post*. His father named him after the lead character in a 1950s TV show called *The Deputy*."

"Huh. Must have missed that one."

"And you call yourself an investigator. Now, what about this Tuco character?"

"It's thinking, give it a minute." He picked up his coffee mug and took a long sip, closing his eyes in pleasure.

"You were in early. Did something pop?"

"You might say that. I got the list of names we were waiting for from yesterday's warrant."

"The juvenile names from Pate?"

"Yes. And right from the get-go, I knew we had a problem."

"What do you mean?"

"The list of names he sent?" Van Cleave picked up the printed list he'd been staring at when she knocked on his door. "It's incomplete. For starters, Emma's name isn't listed, and we know she was there."

Meg whistled. "They wouldn't know that because we never told them about her." She held out her hand. "Can I see?"

He handed her the list. "Who knows who else might be missing? The son of a bitch made sure we gave him time to comb through the list, getting rid of any names that he didn't want on there."

"You think he requested the warrant so it looked like we were forcing his noble hand, but in reality, he was buying time to make sure his list was sanitized. If that's true, then he's guilty as sin."

"Certainly looks that way. Now I need another warrant to seize his electronics and I'll let the geeks at Quantico do the hard digging there. We need to find more than just one missing name. He could claim to have just missed Emma's name by accident. We need actual proof. Then I'll happily slap him with interfering with a police investigation and obstruction of justice."

"You do that, and he's going to know you're on to him.

Wouldn't it be better to string him along for a few days so he thinks you have no idea? What if he's not the only person involved, and nailing him makes others cover their tracks, or worse, bolt?"

"You may have something there. I need to think about the best way to get him into a corner that still works to our advanta—" His computer gave a soft *ding*. "Let's see what we have here." He was silent as he scanned the information on his monitor. "Looks like we won't need those security tapes after all. Not for this identification at least. Although they'll be gold as far as charging this one and being able to trace his business dealings." He turned his monitor so she could see the face displayed on screen. The man had messy dark hair, a thick neck, and a mole at his left temple. "Tuco is an alias. His real name is Dominic Russo, age thirty-five. Dominic is a very bad apple. Multiple arrests. Assault. B and E. Theft. But notice the lack of drug charges. He stayed away from anything that came with suffocating mandatory minimums."

Meg scooted forward to sit on the edge of the chair so she could see better. "Did he go through any reentry programs?"

Van Cleave clicked a few times, then paused to read. "Well, fancy that. He went through the Chesapeake Community Corrections Service Center."

"So that place is definitely ground zero in this."

"Apparently. Now, the question is—did Reed and Russo overlap, and if so, who taught whom the trick about recruitment?"

"Maybe Russo recruited Reed. Maybe that place wasn't all about the victims. It could also have been about strengthening and expanding their business structure. If they were both adults at the time, he would have had lots of time to coerce Reed to his team. It wouldn't have been limited to adult and juvenile mentoring time."

"That's good. That could be something," Van Cleave said. "His team. What if he was using the reentry program to form his team?"

"You mean like it was a pyramid scheme? He was under the guy above him and then he would have several guys leading groups below him?"

"Roughly, yeah."

"That could work. And reentry would certainly house the kind of people who would be more likely to get involved in that kind of scheme. Not exactly the cream of society, if you know what I mean."

"I certainly do."

Meg stood. "I'm going to give McCord another hour to catch up on his beauty sleep and then I'm calling him. I'll see what else he has on Russo or if he's still got feelers out. And I have a lead to follow up on. I've reached out to my old sergeant from the Richmond PD and he said to give him a call later this morning. He may be too far afield to have any expertise on trafficking this far south, but I thought it was worth a shot."

"Absolutely. Departments get involved in each other's cases more than you might think." Van Cleave tapped his index finger on the list on his desk. "We're getting there. The net is slowly tightening."

"I'm just worried it's tightening too slowly and people are slipping through. Undocumented adults far from home with no one to miss them. Kids out on the streets, easy targets for predators. If we don't move fast, lives are at stake."

"Then we need to make sure that doesn't happen. By any legal means possible, we're going to bring down as many of them as we can."

CHAPTER 21

DIY: A type of volunteer rescue where participants improvise and do whatever it takes to help.

Wednesday, July 26, 5:22 PM
Motel 6
Norfolk, Virginia

Meg threw herself down into a padded chair by the balcony doors while Webb propped himself up against the headboard of the bed, stretched out his legs, and crossed his booted feet over the edge of the coverlet.

"Just make yourself at home, you two." Hands on his hips while Hawk milled around his legs, McCord eyed them both.

"Been a long day," Webb said. "This hero stuff is exhausting. Time to take a load off. And she took the only chair."

"You have a good point." McCord sat down on the foot of the bed.

"So?" Meg prodded. "You called and said you had something and we needed to come. We're here. What have you got?"

"Things really started to move when you gave me Russo's

real name. Suddenly I had people coming out of the wood-work who knew the guy."

"Maybe that's why he used the alias. And then an alias for the alias," Webb said. "He was getting too well-known and didn't want it traced back to his real persona and actual track record." Hawk nudged at Webb's hand and he patted the bed. "Come on up, bud."

Hawk didn't need to be told twice. He launched himself onto the bed, turned around a few times and then flopped down with a heavy sigh, pushing his head against Webb's thigh. Webb gave him a good rub and looked up to find McCord staring at him. "What?"

"First you sack out on my bed and then you invite the dog up. What if I didn't want the dog in my bed?"

"You're going to tell me you don't sleep with Cody?"

"And another point to you." He stroked Hawk's head and silky ears. "Maybe your mom will let you stay the night with me. I miss the little guy."

"The 'little guy' is a year old and is still mostly insane. But the best kind of insane." Meg smiled down at Hawk. "And no, you can't borrow my dog overnight because then I'd miss him. Now . . . what have you got?"

"All right, all right." Out of his back pocket McCord pulled a small, beaten-up notepad with a pen jammed down the spiral binding. He opened the notepad and flipped through it a page at a time. "Okay, here we are. So, Dominic Russo is a man cloaked in mystery. You want something, Russo can get it for you. Need a worker? A girl? A contractor? A contract killer? Russo is your guy. This guy seems to be the central hub when it comes to con-nections. If he can't get you what you're looking for, he can find someone who can."

"For a price, I assume?" asked Webb.

"Always for a price. His services aren't cheap either. But

they come with an iron-clad guarantee. Russo's word is his bond. If he says it will get done, it will."

"That kind of dependability could move him far up the ladder of most crime circles," Meg said.

"I get the impression it has. But while he has a reputation for being a jack-of-all-trades as far as procurement goes, he's also a ghost. No one knows where he came from, or where he lives. He just appeared in the middle of all this one day and started clawing his way up the ladder."

"The question then, is who's at the top? And where does he get his people from?"

"I might have some insight there." McCord turned a few more battered pages. "A Short Trip To Hell."

"Are you describing this case?" Meg asked.

"It's a drink," Webb said.

McCord turned around slowly and pinned him with a disgusted look. "You just got kicked out of the Manly Man Hall of Fame. How do you know about a girly schnapps drink?"

"One of the guys on second shift moonlights as a bartender. He can put you flat on your back inside of two drinks. I remember that one. Looks like a girly drink but it's multiple kinds of schnapps mixed with Jägermeister and Red Bull. It's a sledgehammer in disguise and really is a short trip to hell, especially if you mix it with a few different cocktails. But somehow, I don't think you're talking about a kick-your-ass cocktail. What do *you* mean by 'a short trip to hell'?"

"It's the name of a bar."

"Charming," Meg said. "And what does this bar have to do with anything?"

"Remember, these guys don't do business out of a storefront or their own homes. They have a public place they can get lost in or can escape from, with a back entrance. A place where similar rabble will feel comfortable." McCord clapped a hand on Webb's shin. "Speaking of rabble, wanna go out and get some girls tonight?"

"I think the one in the chair on the other side of the room would hurt us both if I said yes to that. Wanna be more specific about what you're aiming for? Because I know you left a girl at home, so that's not your real goal."

"No, but I want to take a run at this guy."

Meg sat bolt upright as alarm streaked through her. "Russo?"

"Yeah."

"You can't do that. You're not law enforcement. Even if you were, you certainly can't do that alone. He's a dangerous man."

"She's getting hard of hearing," McCord said in an aside to Webb. "I don't think she heard me ask you to come along."

"She's not wrong, you know. Going in there on our own, without real backup, could be idiotic," Webb said.

"I can always go solo," McCord shot back. "The most important thing to make this work is *not* being law enforcement. I can do that by myself."

"Going on your own would be beyond idiotic. Fine, I'm in just so you don't hang yourself with this stunt. Don't make me regret it."

"Neither of you are law enforcement," Meg insisted, "so you can't even try this."

Webb sat up and swung his boots to the floor, causing Hawk to raise his head and blink sleepy eyes. "A guy like that will smell law enforcement from a mile away. It's one reason he's so successful. We can do this better than they could."

"I'm beginning to sound like a broken record. You can't do this on your own and without Van Cleave's approval."

"He'd throw off the whole mission. If he looks like a Feeb and smells like a Feeb, he's probably a Feeb. And you certainly can't come with us." McCord stood and started to pace the length of the small hotel room. "I can't walk into a bar like that with a woman—worse, a woman with a dog—and track down a guy to ask about buying a girl for sex. I can walk in with a buddy." He looked Webb up and down appraisingly. "One who looks like he could hold his own in a bar fight. One who's likely been in a few."

"A couple in my day," Webb said. "I held my own. What about you, if things get squirrelly?"

McCord poked his chest with an index finger. "Iraq War, remember? You were here having bar fights when I was dodging bullets and IEDs."

"I spend my days running into burning buildings. You're not seriously questioning my courage, are you?"

McCord grinned. "Nah, just making sure we'll have each other's backs if this goes south."

"Damn straight."

Meg wanted to yank her hair in frustration. "Put the goddamn Y chromosomes away for a few minutes. You're seriously considering going to hang out at this Short Trip To Hell?"

"Van Cleave can't stop us from going to a public place." McCord grinned at Webb. "And you never know who you'll meet at a place like that."

"Which also means we may meet no one," Webb said. "Meg, there's no guarantee that he'll even be there. We're working on the assumption that McCord's intel is correct—"

"Hey!" McCord's expression was pure outrage.

"—and Russo will be there. We may end up spending the night nursing beers and listening to bad music."

"And if he's actually there?" Meg asked.

"Then we're going to approach him and inquire about girls," McCord said. "We'll tell you one hundred percent of what he says and turn the information over to Van Cleave. We're not looking to take him down, just to find out any information that might be useful."

"And if he makes you?"

"He won't, but if by some strange chance he does, we'll defend ourselves."

"With what? You didn't bring firearms. And even if you did, unless you applied to the state for a nonresident concealed carry permit, you can't carry one anyway."

Webb stood and walked over to Meg's SAR pack to nudge it with his boot. "You brought weapons. At least two of them."

"It's illegal in Virginia to concealed carry either my military switchblade or my SAR knife."

"It's not illegal to open carry. That's one weapon for each of us."

Meg flopped back in the chair, crossing her arms over her chest. "It's that easy, is it?"

"It could be," McCord said. He squatted down in front of her so he was at her eye level. "Help us do this safely. We'll let you know when we're going in, and we'll let you know when we're free and clear. We'll be careful."

"We'll have each other's backs if anything goes wrong," said Webb. "And no one uses a weapon unless a life depends on it."

Shaking her head, Meg dug into her pack, pulling out and handing her sheathed SAR knife to Webb and the folded military knife to McCord. "Do *not* get into trouble. I'm not pulling strings to bail you two idiots out of jail."

"Would we do that?" McCord asked. But he quickly

shot up a hand to stop Meg when she opened her mouth. "On the other hand, don't answer that."

Meg certainly hoped there would be no need to go back on her word and make arrangements to bail them out of jail if their cockamamie scheme went sideways.

CHAPTER 22

Trailing canine: A search dog that exclusively follows the scent of a specific targeted individual.

Wednesday, July 26, 10:49 PM
A Short Trip To Hell
Norfolk, Virginia

Webb and McCord stepped into the bar to the rib-rattling thump of 1970s classic rock. McCord scanned the room: Ninety percent of the patrons were male between the ages of twenty and forty, with heavy facial hair, many wearing leather vests with motorcycle club names. Despite the name of the club, McCord was pretty sure there wasn't a schnapps bottle in the place. This was an establishment where beer, bourbon, and whiskey ruled, and metrosexuals weren't welcome.

"You live in D.C. long enough," Webb half shouted, "you forget what a smoky bar smells like. Then it all comes back like it was yesterday."

"I believe that's your designated, isolated smoking room over there." McCord pointed to a room toward the back of the bar, where the door was propped open with a bar stool as a waitress passed through with a loaded tray of drinks. "So much for a separate area."

"They won't give a damn as long as the health department doesn't come through the door. Do you see him?"

"No. And if we stand here much longer gawking, we're going to get made. Come on."

McCord led the way through tables toward the bar as the crack of pool balls breaking echoed from the back of the bar, followed by a masculine yell of triumph. They grabbed two empty bar stools as a brawny, tattooed bartender swaggered toward them.

"What'll you have?"

"Old Virginia," Webb said.

McCord glanced sideways at him, hoping he could hold his liquor if he was starting with whiskey. "Make it two."

The bartender nodded, grabbed two shot glasses, poured whiskey, and pushed the drinks in front of them. Webb tossed a ten down on the bar, and the bartender grabbed it and wandered in the direction of the cash register.

"Bottoms up," said Webb, and tossed back the drink.

"I guess a nice Chablis isn't something you're partial to." McCord picked up his drink, stared at the amber liquid, and then shot back the contents. The whiskey burned all the way down and McCord fought the urge to cough it back up. He thumped the glass down on the bar.

"Not a whiskey drinker?" Webb's eyes were laughing, even though his face was straight.

"Not usually." McCord's voice came out choked with a heavy rasp. "I'll buy the next round and it'll be beer."

"I can live with that." Webb's gaze scanned the bar nearly from one side to the other before shooting back partway. "Don't turn around and look, but I've got him."

"Where?"

"Booth on the back wall, by the washrooms. Bet that's where the emergency exit is. It's dark and less traveled."

"Just like the setup Reed used."

"He was probably taught by the master."

"Is he alone?"

"For now. He's looking at his phone and texting."

"We need to get another round and join him before someone else shows up." McCord waved down the bartender and ordered and paid for two beers. "Ready?"

"Whenever you are."

They picked up their beers and wound their way through the bar to the booth at the back. Without saying a word, McCord slid onto the bench seat opposite Russo, Webb sitting down next to him.

Russo, dark-haired and dark-eyed, with a thick neck and heavily tattooed forearms, looked up from his phone. His eyes narrowed into a mean squint. Everything about him was hard, from the set of his jaw to the bulk of his muscles. McCord hoped they wouldn't find out about that the hard way.

"Can I help you . . . gentlemen?" His voice was a jagged rasp, and the last word carried a sneer.

"We're hoping you can help us," McCord said. "We've been told by a reliable source that you're good at . . . finding desired objects."

"What source?"

"He swore me to secrecy. But he said you could help us out." He raised his beer in Webb's direction, then took a sip before setting it down.

"I can't do business with someone who just walks in off the street. You could be a cop trying to entrap me." He head-jerked toward the front door. "Get gone."

Webb started to get up, but McCord caught his arm, dragging him back down. "Okay, okay. He may never deal for me again, but it's Blackjack Fuller, from the west side."

"How you know Blackjack?"

"We've done some business. Granted that business got interrupted when he got put away for assault on his old lady." McCord curled his lip, hoping it reflected disgust. "Bullshit charge. A man should be able to have a say in his own house without the cops raining fire down on his head. Blackjack certainly agrees, but he has to play it safe while he's on probation."

Russo looked them both over carefully, as if seeing them in a new light. Then he jammed his phone in his pocket. "What are you looking for?"

"Girls," Webb said. He took a long drink of his beer, never taking his eyes off Russo. He backhanded his mouth and put down his stein. "Preferably fresh-faced, if you catch my drift."

Russo nodded thoughtfully. "Young and untouched, got it. What are you looking for? High school? Or younger than that?"

Webb sat back and carefully stretched out an arm across the back of the bench. "I like them young and inexperienced. You can teach them what you like."

"You boys going to share?"

Webb's casual stance froze, his eyes going to slits. "I don't share."

Russo held up a hand. "That's fine, man. I gotta ask or I can't get you what you're looking for."

"I like mine not so wet behind the ears," McCord said. "So, yeah, it's an order for two for as soon as you can arrange it."

"I can arrange something. But it won't come cheap."

McCord pulled out his wallet, extracted a hundred-dollar bill, folded it in half, and slid it across the table under his palm. "Will that do for a down payment?"

"Sure will."

"How do we contact you?"

"You don't. I'll call you. Gimme your number."

McCord pulled his notebook out of his back pocket,

flipped it open to a blank page at the back, wrote down his cell phone number and ripped out the page. He handed it across the table.

Russo glanced at the number, folded the sheet carefully, and slid it into his pocket. "I'll call you. Now if you'll excuse me . . ." He looked at them pointedly.

"You must have other business to do." McCord held out his hand across the table. Several painful seconds ticked by as his hand hung there, untouched, before he pulled it back. "We look forward to your call."

They returned to the bar with their beers, finished them while making inconsequential small talk, and then left. They stepped out into fresh air and McCord breathed in deeply. "God, I *hate* cigarette smoke." They turned south toward McCord's car. "How do you think that went?"

"Fifty-fifty, I'd say." Webb glanced down the deserted street, and stepped off the curb to cut across the asphalt on a diagonal. "You had to give him the guy's name or he never would have bit, but I'm not sure he bought it either way. He may have just gone through the motions to get rid of us. We're not a known commodity, and didn't come through whatever the usual channels are, so he may not want to take a chance on us. He may think we just want to burn him."

"He'd be right if he does. I guess we'll find out if he calls. If he doesn't, my editor is going to throw a hissy fit over the amount of bribery money I've been using for this story."

Webb glanced at him sideways. "That was the *Post*'s money?"

"Sure was. You think my pockets are lined like that?"

They walked on for another minute in silence.

"I feel slimy," McCord said.

"I need a drink not tainted by that hole in the wall. And

a shower. In that order," Webb countered. "These people make me sick. They also make me want to hit something. *Hard.*"

"We're doing what we can. But I wouldn't say no to that drink."

"You're on."

Wednesday, July 26, 11:51 PM
Outside A Short Trip To Hell
Norfolk, Virginia

Meg looked up when the door to the bar opened with a blast of guitar and the pounding of drums and then thumped closed, quenching the sound. She squinted at the single figure standing on the doorstep, digging into the pocket of his jeans. Dark hair, white, about the right build, but in the weak, flickering light outside the bar, it was nearly impossible to see.

Maybe?

She quickly dug into the pocket of the light shell she wore and pulled out a compact pair of binoculars. She quickly focused on the man, but there just wasn't enough light and he was hunched over, knocking something into his hand. What that something was became clear when he raised it to his lips and flicked a lighter to life. For a moment, his face was lit in tones of crimson until the flame went out, leaving just the burning tip of his cigarette glowing red as he inhaled.

Those few seconds were enough.

Russo.

She placed her hand on Hawk's head to find him already alert, his eyes fixed on the man. They were across the street from A Short Trip To Hell, camouflaged in dark clothes, standing in the inky shadow of an alley kitty-corner to Russo's favorite establishment. They'd been there since shortly after Webb and McCord had entered the facility, based on Webb's text.

She'd come separately with Hawk, hell-bent on finding their own way to help. McCord was right: They had no cause to be inside the bar, but every cause to be outside it. Meg had done a little extra snooping. Russo didn't own a car—at least not one actually registered to him—so she wanted to know how he got around. Either he had a car and she'd be able to get down the license plate number, or he lived close enough to his favorite haunt that Hawk could track him on foot. Either way, it would be additional information.

Webb and McCord had left nearly a half hour earlier. Meg was beginning to think she'd missed Russo's exit— several men had gone out, but she didn't think any of them matched his description—or he'd gone out a back exit where she had no line of sight.

Now here he was.

He stepped off the stoop and onto the cracked sidewalk, looked both ways, blew out a puff of smoke, and turned to his right to head away from Meg. She kept the binoculars trained on him as he strode down the sidewalk. He jammed one hand in his jeans pocket and then tossed something carelessly into the parking lot beside the bar. The object rolled under a parked car. Meg took five precious seconds to try to find the discarded item, but it was too dark and too distant.

He just made our job a whole lot easier. Now he can't get away from us.

Russo reached the first intersection and turned right again, disappearing behind a building seconds later. He was moving at a quick pace, likely not wanting to be out in the open for longer than necessary.

Meg jammed the binoculars back into her pocket. "Hawk,

come." She pulled a latex glove out of her pocket and tugged it on as they jogged across the street and down past A Short Trip To Hell. Hawk, out of his FBI vest and on a plain collar and leash to avoid attracting attention, followed her as she stepped off the sidewalk and into the parking lot. Reaching the car, she dropped to her knees, bending over to shine her cell phone flashlight into the gloom beneath the car.

A small, crumpled piece of paper lay beneath. Reaching in with her gloved hand, she pulled it out and then used the edge of her cell phone to press a corner of the lined piece of notepad paper to the car window, pulling the paper flat with her gloved fingers. The only thing on the paper was a phone number, but she recognized it instantly as Clay McCord's. They'd tried to make a deal with Russo, expressed their interest and left contact information, but he either wasn't taking on new clients or he smelled a rat. Clearly, he had no intention of calling Mc-Cord back.

But now they had his scent. She pulled a small plastic bag out of her pocket and bagged the paper before pulling off her latex glove. She offered the bag to Hawk. "Find him, Hawk. Find Russo."

Hawk scented the air for only a fraction of a second and then trotted down the street. Meg slowed him down to an easy walk. With a scent this fresh and undispersed, there was no way Hawk would lose it, and Meg didn't want to stand out, even though neither of them could be visually tagged as FBI. If they were spotted, they'd just look like a woman and her dog, out for an evening walk before bed. The goal would be to stay far enough behind that they were never in visual range.

Russo was likely beyond careful as a matter of necessity and safety. He would be a man with enemies, who would want to avoid being picked off. It might be why he didn't drive a car—a vehicle was just another way to be tagged or a potential death trap if an explosive was planted. She was sure he was carrying, so he likely preferred his chances on foot. He could take a different route each night, cut through green spaces not open to vehicles, and backtrack if needed until he was safe at home.

What he wouldn't expect was a scent dog trailing his every step just minutes behind. He'd never see Hawk, but Hawk could see him as clearly as if Russo was standing directly in front of them.

The route they followed was as convoluted as Meg foresaw. He cut through empty back lots and behind shuttered storefronts. He circled the opera house and bypassed an Exxon station. Then he wove through a huge cemetery, around mausoleums and between headstones. Meg could respect the man's paranoia in thinking that he needed to take these precautions in case he was followed . . . except she was following him, so his paranoia was clearly warranted.

His trail left the cemetery and entered a quiet street, bordered on one side by a long pond on the west side of the cemetery. Meg studied the houses—big, beautiful, two-story clapboards with quaint porches and neatly trimmed boxwood hedges. This couldn't be their end destination. The man she'd seen leave that bar would stick out like a sore thumb in this newly minted middle America.

Hawk apparently didn't think he belonged either because he stayed on the trail that took them down the street, around the corner, over a treed boulevard and up a narrower lane. Streetlights were few and far between in this neighborhood, bathing the asphalt below in a dull, watery yellow haze. Instead of the wide sidewalks in front of the new subdivision, this street was narrow and without walkways. Cheap chain-link fences separated the tiny front yards from the road. Open lots of patchy weeds were scattered down the street, evidence of houses razed from the neighborhood.

This is more like it.

The street was deserted, but Meg expected as much, given Russo's head start on them. Most of the houses were dark, but a few had lights on in their front rooms or up-stairs bedrooms.

Hawk suddenly cut left, heading unerringly up a front walk of paving stones with moss and weeds growing be-tween them. Meg gently pulled back on the leash and Hawk instantly stopped. "Hawk, come." As he angled back toward her, she kept walking past the house, but she couldn't see a house number on the dirty gray siding under the sag-ging porch. Luckily, the next house had a light on beside the front door, illuminating the large black 864 under-neath. Meg didn't look back, but continued down the street, turning the corner to purposely disappear from view in case Russo was watching for anyone tailing him still. Overkill on her part, but if he could be careful, so could she.

She waited a full ten minutes before going back down the street, this time on the far side. She purposefully daw-dled, as if her dog had to stop and sniff every fence post, streetlight, and fire hydrant, and it gave her time to study the house. It was two stories, with every front window dark, and was completely enclosed by chain-link fence. Empty lots flanked both sides of the house. The un-adorned front walkway led to a sturdy front door with no inset windows. The overall air was one of borderline ne-glect and dysfunction.

A movement behind the illuminated front window of a house two doors down on her side of the street caught Meg's eye. She pulled out her phone to glance at the time—12:29 AM. Did she dare?

Hell, nothing to lose.

A soft tug on the leash told Hawk to come along, and he trotted at her side down the sidewalk. Reaching the house, she went up the short walk, up the three steps of the wooden porch, and softly tapped on the door. The noise of a television inside the house instantly muted, so she knocked again. As the squeak of floorboards sounded within the house, she reached into her pocket and pulled out her flip case. She held it out toward the peephole in the front door, hoping the large FBI designation would be clear to the occupant inside.

The door opened a crack to reveal an older man peering through the gap afforded by the chain still locking the door. "Yeah?"

"Hello, sir. My name is Meg Jennings and I'm with the FBI." She looked down at her dog. "This is my partner, Hawk. I apologize for the late hour, but I was wondering if I could ask you a few questions. You don't need to open the door if you aren't comfortable. I realize it's late and this is an unexpected visit."

The man's gaze moved from her to the dog and back again. Then the door closed, and the slide of a chain sounded through the door before it opened all the way. "Come on in."

Meg stepped into a neat and tidy front foyer that opened into a comfortable living room with a silent, flickering TV in front of the wide picture window. "Again, my apologies for the late visit. Your light was on so I wondered if I could speak with you."

"What about?"

"The gray clapboard house across the road. The one with the chain-link fence with the empty lots on either side of it. Do you know who lives there?"

"See him now and then if we happen to be out at the same time. Seen the others who live with him too."

"The others?"

"Men. Boys. Not for long though. They seem to rotate through. I always thought he was running some sort of halfway house for Mexicans. They don't stay long. A few days, a week. Then a new crop comes through."

The hair on the back of Meg's neck rose, but she put extra effort into keeping her tone light and casual. "You've seen these men and boys leaving the house? You think they're all Latino?"

"They look like it. But I've never heard them speak. They come out of the house early in the morning, seven days a week, heads down, always silent. They get in a van and drive away. They come back late. The door shuts and you don't see them again."

"You think it's a halfway house?"

"Might be. Maybe he's trying to help them find work. I always assumed he did, because then they go away and new ones come."

"How many are there at a time?"

"Not sure. Numbers vary. He in trouble?"

"We're not sure, but your information is extremely helpful." Meg pulled a business card out of her pocket, along with a pen. "Would you mind jotting down your name, sir, and your contact information? In case we have any more questions?"

"Sure." The man wrote down his name, address, and phone number and handed the card back to Meg. She handed him a second business card. "All my information is here, including my cell phone number. If you think of anything else you'd like to pass on, please don't hesitate to call me. Again, my apologies for the late visit, but I appreciate the information. You've been very helpful."

Meg said her goodbyes and saw herself out.

She stood for a few minutes in the dark, looking down the street at the dark house. They now had enough corroborating evidence to support Russo's role in possible multiple trafficking rings stretching from the sex trade to illegal farming operations. As soon as she was safely off this street, she was going to get Van Cleave out of bed and was going to lean on him to get a warrant and be here by no later than six o'clock to raid the place.

She'd found a trafficking house. And they were going to save the men and boys inside before they could disappear forever.

CHAPTER 23

Mitigation: Efforts designed to reduce or eliminate search risks, and lessen possible property loss if possible.

Thursday, July 27, 6:14 AM
Washington Street
Norfolk, Virginia

Meg and Hawk stood across the street from the house they'd visited the night before, to watch the operation.

Agents in navy windbreakers with "FBI" in yellow block letters on the back led handcuffed men and boys out the front door. They were a disheveled lot, many of them overly thin and walking unsteadily as if sick or badly malnourished, most with hunched shoulders and lowered heads. Her irritation grew as the stream of people coming out of the house were loaded into an FBI van. These were victims. Why were they being treated so badly?

The stream dried to a trickle and then stopped. *Was that all of them?*

Van Cleave appeared in the doorway, pushing the man they'd trailed last night in front of him. Russo was cuffed, struggling and cursing, calling Van Cleave every name in the book, but Van Cleave's neutral expression never changed. His face remained set in stone as he pushed Russo down the short walk and guided him into a waiting FBI SUV, taking care to ensure Russo didn't bump his head as he settled into the vehicle. But the appearance of calm slipped when Van Cleave slammed the door behind Russo with significantly more force than required.

He's pissed.

Never one to sit back and let others take the lead, Van Cleave had been the first through the door, his agents following behind. It had still been dark, and the house had been caught unawares. Shouts of surprise rang out in response to bellows of "FBI! Hands behind your head!" in both English and Spanish. Meg didn't know how Van Cleave had managed to get a warrant and coordinate the entire op in a little over four hours, but it spoke to his judicial connections and the power of his command that he'd pulled it off. Not a single gunshot had been fired and no one had been hurt.

Meg's gaze was drawn back to the front door as a boy appeared, backlit by the foyer lights. Seen only in silhouette, his frailty was accentuated by the oversized clothes draped over his slender frame. When he stepped onto the front walk, Meg could see he wore no shoes. The female FBI agent leading him down the front walk was gentle with him, her head inclined toward him as she guided him by the arm.

The line started again, threading its way out of the house.

How many of them are there?

Van Cleave paused at the curb as the FBI SUV rolled away from the house, turning on its lights as it picked up speed farther down the street. His eyes followed it until it disappeared from view, and then he stepped off the curb and crossed the street toward them. Beside her, Hawk started waving his tail in happy greeting, his body dancing in anticipation. Van Cleave surprised her by sitting down on the curb beside Hawk, a small smile softening the harsh lines of his face.

He ran his hands over the dog and received an enthusiastic tongue bath in return. Normally Meg would have called Hawk off after just a few seconds, but part of her sensed that Van Cleave needed it. Hawk's joy evidently blunted the sharp edges of Van Cleave's anger.

Meg sat down on the curb beside him, Hawk between them. "That bad?"

"Jesus Christ." Rage tipped every word. "I mean, I knew we were walking into a bad situation, but the number of kids in there is staggering. I thought he'd have half a dozen."

"I've seen more than that walk through the door."

"I bet you have. There are twenty-seven men and boys in total. I had to call a second van to transport them all. They're all immigrants. Usually, in a group like that, it's mostly men, sent out into the fields to do backbreaking work too strenuous for boys. But there were nineteen kids in there."

Meg looked back toward the figures stumbling through the doorway. "I don't see any women."

"Not a one. They don't need them. They're using boys in their place."

"I thought this house was for farm workers?"

Van Cleave lowered his forehead to rest it on Hawk's sturdy skull. "All the men are marked for that, and some of the larger, more mature boys. The smaller boys . . ."

"They're meant for the sex trade."

"Most of them are already in it." His head rose and the

mixture of grief and fury in his eyes had Meg drawing back a few inches. "They're terrified of us. Of the male agents. I had to call for extra female agents to assist. I can't imagine the kinds of abuse they've suffered, but clearly it's all been at the hands of men." The hands resting on Hawk's back balled into fists. "I want to hurt him."

Meg didn't have to ask to know he meant Russo. "I didn't even see it and I can see why you would. You may not have kids of your own, but you have the instinct to protect in spades. It wasn't possible for you to have stopped this before it even started to save them from the experience. But you got them out of it."

"Too little, too late."

"It's never too late. Look at Mary. She thought she was a lost cause and now she's back with her parents and working on rebuilding her life. You know what they say: Where there's life, there's hope. You've given them a chance to have that kind of hope. But why are they all handcuffed? Those are victims, not criminals."

"I agree. However, I couldn't take the chance of any of them getting away. Some of them are scared enough to try to make a run for it, and I don't want anyone getting hurt or chancing anyone getting away and being sucked back into this life because of desperation. I need to get them interviewed and settled somewhere nonthreatening. I need to find out where those kids came from and get them back home if home is a safe place."

Meg sighed. "I can tell you from my years with the Richmond PD that many of these kids ran away from home because it wasn't a safe place."

"Oh, I know. And we'll be prepared for that. CPS will be meeting us and them downtown."

"Good. What's next then?"

"I need the crime scene techs in that house. I think there's information in there about where they've been sending victims to work. We don't want to mess up any evidence and risk an upcoming court case on a technical error, so I'll leave collection to them. There might even be evidence of men and boys who've passed through the house previously. We need to find them, and to pull them out of whatever hell they're in. Lists of their names and work sites will give us that."

"Okay, what's next for you then?"

"A barrel of coffee to make up for not having slept in nearly twenty-four hours, then some paperwork, which will really be time for me to cool down. Then I'm going after Russo once I can trust myself to do it without taking him apart and killing my own case."

"Interrogation? I want in."

Van Cleave's gaze slid sideways toward her. "You're not an agent."

"I'm not supposed to be on this case, period, but I made a promise to a victim—which you agreed to and made happen, I might add—so here I am. I'm an ex-cop, Van, not just some dog trainer off the streets. I can be useful here. I can also be a buffer if you start to lose it. If you think it's going south at any time, I'll pull out and you can send in whoever you need. But I want in, I want to see him go down. I didn't get to see Reed fall, so I think you owe me this much."

Van Cleave stared at her while the dog between them nudged at him with his muzzle. Then his shoulders rose and fell on a sigh. "Fine. But you follow my lead and in- structions, no questions asked."

"Deal."

Meg turned back to the house as the last of the children

were helped into the second FBI van and two female agents climbed in before the doors slid shut. This morning's raid had been a success, but Meg had the feeling that this was only the tip of the iceberg. And like the iceberg that took down the *Titanic*, sometimes what hid in the murky depths was deadliest of all.

CHAPTER 24

Lost Person Behavior: A search strategy based upon known and probable behavior of the missing person.

Thursday, July 27, 1:31 PM
FBI Field Office
Norfolk, Virginia

"Ready?"

Meg stared through the double-sided glass, into the interrogation room beyond. Russo sat in the single chair on the far side of the table, his bound hands chained to the table in front of him, and his angry eyes focused on the mirrored glass opposite him. Staring directly at her, as if he could see her. *Bring it on.* "Ready."

Van Cleave opened the door and strode through to the table. He slapped a file folder down on the table and pulled out his chair with a screech. Meg followed, closing the door behind her and taking the chair beside Van Cleave.

Van Cleave opened the folder. "Dominic Russo, I'm required to inform you that this interview is being recorded. I'm Special Agent in Charge Van Cleave, and this is my colleague Meg Jennings. I'm going to read you your rights again for the record. You have the right to remain silent . . ."

He recited the full Miranda warning. "You can decide at any time from this moment on to terminate the interview and exercise these rights. Do you understand each of these rights I have explained to you?"

Russo nodded curtly.

"Out loud for the recording, please."

"Yeah."

"Having these rights in mind, do you wish to talk to us now?"

Russo let out a bitter laugh. "Sure. Why the hell not?"

"You are currently charged with conspiracy to recruit, sex trafficking of minors, acting in a manner injurious to a child less than seventeen, unlawful imprisonment, promoting prostitution, and human trafficking—providing forced services and involving commercial sex. Oh, and you broke the Virginia Minimum Wage Act for referring illegal immigrants for employment when they lacked documentation. Of course, additional charges could be added as new evidence is introduced into the case. Let's start with the fact that you are essentially running a boardinghouse without a permit, exceeding zoning laws for occupancy."

"I was just trying to help some guys out until they got on their feet."

"You're a hero," Van Cleave said. "The health department is likely going to levy charges concerning the living conditions. Why were there so many people living in that house? A house, by the way, that doesn't belong to you, but is instead registered to Bartlett and Kesell, a shell corporation that we're in the process of tracking down. Why were you there?"

"Like I said, I was just helping out some guys down on their luck."

"Helping them do what?" Meg leaned forward to pin Russo with a hard stare. "Most of them didn't look healthy enough to hold down a real job."

"Whatever we could find for them. I'd help them make connections, help them get on their feet. After that it was up to them."

Meg turned to Van Cleave. "You're right, he's a hero." The look she turned back on Russo said anything but. "What kind of connections?"

"You know, these guys aren't particularly well educated, so whatever jobs we could find."

"Did they speak English?"

"Some."

"I assume you asked to see their papers?" Meg asked.

Russo's expression was all guileless innocence. "That's not what I do. These fine folk arrive at my door, I help them find work."

Van Cleave's index finger tapped the top page in the folder. "You don't check out their immigration status?"

"I'm not ICE. If these hardworking folks tell me they're legal citizens or have green cards, why wouldn't I believe them? I'm sure their employers have a responsibility to check that out."

"And what about the children?" Meg asked. "Some of them looked a little on the young side for Virginia's labor laws. They each have an employment certificate?"

"Don't need one to work on a farm or in an orchard."

Meg and Van Cleave exchanged a quick glance. *His first slip.*

Van Cleave turned a page in his folder. "I see here that you have a few farms that like to take on your workers." He named off several farms, wineries, and orchards.

For the first time Russo looked cautious.

Van Cleave sat back in his chair, crossing his arms over his chest. "You do know we have translators? And my grasp of Spanish is pretty solid. The men and boys were fairly talkative once we assured them you would be in no position to ever harm them again. And that we wouldn't be pressing charges against them, or turning them over to ICE." His fist came down on the table, making Russo jump. "We know what you did. We know how you farmed out— literally—the men and older boys." He leaned in closer. "We found the floor safe with money, drugs, and the records of your sex trade operation. You thought you had those boys terrified into submission. But one of them with more guts in his little finger than you have in your whole body was spying on you, learning your secrets, and told us all about them as soon as he got here. I went back myself late this afternoon and had a locksmith crack the safe. We have clients and transactions. We have the drugs you used to keep some of your victims under your thumb."

Meg laid her hand on Van Cleave's arm to draw his attention. "You forgot to add in the charge of possession with the intent to deliver."

Van Cleave's smile was full of satisfied glee. "My mistake. I did forget." He turned back to the man across the table, who grew paler with each passing minute. "Are you familiar with mandatory minimums for drug charges, Russo? Granted, considering the list of charges you have against you and their combined sentence, that may be the least of your concerns. You're never going to see the light of day again. No prisoner reentry for you." The smile got broader as Russo's eyes went wide. "Yes, we know all about your little recruitment scheme. Luke Reed died before he could tell all, but we found out about it anyway." He looked at Meg. "We could add conspiracy to commit a felony too."

"We absolutely should," she agreed.

"Wait, wait." Russo's hands spread wide until the handcuffs snapped them back. In his sudden rush of panic, he'd forgotten he was bound. "I want a deal."

Van Cleave turned to Meg. "And suddenly he wants to deal."

"Too bad that's up to the district attorney. Not our call."

"Get the DA on the line." Russo's clenched fists hit the table in a rattle of bone and steel. "I'm done talking until we talk about a deal."

"You heard the man," Meg said. "Guess we'll have to talk to the DA."

Without another word, Meg and Van Cleave left the room. Meg nodded to the agent stationed outside the interrogation room door and followed Van Cleave toward his office. He surprised her by turning into the lunchroom instead.

"Coffee?"

"We're going to stop for coffee?"

"At least." Van Cleave glanced at his watch. "Let's give him twenty minutes to cool his heels."

"What about the DA?"

"Already done."

"What?"

He laughed as he pulled out a coffee pod and loaded it into the machine. "I'm so far ahead of him, it isn't funny. You didn't answer—coffee?"

"Sure, thanks."

He leaned against the counter while the machine hissed and dripped out the first cup. "I didn't have a chance to update you. What you don't know is that I called the DA from the car on the way back from the second visit to Washington Street. This is big, Meg, too big for just this one guy. When the whole thing started, I thought we were looking at a sex ring, but now I'm seeing how wide it stretches and into how many aspects of human trafficking. Also into how many major players we might have. Players who we should respect, who should know better. Who are giving up their sworn tenets to uphold the law to make a quick buck." His brows drew together as his jaw tightened.

"For someone who has spent a lifetime trying to stop this kind of exploitation, that must feel like the worst kind of betrayal."

Van Cleave handed her the cup and set up a second. "Pretty much." He looked up and the anger had morphed into determination. "I don't want to get just one guy. I want them all." His hands on his hips, he stared down into the cup as the liquid level slowly rose. "You know, we could have missed the whole thing. If your firefighter buddy . . ." He squeezed his eyes shut and rubbed at his forehead. "Sorry, it's been a long day and it's only just past lunch. What's his name?"

"Lieutenant Todd Webb. And give yourself a break. You've been up since yesterday morning."

"I'm going to have to take thirty at some point today before I walk into a wall or start making mistakes that could jeopardize the case. Anyway, if Lieutenant Webb hadn't caught sight of that van, and if it wasn't a visceral part of the two of you to help the helpless, we would never have caught the thread that led to this entire case. Mary would have died under those bleachers. Emma would have died in the swamp. McCord and Lieutenant Webb never would have made that jackass move to go meet with Russo and you never would have followed him to find that house. Most of those victims would have died."

"Who knew at the time that one chance sighting would have so many ramifications?"

"The ramifications are for the people involved who are steering this nightmare. The rest we'll do our best to save." He took a sip of his own coffee and sighed in pleasure. "Damn, I needed that."

"I'm sure you do. Do you have the okay from the DA to deal?"

"Yes. When she discovered how many charges are levied against Russo, she was happy to swap out a few of the less serious charges. It will sound like a great deal to Russo, but the other charges will put him away for life anyway, so she can be flexible. She understands the bigger picture and she's willing to compromise here to bring down the ringleaders." He glanced down toward the floor. "Where's Hawk today? It's weird to see you without him."

"It's weird to be without him, let me tell you. We're usually attached at the hip. McCord's got him. I wanted to leave him with someone familiar for a few hours, and my sister is too far away and Todd is still helping with the recovery operation. That left McCord."

"He's okay with dog sitting?"

"To progress the case he'll break first? Sure, he is. Any news about our missing girls?"

"Nothing definitive yet, which is why I didn't bring it up, but the Norfolk PD think they've got a line on at least one of them. They're following the lead, hard."

"Then we may catch a break after all." Meg glanced at the clock on the wall. "Think that's enough time?"

Van Cleave pulled out a chair, propped his feet up opposite and wrapped both hands around his coffee cup. "Not yet. I want him nervous and on edge in there. The longer it takes for us to come back, the more uncertain a deal might be in his head."

"Because you're having trouble convincing the DA that it's a good idea."

"Exactly."

When they entered the conference room for the second time, Meg could see that Van Cleave's strategy was paying off. Russo was trying to look cool and collected, but the rattle of the handcuff chain against the table from hands he couldn't hold still gave him away.

Van Cleave sat in the chair and made a show of picking up the papers in the folder and tapping them on the desk to fine-tune the already perfectly aligned edges. He exuded an air of overall dissatisfaction.

"What did he say?" Russo demanded. "Do we have a deal?"

"It's she, and yes, we have a deal." Van Cleave threw the papers back into the folder. "Although she was too damned easy on you, in my opinion. She's willing to drop possession with intent to deliver, acting in a manner injurious to a child less than seventeen, and unlawful imprisonment, as long as you give us names." Both hands landed palm down on the table with a slap. "And I don't mean any names, I mean the people running this organization. Anything else is wasting my time and I'll tell her you weren't going for it."

"I don't know everyone involved."

"Well, let's start with who you do know. And I want details, Russo. You just give me names, with no evidence to support it and are unwilling to stand as a material witness as part of the bargain, then we're done here and you can rot in jail for as long as you live."

"You know about Luke Reed. There's another guy, Vic Hermes. He runs a group of massage parlors—"

Van Cleave pushed back from the table so abruptly it shifted, pinning Russo in his chair on the far side. "We're done here." He looked at Meg. "Let's go."

Meg stood and started to move toward the door.

"Wait!"

They turned to stare at Russo. He sat, hunched in on himself, breathing hard, as if the effort to make the decision was taking a physical toll on him. "Okay, okay.

Mason Pate. He runs the Chesapeake Community Corrections Service Center. He funnels victims to us for a cut of the profits."

The gleam in Van Cleave's eyes was pure triumph. He pulled out his chair and sat down again. "Okay, tell us everything. And don't leave anything out or the deal's off."

The circle was collapsing in on itself.

CHAPTER 25

Clear: A call by a handler to the officials of a canine nose work trial that an area has been searched and no target odor was found.

Thursday, July 27, 4:54 PM
FBI Field Office
Norfolk, Virginia

As she entered the field office, Hawk heeling beside her, Meg scanned the far side of the bullpen, only to find Van Cleave's office with the lights on, but empty.

"Guess he's still in interview. Come on, Hawk, let's take a load off while we wait."

They crossed the office and Meg dropped down gratefully into one of the overstuffed chairs outside of Van Cleave's office. "Hawk, down." Hawk lay down at her feet, looking up at her with luminous brown eyes. "While we're waiting, I want to check in with Emma and see how things are going. It's been a few days since I talked to her, and I bet she'd appreciate a friendly voice." As if understanding the importance of her task, Hawk crossed his front paws and laid his head down on them with a gusty, patient sigh.

She pulled out her cell phone and called up her contact

list, scrolling through it to find the number Van Cleave
had sent her for the cell phone he'd given Emma so she
could contact him anytime, day or night.

More than just trying to close this case for her, Emma's
long-term prospects gnawed at Meg. The girl was eighteen, so juvenile assistance was no longer an option, and
she didn't want the girl back out on the streets, where
she'd possibly go back to her previous life because she had
absolutely no choice.

It had only taken a single short phone call with Meg's
parents, to explain the situation, for a potential solution to
be found. Jake and Eda Jennings were just in the process
of loading up all their newly rescued animals, some of
which would require significant care, and they were more
than happy at Meg's suggestion that Emma help with the
rescue. Meg was grateful to her parents because, for all
Emma's bravado, she knew that Emma herself would require some care. But her mother was an old hand at raising teenage girls, and she knew Emma would be fine, given
a few weeks to settle in and bond with the animals.

If Meg could talk her into going.

Meg sat back in the chair, the phone at her ear, listening
as the phone rang once . . . twice . . .

"Hello?" Emma's voice was tentative.

"Emma, hi, it's Meg." Meg kept her voice light. "It has
been a few days since I touched base with you, so I wanted
to check in and see how you are."

"Good. Lily's been great. She doesn't crowd me or hang
over me. It's giving me time to adjust to the new place."

"Do you like it?"

"I have my own room." When Meg stayed silent, she
continued. "I haven't had a room to myself in . . . well, I
don't know how long. It was weird that first night. Nobody whimpering in their sleep or whispering in the middle of the night. The silence kept waking me up."

"If that place doesn't suit you—"

"No, no, it does. It's just a little strange right now. But not bad strange. And I've met some new girls. For the most part they've been friendly. How's the case going?"

"Good. We're making progress. Nothing I can tell you about yet, but I'm confident we're going to take down more of the ring than we thought possible. No news yet on the missing girls, but local police are investigating some promising leads, and no one has given up hope. Have you heard anything about Mary?"

"I gave her parents Lily's number since Van told me to keep this one secret. They called after her surgery. Everything went well and she's expected to make a full recovery in a couple of months."

"That's great news," Meg said. "You know, I've been thinking. What are your plans when all this is over?" The deafening silence on the other end of the line answered the question for her. "This isn't something you need to do, or, if you think it's not a good fit, you can say so, but I have somewhere you could go. Not only to stay for a while, but to do good work. Work that will make a difference."

"Where?" The single word was full of suspicion.

"Cold Spring Haven. It's the animal rescue my parents run just outside of Charlottesville, Virginia."

There was a long pause. "What would I do there?" Emma asked.

"It's more of a matter of what wouldn't you do. Hand-feed babies of every size, shape, and variety, from kittens to egrets to a litter of Southeastern shrews that were displaced by Hurricane Cole. Help care for sick and injured deer, eagles, and turtles. Feed Auria, our horse, and Jeeves, our emu, the rescue's two permanent residents. Muck out stalls, mend fences, empty and scrub litter boxes."

"You're really selling it."

Meg laughed. "That's life at any rescue, so there's no

point in not being honest. But even mucking stalls can be satisfying because no matter how messy the job, it's all for them. Everything we do is for them. And the animals know it, and pay us back a hundredfold."

"You've worked there yourself?"

"I was going through a bad time a few years ago." She reached for the handblown glass pendant that hung over her heart, rubbing the smooth surface between thumb and forefinger. "I'd just lost a partner, my patrol dog from when I was still on the Richmond PD. Losing Deuce just about killed me. So I quit the force and went back to my parents' to rebuild my life. Within a couple of days of my arrival, someone abandoned a critically ill black Lab puppy on the doorstep. That was Hawk. I nursed him back to health, he helped heal my broken heart, and we've never looked back. It's good work, Emma. Satisfying work. A good place to find your center again when it feels like the world has been yanked out from under you."

Van Cleave suddenly appeared in the bullpen, stalking right past and into his office without seeing her. He slammed his office door, rattling the glass of his windows. He stood stock-still for a moment.

Then he kicked the desk.

Uh-oh.

"Emma, I have to go. Promise me you'll think about it."

"I will."

"Great. I'll call you again in a few days. Sooner if anything breaks in the case. Bye."

"Hawk, come." Meg stood, crossed to his office, knocked on the door, and entered without waiting for a reply. "What happened?"

She found Van Cleave sitting in his desk chair, his right ankle crossed over his left knee, squeezing the toe of his perfectly polished leather shoe. The look he sent her was overflowing with fury. "Absolutely nothing."

"What?" Meg closed the door. "Hawk, come. Sit." She sat in her usual chair opposite his desk and Hawk settled beside her. "Did you not get Mason Pate? Is he out of town?"

"Oh, he's here. He's lawyered up and not saying a word. Nothing. Not to defend himself, not to refute any of my accusations. And he's totally calm. Peaceful even. He's not even breaking a damned sweat!" He picked up a piece of paper, crumpled it into a ball, squeezed it brutally hard, and then tossed it into the blue recycling bin beside his door. It bounced off the rim and rolled three feet away. Van Cleave cursed and hung his head.

"Hawk, fetch the ball. Fetch."

Hawk retrieved the ball of paper. He brought it back to deposit it carefully in Meg's hand. She gave it a gentle toss and swished it into the recycling bin.

"Thanks. Both of you." Van Cleave's foot dropped to the floor and he sat back in his chair, his body limp and wrung out.

"Didn't get that thirty-minute nap, did you?"

"Never had the chance."

"That level of exhaustion sure won't help your day go smoothly. Okay, fill me in. What happened when I went to get Hawk and you went to bring in Pate?"

"Not a whole lot." He loosened his tie and flipped open the top button of his shirt. "I took one of my agents and we went over to the correctional facility. We called first, to make sure he was there. He was, so we went. He's one cool customer, let me tell you. Didn't blink an eye when I told him we were taking him into custody for interfering with a police investigation, obstruction of justice, money laundering, conducting a criminal enterprise, and all the other charges related to human trafficking and the trafficking of minors. Didn't blink when I read him his rights. We got here and he politely asked to call his lawyer. The lawyer gets here and we start the interview but it goes nowhere. He's the perfect client. He shuts up and lets his lawyer do all the talking."

"Perfect for everyone but us," Meg mumbled.

"We get a grand total of nothing. And Mr. Serenity just sits there, all Zen, like he's meditating." His fist thumped down on the desk, making his empty coffee cup jump. "What does he know that we don't?"

"What do you mean?"

"I've been at this a long time. I know when a perp is hiding something. I may not know what it is, but I know there's something. They're nervous, and nerves result in physical tells. But I got *nothing* from Pate. We know he's guilty. Why isn't he concerned?"

"That's a good question. I've never had a perp like you're describing."

"I'd like to give him a drug test. He's got to be on something for that amount of calm."

"Where is he now?"

"We're holding him for now, based on Russo's testimony. I'm also getting a warrant to search Pate's house and workplaces, and to take all of his remaining electronics into custody."

"You have his Harper Group computer, right?"

Van Cleave nodded. "Already at the Computer Forensics Lab. But with what Russo is accusing him of, I doubt he'd have those kinds of records on any work machine. That would be at home. We'll get those too. And I guess we'll have to hit him with more evidence to really crack him." His eyes dropped to the surface of his desk and locked onto a paper bag. "You need to see this."

"A paper bag?"

Van Cleave smiled for the first time since she'd walked into the room. "Not just any paper bag." He opened it up and reached in to pull out a small, spiral-bound notebook with a black plastic cover and backing. "I sent agents back out to Deep Creek Lock Park. It was a needle in a haystack kind of search, but we were unbelievably lucky. One of the guys found it only about thirty feet from the body."

Meg lunged forward to snatch the book from his hand. "It's not."

"It sure is. Reed's notebook."

Meg carefully opened the book, its pages stiff after soaking and drying again. "Do the crime scene techs think they got any evidence off it?"

"You might be surprised by some of the new techniques to pull prints off of wet, porous surfaces. The lab techs took a shot at it and they'll let me know if they can pull a positive ID from it."

Slipping a nail under the edge, Meg turned a page. Handwriting in blue ink ran down the page, lying in a cloud of blue haze where the ink had run. "Some of this is pretty hard to read. That's going to be a problem."

"You'd think so, but I called in a favor." Turning to his computer, he pulled up a file and turned his monitor so Meg could see better.

An image of the book she held in her hands splayed across the screen. "They scanned it?"

"The whole thing, so if it fell apart we'd still have the evidence. Then they did this magic." A single click and the image on screen clarified, the looping scrawl of letters popping from the paper and the smears of ink fading in the background.

Meg couldn't help the small gasp. "That's amazing." She closed the book and set it on Van Cleave's desk as she moved forward, staring at the screen. The words were amazingly clear—names, places, dates, amounts, and payment methods. "My God, Van, we've got them."

"We have a damned good start. It will be even better if we can trace any financial transactions between them, but that's all going to be part of the larger case. That part is going to take months."

"Not the kind of job security anyone wants, but it will all be worth it to slam the door on them one by one for abusing children like that. And maybe, just maybe, the security footage from the tavern Reed liked to hang at will bury a few of the recent johns. Written notes tied to actual video footage would be a real slam dunk."

"We have that footage. We're building a solid case here, Meg."

"I know." Meg sat back in her chair. "You should be proud of the job you and your agents are doing. It's first-class work."

Van Cleave bowed his head in a gracious nod. "Thank you, ma'am. Did you ever hear from your sergeant?"

"I did. He emailed me earlier today, but it got lost in the shuffle. He gave me a couple of names of local PD brass who might be able to help." She pulled out her cell phone, called up her email program, and forwarded the email to Van Cleave. "There you go. Any of the names seem familiar?"

Van Cleave downloaded and opened the message. He scanned the text. "Yeah, I know a couple of these guys. Solid cops. I'll keep them in mind."

"If you need to contact them, drop Archer's name. That could help open some doors. Now, you." She punctuated the word with a stabbing index finger. "You're done for the day. More than done."

Van Cleave heaved a big sigh and tipped back in his chair, his head tilted back against the headrest. "I think you're right."

"Do you need a lift home?"

"No. I can get myself home, but I swear I'm having a scotch with dinner with my beautiful wife, going to smoke a pipe to relax for a few minutes, and then I'm falling into bed. My wife will keep everyone at bay unless it's a life-or-death emergency."

"That sounds pretty good."

"Doesn't it?" He rubbed his face with his open right hand. "I'm about ready to drop."

"We'll get out of your way then. Hawk, come." Meg stood, Hawk following suit. She turned at the door to look back at Van Cleave. He looked like he'd aged a decade in the past few days alone. "You're sure you're okay?"

"Definitely, go."

"See you tomorrow then."

Near the outer door, she glanced back into Van Cleave's office. He was on his feet and reaching for his suit coat.

He'll be fine.

She looked down at her dog. "Come on, Hawk. Let's go see Todd and Clay."

She wanted to run today's case advancements by them. Webb was a purely logical thinker, where McCord drew from his myriad experiences to spin a bigger picture.

Together, they might be able to make some sense out of the day.

CHAPTER 26

Head snap: An abrupt change of direction by a scent-work dog when it crosses a scent plume.

Thursday, July 27, 6:13 PM
Motel 6
Norfolk, Virginia

McCord's voice carried through the cheap hotel door even before she knocked on it. The voice stopped momentarily and then the daylight leaking through the peephole disappeared for a few seconds before returning as the viewer stepped back.

McCord opened the door, pulling it wide. "Come on in. And say hi to Cara while you're at it."

"She's on the phone?"

"Skype." He pointed at his laptop on the desk.

"Hawk, come." Meg stepped into the room, and walked past the bathroom to find Webb stretched out on McCord's bed. The muted TV was on in front of him, showing the Washington Nationals in the outfield at Nationals Park. "Hey, didn't see you there." She circled the bed to his side, bent down and pressed a quick kiss to his grinning lips.

"Hey! Knock it off and come say hello to your sister."

Meg turned at the sound of Cara's voice. "Spying again, are you? Been doing that since you were old enough to toddle after me."

Cara's smile on screen was pure triumph. "You never could get away with anything while I was around."

Chuckling, Meg turned back to Webb. "How did it go today?"

"Good. They're only going to need me for one more day, then they're releasing me at the end of tomorrow. I'm back on shift at DCFEMS on Monday."

"And thus endeth your vacation."

"This was *not* a vacation." He gave her shoulder a gentle shove. "Go talk to your sister, then we can catch up."

Meg rose and moved to the chair in front of McCord's laptop. "Hey. How are things at home?"

"Good. Where's my main man?"

"I assume you don't mean McCord."

"I'm right here, you know," McCord said. "I can hear you."

Meg tipped the laptop to where Hawk had jumped up and settled beside Webb.

"There he is. Hey, Hawk." Cara waved into the camera.

Hawk's head rose and he looked in the direction of the laptop, clearly mystified that while he could hear Cara, he couldn't smell or see her.

Laughing, Meg set the laptop back on the desk. "Now you've confused him."

"That always amuses me. We've been confusing Cody all week in exactly the same way. Speaking of which . . ." Cara tipped sideways and the screen was filled with the snout of a bobbing golden retriever.

"Hey, Cody," Meg said. "Who's a good boy?"

The screen abruptly went black as Cody lunged toward the camera, and then the dog was gone and Cara sat alone again.

"I swear that dog never stops moving," Cara said. "It's good to actually see you instead of just catching you by phone. How's your case going?"

"It's coming . . ." Meg's tone was anything but sure.

"That doesn't sound very reassuring. What's going on? Last time we talked was a couple of days ago and you'd just been to that bar where the guy running the sex ring used to do business."

Meg ran her hand through her hair. "God, that seems like a lifetime ago. When was that? Tuesday? So much has happened since then."

"How much can you tell me about what's going on?"

"We have two arrests on public record, so I can certainly talk about those." She filled Cara in on the previous few days, including Webb and McCord's visit to A Short Trip To Hell, her tracking of Russo after, and the op and the arrests that followed. When she got to today's arrests, she noticed that Webb and McCord had stopped paying attention to the baseball game and now had their attention firmly fixed on her. "So, while Russo is scared to death and is willing to sell his soul to make a deal, Pate considers it a minor inconvenience."

"Jail is a minor inconvenience?" said McCord. "This is a guy who runs a private prison, he should know better. I've interviewed my share of inmates. Prison is brutal."

Meg carried the laptop over to the bed and sat down on it, cross-legged, beside Webb, giving her dog a gentle shove to give her more space. "Shift it, Hawk. Stop hogging the bed." She placed the laptop on the far corner so it was like the four of them were sitting in a circle. "Then what is it that he knows that we don't know?"

"Maybe he thinks Russo is an unreliable witness," Webb said. He looked at McCord. "What you do think? We met him. He might provide drugs to his vics, maybe even take them himself, but Russo seemed pretty solid to me. Totally in control of the situation."

"Agreed," McCord said. "But we don't know what their business arrangement is, or how much contact they had. Maybe Pate thinks he can discredit Russo as a witness? What evidence do you have besides that?"

"The fact that he left Emma off the list of juveniles that went through his facility. The tech boys are still going through the computer data and cross-referencing it to known victims. The problem there is if a certain girl is not a known victim, then she could be left off the list and we'd never make the connection. We only made the connection with Emma because we had her full story."

"That's not going to be enough to hold him. Any decent lawyer would get him out of that error." McCord made air quotes around the word "error." "What if he's not worried because he's assuming he'll go to his own facility? Once he's there, he'd expect to be treated like royalty."

"Not buying that," Webb said. "First of all, he shouldn't go there at all simply because he'd managed that facility. And even if some miracle occurred and he was sent there, he'd still be confined. He might have some luxuries provided to him on the sly, but he'd still be a prisoner. It wouldn't be the same. I'm assuming this would be a pretty hefty jail sentence?"

"Definitely." Without looking, Meg's hand dropped to scratch behind Hawk's ear and his tail thumped in response. "Even a prisoner with luxuries would be a prisoner for far too long."

"Keeping that in mind," Cara said, "what if it's not the prison at all? What if he thinks he's never going to get there? Never going to be convicted. What's his get-out-of-jail-free card that could happen before that? The trial? The world's best attorney?"

The idea hit Meg so hard she actually jerked. She turned

to face Webb, who stared at her curiously. "Not the attorney. Too much uncertainty in how the trial might go. But what's better than an attorney to get you out of a trial?" When three blank faces met her gaze, she said, "A judge. A judge you know will bail you out of a situation."

"You think he has a judge in his pocket?"

"What if he's had one in his pocket all along?" She paused for a second, staring down unseeingly at her dog as the puzzle pieces started to fall into place. Then she looked up. "The amazing thing is that Pate dropped this point on us the first day we met him, but it didn't penetrate until now. So, we have people being arrested for various crimes, getting their day in court and being sent away. We have those same people being assigned to one specific reentry program. Now, how do people get there? A social worker can recommend the program, they can request it themselves or . . . a judge can specify both the treatment and the facility as part of the sentence."

"And there it is." McCord sat back against the headboard. "Jail here for X amount of time, followed by reentry here for Y amount of time. It's genius if you're thinking what I think you're thinking."

"I think so, and you can thank Cara for steering me in that direction." She looked into the webcam. "Leave it to you to always find a pattern in something."

Cara grinned widely. "We all have our skills. I just get to help on the quiet, and then watch you bring down the bad guys."

"Let me make sure I'm following," Webb said. "You're suggesting a more complicated setup. You think you've got a dirty judge who's getting some sort of kickback for sending select perps and kids to a specific reentry program. In this case, one run by Mason Pate. The judge is sentencing the kids and then specifically targets them, giving Pate recommendations on who would be vulnerable as a victim or would make a good ringleader, based on their criminal past. Pate is heading the trafficking operation, and he's using his private facility to single out those ringleaders and victims, or identify new ones, depending on who gets sent in. He makes sure they get thrown together and connections get made. The trafficking rings expand, the judge gets a finder's fee, and Pate gets a significant cut of the overall operation's profits?"

"Jesus Christ," McCord breathed. "It all makes sense. All the dots connect, including Pate specifically trying to keep certain minors out of the picture."

"More than that," Cara said, "he could be betting that whoever this judge is, he's going to make sure he gets Pate's case, which he'll then throw out of court for some reason."

"He could use a technicality," McCord said, "but a better way to handle it would be deciding that the evidence wasn't strong enough and finding Pate not guilty. Or influencing a jury, if there is one."

"Or allowing, or not allowing, certain statements or evidence to become part of the court case. He could totally steer the case away from Pate. Once found not guilty, the Fifth Amendment says he can't be tried again for the same offense," Meg said. "Double jeopardy will save him." She pulled out her cell phone. "I need to call Van Cleave." She winced. "He said life-or-death emergency only, but I think this qualifies. If I'm lucky, he's still drinking scotch and having dinner with his wife." She looked toward the laptop. "Cara, stay with us, but we can't let him know you're listening or that you contributed."

Cara waved away her sister's concerns. "I know the routine. Do it."

Meg called up Van Cleave's cell number and dialed it, putting it on speaker and holding the phone out on her palm in the middle of the group.

It rang for so long, Meg was surprised by his live voice instead of voice mail. "Van Cleave." The words came out as a growl.

"Van, it's Meg. I know you're finally home, but I wouldn't be calling unless it was really important. I need to run something by you. It'll be worth your time."

A sigh heavy with exhaustion carried down the line. "Shoot."

"I'm here with Todd Webb and Clay McCord. After your unsuccessful round today with Mason Pate, we've been turning over some potentials and we have something we want to run by you." She summarized their theory and then sat back, waiting. Seconds ticked by. Meg glanced up at Webb, who returned a pointed look and shrugged.

"God damn it!" Fury exploded from the phone, followed by rapid footsteps, the sound of glass solidly striking wood, and then typing.

"Van?"

Typing. Silence. More typing. A mumble. Keystrokes again.

"Van?" Meg said it a little louder this time. "Everything all right?" A few more seconds of silence, then the squeak of a desk chair. "Van!"

"Bloody hell. I think you got it."

"We did?" Meg reached out blindly for Webb, caught and held on to his thigh. "What did we get?"

"I logged on to the system from home so I could run some quick searches. The same judge sentenced Emma, Reed, and Russo to go to the reentry program. That *specific* reentry program."

"He did it at the time of sentencing?"

"He did."

"Yes!" Meg pumped her fist in triumph. "Van, we need to find out who else he sentenced to go there. And we need access to his banking records."

"Oh, don't worry, I'm already ahead of you there."

"What's his name? The judge?"

"Marcus Fairfax." He heaved out a big sigh. "And now reality and caution are starting to rear their ugly heads. We need to keep in mind that this could just be a judge who's convinced the reentry programs do serious good and, as a result, he tends to order inmates there near the end of their sentence."

"You don't seriously think this is a coincidence?"

"No. But it's experience talking. When you're knee-deep in an investigation, you're always looking for links, and sometimes you look too hard. That being said, we will consider the possibility that he may be connected somehow. I don't have any problem going after a dirty judge—and that's a big assumption that he is—but to even make that attempt, we have to be beyond certain. Right now, we're just tossing out the possibility of a connection. If we go after this guy, we have to be one hundred and ten percent sure. It can't be something that could be chalked up to coincidence."

"Agreed. A few prisoners could be sent to the reentry facility, as you said, by a judge who thinks that reentry programs show promise, and he wants to throw a bunch of people at the system to really try it out. But if he really is involved somehow . . ."

"Then I will cheerfully take him down. I don't care what your rank is. You break the law, you get me on your back."

"There's the white knight I've come to respect. We have to be sure, but then we need to take him down if it's him."

"With you, all the way."

"What's our next step?"

"The financials are going to be the key. If we can tie him to kickbacks, and if we can find that they're coming from Pate or the Harper Group, then we'll slam that door behind him hard. Thank you, all of you. This may be the break we need. If we can identify Fairfax as the source of both the vics and the ringleaders, we'll be able to trace them to new locations and unknown victims." There was a pause filled with the clinking of ice cubes. "I'll settle better now with this blank filled in, but I have to get some sleep. I'll hit this first thing tomorrow, I promise."

"Good enough for me. Get some rest."

"God willing." With a click, he was gone.

With a shaky laugh, Meg dropped her phone on the bedspread. "It's official. You guys are awesome."

"It was your breakthrough," McCord said.

"Yeah, but I never would have had that without Cara lining it up for me and you guys setting it up for her. Teamwork. We've proved time and again we work better together. It never gets old."

Webb put his arm around her and pulled her in as McCord lifted the laptop over Hawk's head to speak to Cara directly.

Meg looked around her, studying the faces of the people she'd come to depend on as steadfast friends and helpers.

No, she had that wrong. Not friends.

Family.

CHAPTER 27

High Value Reward: A reward that a working dog finds highly motivating—bacon, steak, a living search object, etc.

Friday, July 28, 7:22 AM
Motel 6
Norfolk, Virginia

Meg woke to the insistent ringing of her cell phone. She opened her eyes to a strange room cloaked in shadows, but the comfort of a familiar scent.

She rolled over and grabbed her cell phone after a few clumsy misses. "Jennings." The single word came out hoarse and scratchy, so she cleared her throat and tried again. "Jennings."

"Meg, I'm sorry I'm calling early, but I need you ready to roll."

Meg's eyes snapped open as sleep fell away. *Van.* "What happened?" She squinted at the bedside clock but only got a red blur. "What time is it?"

"About twenty after seven. I know it's early, but I wanted to get a warrant from one particular judge, and the best place to nail him down is during his dawn run. He's predictable, always takes the same course. I thought I'd join him."

"After the last few days you had?"

"I was in bed by shortly after seven last night. I ate and pretty much lost consciousness. By five I was awake. I did some more research this morning, and by six had my Nikes on and I met him partway. By seven I had my warrant signed."

"We're doing this then?"

"Damn right we are. The warrant covers Fairfax's home and office and includes all his electronics. We can also go after his ISP if we need to dig further. We'll go in two teams; I'm heading the team to his house. I thought you'd like to join me."

"I would. Text me the address."

"Will do. Be there at 9:00 AM."

"You don't want to start earlier?"

"And risk Fairfax actually being there? You know the law. We have to knock and wait a respectable amount of time. After that we can make a forced entry. In this case, I have an agent who could make a career breaking and entering with his lock-picking skills, so we'll go in that way. By nine, Fairfax, who lives alone, should already be at the courthouse. Which reminds me. I found another commonality while I was comparing cases this morning. Not only did they all have the same judge, they all had the same prosecuting attorney. That made me dig further. There are a lot of convictions with this combination of prosecuting attorney and judge, and many of those sentences included the Chesapeake Community Corrections Service Center. That gives us a pool of inmates to track down."

"It's the prosecuting attorney who recommends the sentence for the judge to rule on, right?"

"Yes."

"You think he's involved too?"

"I'd say we have a good chance. The house of cards is

falling in on itself. Again, not enough evidence to accuse him, but definitely enough to get a warrant. I hope to have enough to make the accusation later today. Now get up. See you in an hour and a half." Van Cleave hung up.

Meg put her cell phone back down on the table and rolled over again to limply collapse. Warm arms came around her.

"Good morning." Webb's voice was a low rumble.

"Morning." Smiling, she leaned over and kissed him. "Sleep well?"

"Like the dead. You exhausted me."

Laughing, she rolled her head off his shoulder to lie on her back. She glanced sideways at him. His dark hair was standing up in every direction and stubble darkened the line of his jaw. He looked sleepy and sexy as hell. "We exhausted each other." Laying one hand on his chest, she ran it down under the covers. "I have to meet Van for a residence search at nine, but if we're quick, we have time for round two."

"Round two? Try round four." In a lightning-fast move, he rolled over her, trapping her body beneath his. "Maybe we'll fit round five in there too. We firefighters are a pretty inventive lot and we know how to make do with whatever time we're given."

She was laughing when his mouth came down on hers, and she forgot all about victims, searches, and investigations.

CHAPTER 28

Multiple Hides: A search area containing more than one source of odor.

Friday, July 28, 8:58 AM
Bar Harbor Drive
Norfolk, Virginia

The winding driveway leading to the house was already full of FBI vehicles, so Meg parked her SUV against the rounded edge of the cul-de-sac. She hopped out and opened the back door for Hawk. He jumped down and stood still while she snapped the leash onto his FBI vest.

They walked past the cars to the group of agents clustered around Van Cleave. Van Cleave was finishing the last of his instructions when he noticed her.

He stepped out of the group. "Good, you're here. We're just about to get started, but I wanted to update you first."

"You have something new?"

"Norfolk PD has found two of the three missing girls. They were staying at one of the Norfolk community shelters until an officer thought to check there."

"Smart girls. Free food and lodging, and the safety of being nothing more than faces in an anonymous crowd.

It's probably the most normal few days they've had in a long time. They're okay?"

"They're physically unharmed and are now tucked away in a safe location. They're also working with Norfolk PD to help locate the last girl." He grinned. "Things are turning around for us. I've got a good feeling about this. We're going to tie this one up tight."

"Music to my ears. Go to it. We'll stay out of the way until you give the okay to go in."

Meg pulled back to stand near the line of virtually identical black SUVs as Van Cleave and his group of agents mounted the steps. Van Cleave rang the doorbell, waited ten seconds, then banged on the heavy front door with his fist, calling, "FBI! Open the door. We have a warrant to search the premises." He then stepped back and waited.

He met her gaze over the heads of the agents standing on the steps below him and grinned.

No one home. Just like he planned.

While they waited, Meg studied the house. It was magnificent in its own way—three stories of blinding white clapboard with a square front porch flanked by twin garage doors. Over the porch, a three-sided projection extended from the house, each level a line of curved picture windows rising to the roofline. It was a beautiful house, but Meg couldn't feel any warmth from it. Even from a distance it felt cold, sterile.

Van Cleave waited a full five minutes and then repeated the doorbell, the banging, and the announcement. When there continued to be no response, he motioned for one of the men to come forward. As the agent dropped to his knees and went to work on the lock, Van Cleave made a phone call after pointing out the small sticker beside the front door that identified the alarm company.

Probably to let them know the FBI has a warrant to legally enter. Maybe sending a copy of that warrant to prove it so they'll shut off the alarm and not tell the owners.

Within a couple of minutes, the door was open, the alarm silenced, and agents were flooding into the house. Meg could hear them announcing themselves as they swarmed upstairs, their dark-jacketed forms flowing past the windows. Five minutes later, Van Cleave appeared in the front door and waved her in.

They jogged up to the front porch and stepped into a small foyer that opened up to a grand staircase leading over their heads to the main floor.

"Hawk, heel."

Meg and Hawk followed Van Cleave up the stairs and found themselves in the windowed projection looking out over the mass of cars winding away from the house. Then they rounded the corner of the staircase and walked into a large, open-concept living space.

It was elegant and neat as a pin. And as cold and sterile as the outside of the home. Almost everything was stark white—from the walls, to the decorative columns that separated the dining room from a living space full of white sofas and chairs, to the cabinets in the kitchen. Only the odd splash of color broke the chill of the snowscape: The kitchen counters were pale pink marbled with black, the cushions of the rococo dining chairs were midnight blue, and the throw cushions on the couch were blood red. Other than that, sterile white covered every surface.

"Great living space, isn't it?"

Meg sent him a side-eyed glance. "Please tell me you're kidding."

"Definitely. The house is an ice palace. Seems kind of unusual for a man living on his own."

"Maybe it says something about his personality. Cold and detached. In it for the money."

"Which he evidently has plenty of. One thing I can't fault him for is the view. It's pretty spectacular."

Meg wandered to the far end of the living room. The floor-to-ceiling windows had no drapes to warm them, but it also allowed for a panoramic view of the expanse of the Elizabeth River. Sunlight flashed on flowing water, but even days after the storm, the river still looked churned and murky, and debris scattered the backyard. The dock at the end of the walkway to the river hung at a drunken angle, as if it had been yanked from its moorings by the rage of the river.

"The house survived the storm, even if the outside took some damage. I'll bet before the storm, it was a pretty nice spot."

"And will be again. Whether it is for Judge Fairfax remains to be seen."

Meg turned away from the windows. "What's been found so far?"

"They're going through a room at a time, but I brought one of the computer nerds with me and she's already hard at work on getting onto his computer."

As if on cue, a yell came from upstairs.

"That might be her now. Let's go up."

An additional flight of steps carried them to the bedrooms, which blessedly held some color in the form of linens and paint.

"Where do you want me?" Van Cleave called out.

A blond head popped through a doorway at the far end of the hall. "Sir! Down here!"

The room was set up as a study with a heavy wooden desk, and book-stuffed shelving units that covered every piece of wall not taken up by windows or the door. Additional stacks of books were piled on the judge's desk. The agent sat in front of a wide high-definition monitor, her hands flying over the keyboard.

"What have we got?"

"Full access to his system, for a start." She glanced up. "For someone who spends his day dealing with the seedier sides of life, he had a really weak password. He should have known better."

"You'd be amazed at the number of law enforcement officials who know what it's like out there and still have an it-can't-happen-to-me attitude. What's on his system?"

The agent noticed Hawk and lit up with a brilliant smile. "Hey, big boy, you're a handsome fella." She tilted her head up to Meg and extended her hand. "Agent Sylvia Stiles."

They shook.

"Meg Jennings. And this is Hawk."

"Well, isn't he a ray of sunshine on this case. Are you the handler and dog who found the first victims?"

"That's us."

"Good job." Stiles turned back to the computer. "The it-can't-happen-to-me attitude was in full swing here, because Fairfax has done nothing to hide his activities. Well, he's using an anonymous email address, but it's still coming into this computer, filtered through his own ISP. We'll be able to get full records from them about all this traffic. But what I have here is evidence of the whole scheme. He's in the circuit court, which tries the serious adult criminal cases and all felony juvie cases for fourteen-years-of-age and up. He has no control over who comes into his courtroom, but it looks like he and the prosecutor, Henry Fisher, a deputy Commonwealth's attorney, are considering the cases that come before them and are hand-picking certain defendants."

"You can track all that?" Van Cleave asked.

"He's got spreadsheets, for God's sake." There was no mistaking the disgust in Stiles's tone. "It's the most cold-blooded thing I've seen in a while. He tracks everyone who goes through the courtroom. Some defendants go through more than once and get picked the second time, but not the first."

"Maybe not vulnerable enough the first time?" Meg suggested. "Or not hardened enough, if it's someone being picked as a ringleader."

"He doesn't give reasons," Stiles said. "Only black-and-white selections."

"He's probably taking Fisher's suggestions as a pool, and then making his own call during the trial itself. Fisher may also be encouraging or even pressuring defendants to plead out so they can end up in the right facility. And keeping in mind that drug cases and more minor felony charges won't require a jury, Fairfax is literally judge, jury, and executioner on those cases. Between the two of them, they can select exactly who they want, and funnel them right into their little setup."

"And once Fairfax makes a decision to send a defendant to the private facility, he's letting someone know. Emails go out to an address associated with a company I've never heard of before, but between the ISPs, we should be able to trace it."

"What company is that?"

"Bartlett and Kesell."

"Really . . ." The word came out as a drawl. Van Cleave looked over at Meg. "That's the company that owned Luke Reed's house. It's going to take some fancy electronic tracing, but I bet that leads back to Pate if we can dig through enough layers. Connect the dots, Stiles. Carefully and legally. This has to stick."

"Oh, it'll stick. Don't you worry there. There's also references to other aliases and several other trafficking arms—the sex trade, agriculture, massage parlors, domestics, construction, landscaping. And probably others I just haven't found yet. Definitely there are references to other contacts, but it's going to take a little more time to give you names there. There's no doubt, this is *big*."

"I've been saying all along that it's going to come down to computer forensics and financials. Has he made any notes about financials?"

"Oh yeah. He's exacting, this judge. Extremely detailed. He's been at this for a while and hasn't been caught, so he must think it will never happen. His emails and his offshore banking transactions all go through his ISP. He really didn't think anyone would look at him, because he's respected, with a squeaky-clean reputation as a hardliner, but one who calls his shots clearly and fairly."

"He can do that," Meg reasoned. "He's got a big enough pool of potential victims and ringleaders to choose from, that his verdicts and sentences don't look out of place. And he could use some defendants as decoys, taking people with identical charges and nearly identical cases and not sending them to Pate, to cover his tracks. Then nothing looks suspicious, but in reality, he's cherry-picking defendants to line his own pockets."

"Son of a bitch," Stiles muttered.

"On the bright side," Van Cleave said, "I think we're going to add a few more federal charges into the mix. Tax evasion—because there's no way he's declaring this income—and money laundering. There are penalties for extrajudicial compensation, and I'm going to slap him with every one of them."

"How do you want to play this?" Meg asked. "Are you satisfied you have enough evidence to take Fairfax into custody?"

"Fairfax for sure. What about Fisher?"

"We have enough to take him into custody now, get a search warrant, and gather more evidence before he starts screaming habeas corpus. At the beginning, he's mentioned as H. F., and it's clear he's a prosecuting attorney. A simple check of the Norfolk Commonwealth Attorney's Office told me he's the only attorney with the initials H. F. Cross-referencing of recent public criminal cases tried by Fairfax link Fisher by name. Later emails refer to him as Abe." Stiles rolled her eyes. "It's like they think no one watched TV in the 1970s."

Van Cleave chuckled cynically. "Abe. Abe Vigoda. Fish from *Barney Miller*. Fisher." He threw Meg a pointed look. "More aliases."

"I'm so done with the TV and movie aliases. We'll take them both into custody then?"

"If Stiles is sure this is enough to hold them—"

"I am," Stiles interrupted.

"Then yes, we're going after both." He shot back his cuff and looked at his wristwatch. "And look at that. By the time the team organizes, we'll be arriving at court just before the noon recess." His grin was pure calculation. "It just so happens that both Fairfax and Fisher are in court today. Together. Trying a drug-possession case."

"You'll get two birds with one stone and possibly cut their next recruitment off at the pass," Meg said.

"That is absolutely my intent. Thanks, Stiles. Pack all this up and take it back downtown and work on it more there. The warrant covers the ISP, and I've already sent a team over there, so that information should be coming through soon for you, as well." He turned back to Meg and Hawk. "We're going to head downtown. Coming?"

"Oh, you bet. I wouldn't miss this."

"This is the part I enjoy the most. Nothing more fun than bringing in the bad guys. Let's go ruin their day."

CHAPTER 29

Finish: A statement by the handler to a canine scent-work trial official that the dog is unable to find additional sources of odor.

Friday, July 28, 11:14 AM
Norfolk Circuit Court
Norfolk, Virginia

Meg met up with the group of agents who would be staging the arrests in the foyer outside courtroom 12. They clustered down the hallway, away from the heavy wood double doors that led into the courtroom. Hawk was still with her, so she stayed on the outside of the group, Hawk sitting patiently at her side.

"You're sure this is the best way to do this?" one of the agents asked Van Cleave. "You don't think it would be better to wait until he's in chambers?"

"It would be more private for Fairfax, but then that separates him from Fisher. I want them both. I also don't want him to have any hint of trouble brewing or he'll be in the wind. He has plenty of offshore resources, has no family here, and would disappear before I could snap my fingers. No, this is the only way. I realize it's going to cause a mistrial in this current case, but that would happen anyway, as the defendant is going to be needing a new prosecutor and a new judge." He craned his neck, looking through the faces surrounding him. "McCarthy? Where's McCarthy?"

"Here, sir." A short, slightly portly man in a traditional black suit stepped between two other agents to the front of the group.

"Good. We've gone over your role. You go right to the bailiff and make sure this thing doesn't become a real mess. He's a sheriff's officer and he's going to be armed. We don't want this getting out of hand. Make sure the bailiff stands down so we can do our jobs."

"Yes, sir."

"Excellent. Everyone else knows what to do? Close off the back and side doors, hold the defendant so he doesn't get away in the confusion, keep the courtroom calm. I'll take Fairfax. Baxter, you take Fisher."

A tall, blond man at the front of the group nodded. "Ready when you are, sir."

"Jennings?"

"Here. With Hawk."

"You come in last. Stay by the main doors to keep anyone else from bolting. No one will get by Hawk, and that will also help keep people out of the aisles. Okay, let's do this. Court has been in session since nine thirty, and he could be breaking for lunch recess anytime. Earpieces in, go get into position. I'll give the signal to move in."

Meg and Hawk stayed with the agents going in the main doors at the back of the courtroom while other groups broke off to man their respective doors. Van Cleave waited until the corridor had been quiet for a full sixty seconds before giving the signal. "All groups . . . on my mark. GO!"

Agents streamed through the doors into the courtroom. Cries of alarm came from the viewers at the back of the courtroom as several people shot to their feet in surprise.

The defendant, a young black man in an orange county-jail jumpsuit sat at a table near the front of the room, accompanied by his lawyer. Two lawyers sat at the other table. Meg bet the younger man on the end, dressed immaculately in an impeccably tailored suit—probably Italian—was Fisher.

Despite the shouts, Van Cleave walked up to the bench while, behind him, McCarthy was making a direct line for the uniformed Norfolk sheriff's officer, who already had his hand on the butt of his gun. McCarthy had his flip case open to show his identification and was already talking from ten feet away. The officer's eyes darted from McCarthy to the other agents, finally settling on Van Cleave. His shoulders relaxed and his hand moved away from his firearm, but Meg noted that it didn't fall to his side. The officer was prepared to act if needed; the question was, in whose defense?

At the front of the courtroom, Fairfax pounded his gavel on the block. "Order! Order! Sir! What are you doing? Get out of my courtroom!"

Ignoring him, Van Cleave kept coming, pulling out his ID even as he announced himself. "FBI Special Agent in Charge Walter Van Cleave. Judge Marcus Fairfax, you are under arrest for conducting a criminal enterprise, conspiracy to recruit, conspiracy to commit sex trafficking of minors, promoting prostitution and money laundering. You have the right to remain silent—"

Fairfax shot to his feet. "You're insane. You can't do this."

Van Cleave had his handcuffs out now and was stalking behind the judge's bench. "Watch me," he snarled.

Fairfax whirled toward the bailiff standing at the door. "Thompson. Stop this. Take these men into custody."

The officer simply took a step back until his back bumped

against the wall behind him. McCarthy's mouth moved to form the words "thank you" to the officer.

Van Cleave took advantage of the judge's half-turned position to snap a cuff on his right wrist, wrenching his hand behind his back as he muscled the other arm around and closed the second cuff over his wrist. He gave Fairfax a push backward into his chair. "Do yourself a favor and stay down."

But Fairfax was trying to get up again, cursing Van Cleave.

Van Cleave put one hand on Fairfax's shoulder and pushed down, hard, and then leaned in. Meg couldn't hear what Van Cleave said, but she could imagine him finally loosening his iron hold on his vitriol and hammering Fairfax with a detailed list of his transgressions and what had happened to the children he'd sold for his own profit.

When Van Cleave straightened, Fairfax's face was sheet white.

"You have the right to remain silent." Van Cleave finished reading the full Miranda warning and then turned to Agent Baxter, who stood with several other agents grouped around Deputy Commonwealth Attorney Fisher. "Baxter, he's contained?"

"Yes. And he's been read his rights."

"Excellent." Van Cleave turned to the courtroom. "My apologies, ladies and gentlemen, for the disruption this morning, but we had no choice." He looked at the assistant prosecuting attorney. "You'll need to start this trial again with a new judge. Bailiff? If you could return the defendant to his cell, the prosecution and the court will require some time to reorganize." He looked down at Fairfax and a smile slowly curved his lips. "This judge will never sit at the bench again. But he'll be back, soon, for his own day in court."

Van Cleave looked down the main aisle of the courtroom to where Meg stood with Hawk, blocking the back doors. She grinned back at him. Justice was blind, but this time she saw her way to uplifting the victims and bringing those responsible to their knees.

For Emma and Mary. For Celia and Leah, gone too soon. For the men and boys rescued only the day before. For most, their journey was far from over. But it was the beginning of healing and finding their way home.

CHAPTER 30

Move-Up: The ability of a dog team to compete at the next level in a multistate trial if they pass the entry-level competition on the first day.

Sunday, July 30, 11:07 AM
Cold Spring Haven Animal Rescue
Cold Spring Hollow, Virginia

Meg glanced in the rearview mirror as she turned into her parents' long, winding driveway. McCord, with Webb riding shotgun, pulled into the driveway behind her. She turned her eyes forward to the long, rambling ranch house at the end of the driveway, encircled with a welcoming wraparound porch. The tall lines of the big red barn rose behind it, and fenced paddocks stretched into the distance in all directions.

Home.

She and Cara might have their own place now, but home would forever be where her parents lived and worked so hard within the rescue community. Where they now would open their home to an exhausted, abused, lonely girl, with no one of her own to depend on as she tried to adjust to her new reality.

She looked sideways at Emma, who sat in the passenger seat beside her. The girl's eyes were like saucers and her mouth sagged open. Meg tried hard not to smile. She understood the wonder of the rescue, but didn't want Emma to misconstrue her reaction as poking fun at her.

"Welcome home," she said quietly. "You're sure you'll be okay out here? It's pretty far from the hustle and bustle of city life."

"I've lived the city life," Emma said. "It's not all it's cracked up to be."

"Working with animals is its own therapy, let me tell you." Movement out her side window caught Meg's eye. "Uh, Hawk. Auria is already waiting for you. Emma, look left."

The girl gasped as she realized a bay mare was galloping to catch up to the SUV, and then settling into a matched run with it.

In the back, Hawk let out a happy bark. The horse whinnied back.

"That's Auria. She and Hawk are best buddies. They both started out at the rescue together and they're inseparable when we're here."

Up ahead, her parents stepped out of the house, followed by . . . Cara? Yes, that was definitely her sister, with Saki at her side, and Blink poking his head around her mother's legs. And the yellow streak running in circles on the porch was Cody, McCord's golden retriever.

"Looks like the whole family is here to meet you. That's Mom and Dad. And the one who looks like a carbon copy of me is my baby sister, Cara. Mom must have told her we were on our way in. Cara and I live with our dogs in Arlington, but it's only a couple of hours to get here, so we drop by when we can."

"She came to see you?"

"She's dating Clay McCord—the reporter—in the car behind us. He went to North Carolina to cover the hurricane, so he's been gone for over a week." She chuckled. "I would bet he's probably a bigger draw than me."

They pulled in close to the porch. Meg let Hawk out and stood back as her dog shot through the gate her father held open and into the paddock to dance happy circles around the mare. Bracing one hand on the roof of the car, Meg bent down and looked in. "Ready?"

Emma took a big breath, clutched the bag she held on her lap, and nodded.

"Come on out then." Meg shut both open doors on her side and circled the SUV to meet her parents, sidestepping Cody as he shot past, finally released by Cara once Mc-Cord's car was parked. She hugged her mother first, then her father. Turning, she found Emma standing by the SUV, looking around uncertainly.

Meg stepped to the young woman, put an arm around her waist and drew her forward. "Mom, Dad, this is Emma. Emma, these are my parents, Jake and Eda Jennings."

Emma gave them a shy smile. "Mr. and Mrs. Jennings. Thank you so much for offering a place for me."

Eda stepped up and drew the girl away from Meg to give her a hug. "Welcome to Cold Spring Haven. And just Jake and Eda will do. We're so pleased you're here with us. Do you like iced tea? I've got some on the porch. And maybe after you're settled, Meg can take you around to show you the rescue."

"That sounds nice."

"Let me take your bag." Jake lifted the bag from her hands and then held his out to shake. "Nice to meet you. Meg told us some amazing things about you. Now, come on up. Eda baked pound cake and slapped my hand when I tried to sneak a piece because you get first honors. I can't eat until you do."

His wife fixed him with a mock glare. "Jake, you're terrible."

Jake winked at his wife and then led the women up to the porch, where he left them to take Emma's bag up to her room. Eda settled Emma in a chair, got her an iced tea and a slice of cake, and introduced her to the petrified Blink, who cautiously inched forward to sniff Emma's extended hand.

She's going to be just fine.

Meg turned back to find Cara and McCord locked in an embrace as Webb pointedly looked in any other direction and Cody did his best to push between them. "Hey!" she yelled with a wide grin. "Knock it off and come say hello to your sister."

Cara pushed away from McCord, smiling at the echo of her own words from days before. "Guess I deserved that." The sisters hugged and broke apart, laughing. Cara's gaze darted up to the porch, where Blink was standing by Emma's knee, allowing her to stroke his back, and her eyes went solemn. "You think she's going to be okay here? She's had a tough go of it so far."

"She has, but the rescue will be great for her. Mom might be a little out of her league because this girl will have issues that we never had, but she'll rise to the occasion. The hard, honest, physical labor of the rescue will do Emma good in the short term, and who knows? It might even point her in a new direction."

Barking attracted their collective attention. Saki was standing on her stubby back legs, her front paws braced on the cross posts of the paddock fence, watching Hawk and Auria race around as Cody bulleted up and down the fenced perimeter.

"Do we dare let her in?" Cara asked.

"She's never shown interest before, but why not? Auria is insanely careful about where she puts her feet when a dog is around." Meg turned to the dancing golden retriever at her side. "What about you, Cody?"

As a group, they walked to the paddock and Meg opened the gate. Cody went through in a yellow blur, then Saki trotted through toward Hawk and Auria, to join the chaotic chase.

"Cody never stops moving, but it never fails to amaze me how fast Saki can run on those short little legs. She's greased lightning."

"She's a special girl, my Saki. Therapy dog extraordinaire, and spunky as hell."

Meg closed the gate and joined the others at the fence, slipping between Cara and Webb. She propped her elbows on the fence railing to watch the happy exuberance inside.

McCord poked his head around Cara. "So . . . now that the case is officially closed . . ."

Meg rolled her eyes and pointed a finger accusingly at McCord. "Look, Mr. Reporter, I haven't forgotten you have first crack at this story. I've already put the request in to Craig; I'm just waiting for him to get back to me. Then you'll get the green light."

"I'm just saying I have the story mostly written and it could go out as a headliner tomorrow morning." McCord rocked back and forth and innocently whistled a tune until Cara elbowed him in the stomach, the notes disintegrating into a gasping indrawn breath.

"A deal's a deal. If I don't hear from Craig in an hour, I'll contact EAD Peters myself. You'll get your story." Meg turned around and leaned on the fence, her gaze passing over the rolling hills of the farm and finally coming to rest on the trio sitting on the porch.

"We should go join them," Cara said. "You've given them a few minutes to get to know each other without a crowd looking on."

"Was I that obvious?"

"To me, yes, but considering we think alike and I would have done the same thing, maybe not to anyone else." She looped an arm around McCord's waist. "Hungry?"

McCord grinned down at her. "I could eat."

"You can always eat."

"Isn't that God's own truth." He gave her a squeeze and led her toward the house, his head bent low to murmur something private. Cara tossed back her head and laughed in response.

Meg held out her hand. "Well? Shall we join them?"

Webb wove his fingers through hers. "You know, bringing Emma here was a great idea."

"I wasn't sure it would work. It's going to be a big change for her. But it will take away the need to do anything to support herself, all while making sure she's safe. And she won't have to worry about anyone looking for her, now that the trafficking ring has collapsed and the ringleaders are dead or arrested. It will give her a chance to heal and find her bearings again." Her smile faded. "It worked for me after I lost Deuce. There's a peace to be found working with animals, which you can't quite find anywhere else."

"Then it's a real gift you've given her." He lifted her hand and kissed the back of it as they stepped onto the front walkway. "You're back to work with the team this week?"

"Craig is expecting me tomorrow. It'll be good to be back. This may sound stupid, but while putting those guys away was satisfying, it's just not the same as our search-and-rescue work."

"It's not stupid at all. Saving lives is its own reward."

"Of course you get it." She gripped his hand. "More than that, you get me."

Hand in hand, they walked up the porch steps to join their ever-expanding family.

AUTHOR'S NOTE

The idea for this novel came from several sources—personal experience with local hurricanes, research into real-life rescues and recoveries by National Disaster Search Dog Foundation teams, and media reports of both tragedy and the triumph of everyday people's amazing courage and resourcefulness during natural disasters. This manuscript was completed prior to the 2017 hurricane season. As a result, any similarities to the tragic story of the Saldivar family, who lost their lives when their van was washed away at a low-water crossing during Hurricane Harvey, are sadly coincidental.

ACKNOWLEDGMENTS

My heartfelt thanks goes to a group of wonderfully talented publishing professionals who helped transform this novel into its final form: My agent, Nicole Resciniti, for always standing by, ready to assist with any book or career direction question. My critique team—Lisa Giblin, Jenny Lidstrom, Rick Newton, and Sharon Taylor—for skillfully juggling character, technical, and plot points, and always finding the time to fit me in between insane home/work schedules and catastrophic forest fire deployments. And Esi Sogah, for your eagle eye in always being able to pinpoint issues, big or small, to help turn a draft into a shiny final product. I'd be lost without each one of you, so thank you!

Keep an eye out for more
F.B.I. K-9 Mysteries
Coming soon
And don't miss the first two books
In the series
LONE WOLF
and
BEFORE IT'S TOO LATE
Available now wherever books are sold